FOURTH RITE

A Reverse Harem Tale

Lovin' the Coven
Book 4

Jacquelyn Faye

∞ Untold Press ∞

Fourth Rite
A Reverse Harem Tale

Lovin' the Coven, book 4

ISBN-13: 978-1-945893-10-0

Published by Untold Press LLC
114 NE Estia Lane
Port St Lucie, FL 34983

www.untoldpress.com

PRODUCED IN THE UNITED STATES OF AMERICA

10 9 8 7 6 5 4 3 2 1

Dedication

This one goes out to Jason Mamoa's abdominal muscles. You are beautiful, you are strong, and gosh dang it all to heck,

I LOVE ALL SIX OF YOU!

You're the only harem I need.

Chapter 1

The feathered end of the arrow hit the ground without a sound. The end with the wickedly-barbed, silver tip chimed like a bell as it struck the cracked sidewalk. I stood in the middle of the sidewalk, eyes transfixed on the arrow that had almost sent me to the afterlife.

That was amazing. I can't believe you caught that…

Shouldn't we be chasing the elf instead of staring at the stick?

I transferred my gaze from the arrow back up to my demon familiar, the one who had caught the elven archer's arrow in his mouth and snapped it in half with his incredibly powerful jaws. *You want to live? Chasing an elf isn't a good idea. You think he's good with a bow, you should see them with a blade.*

Lord of the Rings good?

Dread Pirate Roberts good. Even left handed.

Who?

Never mind. I reached down and picked up both halves of the arrow off the ground. *Dar?*

What?

I shoved the arrow in my jacket pocket, letting the magic swallow it and effectively making it disappear. *This stays between us.*

The German Shepherd's eyes narrowed, and he huffed. *Might I ask why? Somebody did just try to kill you.*

We have new coven members coming in every day. Josie's mom and Shea will be here any moment. I don't want to start a panic.

What if the elf does?

I left his question unanswered. *Do this for me. Please. You know how they can get when I'm in danger. Honestly, I can't handle it right now.*

Yes, Master.

No. Bad doggy.

His sigh was very human-like. *Thank you.*

For? I rubbed his head.

Saving me. Another hour in Gehenna and I might not have made it back to you.

Well, you saved me, so that makes us even.

The door to the diner opened and chimed, letting out a waft of warm, burger-scented air.

Yuki stepped outside and shoved her hands in her pockets, turning her face up to the sun and smiling. "I still can't get used to that."

Her smile made me happy. "You get used to sleeping at night, yet?"

"Kind of funny. I don't need much sleep. When the sun was up, I was out. Literally dead to the world. Now that I'm not, I only sleep for a few hours and I'm good to go."

"And you don't even drink coffee. People would die, if it were me."

Yuki didn't laugh at my joke. She wasn't even looking at me. She was staring at Dar and frowning. I tried to act innocent when she shifted her gaze to me.

"Seriously?" She put a hand on her hip and cocked her stance.

I flicked Dar on his snout. "Did I not just get through telling you to keep your mouth shut?"

She's your familiar, too. If you're going to be stupid, it's up to us to keep you from getting perforated.

Yeah. What he said. Yuki gave me a disgusted look.

"Stay with Dar. I'm going to go pay the bill."

"What are you going to pay him to do?" Yuki wiggled her eyebrows, shifting gears and going from zero to perv in three-point-eight seconds. She needed to quit hanging out with Jimmy.

I grinned at her and went back inside. Jimmy was mopping the floor and Chief was carrying a tray of broken dishes to the counter while Nana sat in the booth, sipping tea.

"Thanks for cleaning up. I felt horrible."

"Yeah, well sometimes hellhounds just fall from the sky. What you gonna do?" Jimmy paused and leaned on his mop.

"You mean German Shepherds," I reminded him softly.

"Yeah. I think everybody in the diner saw what really happened. But kudos for the wishful thinking."

I turned my head and caught everybody staring. They quickly lowered their eyes and suddenly found their meals *very* interesting.

Might as well get 'I'm a witch T-shirts' made for everybody.

I'd planned on bringing everybody out eventually, but things were progressing a little *too* quickly. Hopefully, things would be a little quieter for a while. I could use the vacation, and I'm sure the good people of Cedar Falls could stand a little dose of normalcy. It was bad enough the town had been attacked by demons, people suddenly announcing themselves a coven of witches might just push them over the edge.

"Shit," I said with more than a little worry.

"Nope. None of that. Just some broken dishes. At least he's house broken."

"Don't start. I have a headache."

9

"That's what she said." He bowed at his humor.

I shot him a dirty look and headed for the counter. "Sorry about all that," I told Marge with an exasperated sigh.

"No worries, sweetie. Can I get you a coffee to go?"

"I'll love you forever. More."

She winked and poured some coffee in a paper cup and slapped a lid on it for me. "Pretty dog."

"Thanks. That's Dar."

"Dot, how did he get into the restaurant?" She slid the coffee over to me.

I leaned forward and whispered, "Do you really want to know?"

She thought about it for a minute and sighed, shaking her head. "Maybe someday."

"Well. I can give you the simple answer. Magic."

"That works."

"How much do I owe you for lunch and all the dishes?"

"Here's the bill for lunch, but your boys worked off the dish debt."

I slipped my card into the black plastic bill holder and handed it to her. "Guess I'll just have to make it up to them later."

"Let me know if you need any help!"

Lunch threatened to make a return appearance. Picturing Marge naked was *not* something that should be done on a full stomach, empty stomach, or any other kind of stomach. Just no. "I don't know about all that, but I might sell the mouthy one to you cheap."

"The one with the gun? No thanks. I'll take the skinny, purdy boy."

"Oh, stop. They're both pretty."

"How do you handle two of them?"

"Three…" I let it slip without even thinking about it. I needed to have my brain to mouth filter changed. There was a big, gaping hole in it.

"Three? Don't tell me you and Jason…"

My blush was all the answer she needed. At least our conversation had taken place in hushed whispers. It was bad enough the occupants of the diner saw my demon dog fall out of thin air. If they had an inkling that I had three boyfriends… Yeah. Being called a witch would be the least of my problems.

"Maybe."

"Oh, dear Lord, girl!"

"Let's just keep that between us."

"Yeah. Don't need anybody else knowin' your business. Specially, if you come in here walkin' funny."

That blush I still had on my cheeks turned into a beacon of embarrassment for all to see. I took several deep breaths as I waited patiently for her to ring me up.

She put the receipt for me to sign down on the counter, pulling out a pen from her pocket. "Hard to believe that just a month ago, you rolled in here and I warned you about not breakin' Chief's heart."

I smiled fondly at the memory. Josie and I had just gotten into town and were starving. Chief had come in to pick up his food order and I instantly fell in love with his ass in jeans. I'd asked Marge for his number and she told me to go easy on him. He had tragically lost his wife and wasn't looking for a relationship. Oh, how the mighty had fallen. In love. With him. I hadn't said the words to him, yet. But I planned on it. If he ever stopped pissing me off long enough to actually tell him. Glancing over my shoulder, just watching him talk to Nana made me smile.

"You got it bad, huh?"

I turned back to Marge and grinned, before leaning over and signing the bill. I gave her a hundred-dollar tip to pay for the dishes or treat her to something special. She deserved it, either way.

I pushed the receipt and pen back to her. She immediately scribbled out one of the zeros. "Nice try, darlin'."

"Damnit, Marge."

"I might have been born at night, but it wasn't *last* night."

"What?"

"I don't know. My mother used to say it."

"Okay, then."

She cackled and punched in a few more buttons on the credit card machine. "See ya, sweetie."

"See ya," I said and went back to our table.

"You guys ready?"

"Guy?"

"Figure of speech, Nana."

She harrumphed and slid out of the booth, Chief offering her an unneeded hand. She might have seen nearly a thousand years, but she could probably still outrun me. She even made me jealous watching her ride her broom. I couldn't do a pull-up to save my life.

"Thank you, William."

As soon as his hand touched hers, my hackles rose. It was ridiculous, I know... She was my freaking grandmother, but Chief was mine. Managing to swallow it down, I flashed them both a fake smile and grabbed Jimmy's arm. "Ready?"

"Um... Yeah?"

I pulled him out the door.

Dar stood up and took position in front of me, already in guardian mode. Yuki was looking *everywhere* but at me. They were being about as subtle as Josie when she flirted. Her idea of subtle was bashing someone in the face with an I want to fuck you brick.

12

You guys want to tone it down a bit?

No. Dar's voice left little room for argument.

He's long gone and not going to take another shot with this many people around.

You willing to bet our lives on that?

And there it was. They were worried about me, but I needed a reminder that it wasn't just my life on the line. It was all of ours. If I died, so did they. Dar had resorted to playing dirty.

Fine. Guard away.

"Well, I need to get back to work."

I turned back to Chief and nodded. "Be careful."

"I will. See you tonight?"

Jimmy, since his accident, was still on administrative leave. He had broken his back when a truck fire exploded, and been miraculously healed, by me. At least it gave him the opportunity to spend the day with me. Later that evening, the three of us were meeting for dinner. They absolutely refused to tell me where we were going but I vetoed Italian. It would be a few weeks before I could set foot in there without blushing myself to death. "Yep."

He gave me a small smile and turned me around, gently caressing my lips with his. "Have fun."

"You, too. Put a hurting on all that paperwork."

"You have no idea. The mayor is on my ass about the demon attack. I don't know what to tell her."

"Her?"

"Yeah."

I stared at him for a moment.

"You...okay?"

"Yeah. Why wouldn't I be?"

"You just seem a little shocked."

"Surprised that the mayor is a woman."

"Well, it is the twenty-first century. I hear you guys can even vote now."

"So… Do you often have dealings with the mayor?"

"Yeah…" He nodded slowly.

"Is she pretty?"

What in the fuck is wrong with me?

Even Dar looked over his shoulder at me. Jimmy chuckled beside me and Nana cocked an eyebrow. It was at that moment it wasn't just me who thought I was a jealous psycho. Everybody did. It was almost a relief.

Chief took a deep breath and nodded. "Would you like to meet her? She's actually a decent human being, for a politician. She's even been asking about you. It's not every day that a well-meaning stranger moves into town with lots of money and starts buying properties and helping the locals."

I blushed once again. Wanting to say no, and that I trusted him implicitly, I said, "Yes. I do want to meet this woman."

Seriously? What in the fuck is wrong with me?

"Okay. I'll introduce you sometime."

"Okay."

"All right."

"Yep."

"Dot?"

"Yes?"

"Switch to decaf," he said with a wink and headed for the station.

I sighed, wanting to call him back and apologize. At least I knew I had a problem, and that was half the battle. Turning to Jimmy, I put my head against his chest. He patted me on the head.

"You okay?"

"No. I feel stupid. I don't like feeling stupid."

"Want my honest opinion?"

"I don't know. Do I?"

"I think it's hot when you get jealous, and I'm pretty sure Bill does, too."

"Really?"

"Really."

"Good, because I can't seem to quite control it."

"You should see your mother, dear. They don't call her the Bitch Queen for nothing."

"Yeah. I'm pretty sure you're the only one who calls her that, Nana."

"Hmm. You may be right. Well, I have a house to put together. You children behave yourself."

"Don't blow anything up," I called after her.

"It's Friday. I only blow things up on Tuesdays, Child."

With a cackle, she was off. I'd probably take the secret to my grave, but I was grateful. Grateful she had moved and was around in my life. It made me less homesick, probably because the resemblance to my mother in looks and attitude were uncanny. I couldn't tell her that, either. She'd probably blast me from the face of the earth.

"So, where are we headed?"

"Store. Want to see how Jason is doing."

"You just want to look at his ass."

"You probably do, too."

"I've seen it. It is quite impressive."

"You're an impressive ass, too, sweetie." I patted his arm.

"Um…"

I laughed as we walked the few doors down. He put his arm around me, and I snuggled into his warmth while ignoring Dar in front of us. He had taken point and left the almost overbearing presence of the overprotective vampire to cover our rear.

"Seriously. What is going on?"

"What?" I looked up at him innocently.

15

"Your familiars look like they're waiting for more demons to show up and try to eat us."

"I have no idea."

He narrowed his eyes, but let it go.

He pulled the outer door to the bookstore open for me, the inner door was propped open and I gasped as I got a look inside. Over half of the bookshelves were already in place, un-sanded and un-stained, they were still impressive looking with their naturally dark wood.

"Holy shit," Jimmy said what I was thinking.

"Yeah."

Freddy Johnson had said the shelves were going to be a couple of weeks to install. It had only been a few days…

"Hey, Dot. Whatcha think?" Freddy saw me before I saw him. I walked into the store and saw him in the corner with a couple of workers, fitting a shelf.

"It's beautiful! Holy crap, they're going up fast."

"Well, I thought it was going to take a while to find enough of the same wood. Turns out the lumber mill was filling a *huge* order that was cancelled at the last minute. You *were* in luck."

I smiled, knowing the truth. When he'd told me what he was doing, I may have cast a little bit of a luck spell on him. I was glad to see my magic wasn't getting rusty.

"Isn't that strange."

"Yeah," he said with a chuckle. "You might have the keys to the place next week. Better go check on your boy, though. He was fighting with the licensing department last time I was in the kitchen."

"Oh, boy."

I headed back, Jimmy and my familiars in tow.

Jason was sitting at a makeshift table in the middle of the kitchen. "Hey, handsome."

"Dot!" He stood up and the chair shot back, bumping into the wall and leaving a faint mark on the fresh paint.

"Easy, tiger."

"Sorry. You scared me."

"I have that effect on people."

He gave me a droll look and rolled his eyes. "What are you doing here?"

"Came to check on you. Freddy said you were threatening the nice ladies in the licensing department?"

He grabbed the chair and offered it to me. I shook my head and held up my hand. He turned the laptop to me and sat back down.

"They're claiming that we need to have separate licenses for the bookstore and the coffee shop, which is in a *completely* different world because it's food service. I really need Josie to come by and fill out the forms because it's her ball of wax."

"Oh. That's nothing major. She's at the furniture place. I'll have her park her butt here when she's done."

"That works. Thanks."

"Deep breaths, Jason."

"Yeah, yeah. Just panicking because Freddy is ahead of schedule and I don't want to slow you down."

"Uh… We're witches. Not a problem. Rest of forever and all that."

He nodded, his tense shoulders relaxing with some of the pressure off him. "Well, the good news is you're all incorporated. I made myself a manager, so I hope you don't mind. Unfortunately, First Moon is already a corporation, so now you're Lady of the First Moon, Inc."

"That's kind of sexy," Jimmy said with a grin.

"I like it, too," I told him and walked over, leaning against him as I looked at what else was on the laptop. He had gotten waste management all settled, created accounts with book distributors and food service suppliers. The more I flipped through his open tabs, the more impressed I got. He was doing a fantastic job. "Wow. You've been busy."

"Not busy enough. There's still a ton of shit to get done. I've been working on a…planogram? For the layout of the bookstore. Have time to take a look?"

"Email it to me. I'll look at it tonight."

"Okay."

"What are your plans tonight? Want to come to dinner with us?"

He blushed. "Uh…"

"What?"

"I'd love to. But I have class tonight."

Blinking in surprise, I grinned and hugged him. "Already?"

"Yeah. Classes were just starting up."

"What are you studying?"

"Business management."

I couldn't help it. I sniffed and a tear leaked out, I was so proud of him. "See! Now, even if you get sick of my weird ass, you'll never step foot in another factory again, unless it's to run it!"

He stood up and looked over my shoulder, shy because Jimmy and my familiars were in the room. He leaned over and whispered in my ear, "Like I could *ever* get sick of you."

I pulled his face to mine and kissed him. Hard.

"Hey," he said after pulling away. "Not allowed to kiss me when I'm on the clock."

"You're my boyfriend. I can kiss you whenever the damn hell I want."

"Uh. I am?"

I blinked in confusion.

Woah. Way to jump the gun. I could have kicked myself. *I just assumed…*

"Did you not want to be my boyfriend?"

"Gosh, I don't know. It's so sudden... I mean I like you, but– I'm kidding!" He must have seen the look in my eye, or noticed I stopped breathing. My heart started beating again and he started choking from laughter.

"You're a funny man. Remind me to kill you last."

"Welcome to the club," Jimmy said with a grin over my shoulder.

Chapter 2

"Can I get you something to drink?"

"I'd love a glass of wine!"

I bet you would.

Instead of saying the thought out loud, I just gave her a sickly-sweet smile. Miranda Barton, Josie's mom, wasn't the brightest bulb on the string, and probably thought it was genuine. What I really wanted was a meteor, preferably planet-killer sized, to come down and kill the dinosaur in my living room and put the rest of us out of our misery.

Not that she looked like a dinosaur. Even with her stubby little arms, she was far from it. We were witches. Once we hit our mid-twenties, we stopped aging. Miranda's problem was she wasn't very pleasant looking when she hit twenty-five. She was a witch and she made what she was into who she was, with a vengeance.

I tried not to stare at the pointy, purple hat, green and orange striped leggings, purple dress, and green-tinged makeup. It was almost Yule and she was dressed for Halloween. I was pretty sure she owned ten outfits and they were all the same. Hers was the house that the kids avoided on Halloween. Christmas, weekdays, and weekends, too. Any ball accidentally kicked in her yard was lost forever.

Miranda was the reason Josie practically lived at my house growing up. And probably why she moved four states away with me.

"Would you like anything, Shea?"

"Two glasses of wine?"

I nodded at him, knowingly. He had shared the expense of a moving truck with her and had subsequently spent almost twelve hours trapped in the cab of a vehicle with the crazy witch. He looked like it had been twelve days. "Sure thing."

"I'll get it, Dot," Yuki said and headed for the kitchen, cutting off my escape route. "Would you like one?"

"Please."

Want me to put some arsenic in hers? Yuki asked silently.

I snorted, drawing a confused look from Miranda. *Don't bother. Probably not strong enough to kill her.*

How in the hell is Josie related to that?

Human father. She probably got him drunk and took advantage. Maybe he was hot?

"So, did you find places yet?" I said to make conversation. *Please say yes. Please say yes.*

"I have taken an apartment not far from here," Shea answered.

"I'm going to find Josie and I a cute little house. How is the real estate market, dearie?"

Oh, boy. This isn't going to end well…

Josie needed to hurry her ass home. I'd left her and Candace at the book store. She'd promised to hightail it home as soon as she was done, but I had a feeling she'd left me to do her dirty work.

"Miranda… Josie is planning on staying here. Her and her significant other are quite happy. Why don't you find an apartment, too? It would be easier for you to take care of by yourself." I'd specifically left out the word 'girlfriend' on purpose. She might have expected me to fight the housing battle with her mother, but I'd be damned if I was breaking *that* news to the crazy old bat.

"Oh, don't be silly! Of course, she's going to want to move in with me."

"No. She really doesn't." This was going to be harder than I thought.

"But, why?"

Oh, I don't know. Might be because you're a control freak and take the witch thing a tad too far? Maybe? "The whole *point* of us moving away, other than being driven here by the goddess herself, was to strike out on our own. It was time to become independent witches. Do you think I would let my mother move in with me?"

"You're hardly one to talk. Isn't your grandmother here?"

"In her own house, yes."

"Really?" Her voice rose twenty octaves.

"Really."

"Oh. I did not know that. Do you think she would be interested in a roommate?"

I started chuckling to myself. Evilly. Inside. "Honestly, I don't know, but you should *definitely* ask her, Miranda."

It was totally worth it. Shea's hood fell back, and he looked like he was going to shit a familiar. Even Yuki dropped a wineglass, the shattering sound a prelude to the fireworks that were going to happen when Miranda popped the question to Nana.

"I definitely will!"

Sometimes, I really loved being me.

Until the thought of Nana turning me into a three-petered puppy crossed my mind...

Yep. Still worth it.

Yuki brought some wine over to get us started. "I'll go clean up the mess. Sorry about that, Dot."

"No worries." I shot her a grin.

Dar, who had been sitting next to me, guarding me from the Miranda, gave up and lay down, head covering my feet. *It was nice knowing you. Your grandmother is going to vaporize you.*

I'll just plead innocence. How was I to know she would ask?

Evil.

And its name is Dot, I said with a grin.

"Well, I can recommend the local motel until you get situated. I'd offer you a place here, but we're full. I should add a second story."

"Oh, I don't mind the couch, dearie."

Fuck me. This is never going to end.

"I can stay in your room, Master. Miss Barton can stay in my room."

"Master?" Miranda asked confusedly.

"She's my other familiar." *What are you doing?* I asked Yuki separately.

She's not going away until she has a place. I really don't want to walk out of my bedroom and see that sleeping on the couch. Please?

"You have a vampire…as a familiar?"

"Yes, Miranda. And a…hellhound." I pointed at Dar, not wanting to let her know he was a *demon* who could transform into a hellhound. Not that I knew what he was anyway. Even Nana had never seen his kind before, and I was pretty sure she was from hell, too. I knew my mother was the devil.

"What? How is that possible?"

"Magic."

I looked back at Yuki. She was pleading with her eyes.

Fine. But if you snore, I'm pushing you off the bed.

Yay!

I rolled my eyes.

24

The front door opened, and Josie peeked in. "Hi, *Josie*," I said loud enough for both her, and her charming mother, to hear. Just in case she wanted to run away.

"Hey…Dot. How's it going?"

"Your mom is here," I said, pointing in her direction. Josie could see me from the front door, but not Miranda or Shea. "Come say hi."

"Mom?" Josie tried to sound surprised.

Miranda got up from the couch. "How's my widdle Josie Wosie?"

You're fucking kidding me. Dar lifted his head and stared at the woman, doggy disgust evident on his face. He made a gagging noise that I'm sure had absolutely nothing to do with hair balls.

On second thought, I'll go stay at Nana's. Yuki's mental voice sounded a lot like Dar's gag reflex.

Oh, you're not going anywhere. Either of you.

I'd tell you to send me back to Gehenna, but I'm reasonably sure she might be native to that plane. She smells like a pit fiend and probably farts like a balor.

I spit wine.

Josie walked in with a very afraid-looking Candace hiding behind her. "Hi, Mom. Missed you."

With every bullet apparently. Yuki added.

Yuki!

What? Please. I thought my father was scary…

I think I win that award. I said haughtily.

True story, your mother is *scary. But, this woman…*

She's more annoying than anything.

"So, is this true? You don't want to move in with your mother?"

"It's not that I don't *want* to, Mom. Dot would be completely and utterly lost without me."

I decided to let it slide. If it made her life that much easier, so be it. Apparently, there were no limits what I would do for a friend.

"She cooks like Madeline!" Josie added, almost as an afterthought.

Except that.

"Wait. What?" I stared at her, forming the words for my frog spell. She could get away with a lot of things, but saying I cooked like my mother…

She looked over her shoulder at me and winked.

"Well, I suppose… She obviously needs *someone* to take care of her. And since her grandmother refuses to live with her, not that I blame her, I guess it's up to you."

I poured my glass of wine into my face hole, sucking it down in one swallow. It was going to be that kind of night.

Yuki got up to get me a refill. *Don't forget you have dinner plans. Don't get shit faced.*

I flipped her off when nobody was looking. *Don't tell me what to do.*

Thanksgiving was her only reply. It was enough. One more glass wouldn't hurt, though.

"So, where is this 'significant other' I've been hearing about?"

Oh, boy. Here we go. Don't chicken out, Josie.

"Um…"

There was a moment of silence while Josie internally debated introducing Candace to her mother. I was starting to sweat when she finally took a deep breath and stepped to the side, putting Candace in full view of her mother.

"Well, where is he?"

"She. Where is she. Mom, this is Candace. Candace this is my mother."

"Hello, Miss Barton."

"You?" She turned her confused glance to her daughter. "Wait. You're gay?"

I quietly sucked in a breath, ready to jump in.

"Yeah."

"I can't believe I never knew?" She peeked around her daughter and looked at me.

"No. The sleepovers were just sleepovers." I shook my head and held up my hands.

"You, I could believe. But I'm shocked that my daughter likes girls. She was always so popular and boy crazy."

"Mom…"

"Oh! I'm sorry. It's a pleasure to meet you, dear!" She got up and gave Candace a hug.

Thank the goddess.

"Pleasure to meet you, too, Miss Barton."

"Call me Miranda! Oh, my Lady. You're adorable. You're over eighteen, right?"

"Mom!"

"I'm just checking! She looks young. Especially with those pointed ears… Wait. You're fae?"

Candace nodded.

"Oh, my Lady!"

Shea shuddered and gently rubbed his ear.

Poor Candace. I guess it's better than the alternative.

"You want to take the truck to your place and unload?" I asked Shea, wanting nothing more than to get the hell out of my own house.

He seemed surprised by my question, glanced around, and nodded emphatically. "Please?"

"Come on. We'll let these three get to know each other."

Josie shot me a dirty look and I took great pleasure in ignoring it. "Miranda, have Josie show you where Yuki's room is."

"You're staying here, Mom?"

Miranda blinked. "Just until I find a place."

Josie pulled out her phone. "I'll introduce you to the real estate agent, tomorrow. I should probably go call him *right* now and set up an appointment or something."

I chuckled. "Come on, Shea."

He nodded and practically leapt from the couch. Dar got up and Yuki grabbed my jacket for me.

"Need an extra pair of hands?" Candace looked *desperate.*

"Of course! Come on, sweetie. We'll let Josie and her mom catch up."

Josie's face screamed, *Betrayal!*

"I'll have her home before dinner. I'm going out with the guys tonight."

"Uh. Okay. Thanks, Dot."

"You're welcome!" I put on my coat and herded my herd out the door. Shea pulled out a key ring and headed for the driver's side door of the large moving truck. "You can drive that thing?"

His hood nodded.

"Okay, we'll follow you in my car."

The drive to his apartment only took a few minutes and was down some side streets I'd never seen before. While the neighborhood wasn't exactly posh, it was nicer than most of the areas in Cedar Falls. By far.

"I wish I had known these were here."

"Do you not like your house?" Candace leaned forward between Yuki and me.

"Yes. But this is a pretty nice neighborhood."

"Yes. Doctor Shapiro lives in that house over there."

I looked up, catching her gaze in the mirror. "How do you know that?"

"Christmas party."

"He's a pretty nice guy. For a doctor."

Candace nodded enthusiastically.

"Do you miss working?" When she'd been kidnapped by the evil witch trying to slaughter the vampires, she'd been placed on leave, too.

She shrugged, noncommittally. "Sometimes. I've been there almost ten years. People were starting to take notice of my not aging. It was almost time to move on, anyway."

"That might not be necessary... With the demons and Dar at the diner, we might be out of the closet, anyway. People are going to start talking. It will be interesting to see how all this plays out."

"Interesting."

"Sure. Let's go with that."

Shea pulled into the apartment complex and made a right, parking in front of the first building. I slipped into one of the few open parking spots, relatively close to the truck. By the time we made it back to him, he had the back door open and was sorting through the contents.

"You relieved to be Miranda free?'

"You have no idea. That woman is certifiably insane. I'm amazed her daughter is as stable as she is."

"You're welcome. I raised her as my very own."

"Aren't you two the same age?"

"Well, yes. But, you don't think the woman with striped leggings and a witch hat is responsible, do you?"

"No. You did an excellent job, Lady."

"Call me Dot, Shea."

"Is Shea the fae blooded witch you told me about?" Candace asked curiously.

"I am," he said and pulled back his hood.

Seeing them together was like night and day, which made sense. Shea was a shadow walker. His blood gave him the ability to travel from place to place in our world through the realm of shadow. Candace, with her golden hair and lustrous skin, looked like the sun incarnate. They were both absolutely beautiful, but in different ways.

Shea's hair was much darker, brown bordering on black. His features, while not masculine in the slightest, were far more angular than Candace's delicate, rounded features. Even their eyes were dissimilar. His were shaped like almonds and had an upward tilt. Hers curved more but were tilted under a straighter brow.

"Twinsies." Yuki chuckled next to me.

"They do look quite a bit alike, but they're Ying and Yang."

"Literally."

They both turned to regard Yuki and I, before focusing back on each other. Candace shyly stepped forward and offered him her hand. He bent down and took it, squatting in the back of the packed truck.

"Hello."

"Greetings, Candace."

I half expected sparks to fly from their fingertips when they touched, or something like that. It was almost a disappointment to see them acting normally, even shyly.

Until Candace gasped.

"*Unseleighe sidhe*!"

He held up his hands. "Aye. My father."

I spoke Irish. Without a doubt, she had just called him an elf of the dark court. He was a shadow walker. I wasn't that shocked.

Candace turned and gave me a worried expression. I shrugged my shoulders at her. "I have a demon and a vampire as familiars. Not too worried about the flavors of elf blood running through your veins. Yuki might, but I'm not."

"Hey! I'm not going to eat them."

"Why? It would be like a chocolate *and* vanilla sundae."

"I *am* kind of hungry."

"When was the last time you ate?"

"A few days ago."

"Do you think you'd still be welcome to feed with George and the other vampires?"

"Probably not."

"So, I need to set something up with your father."

Yuki blushed, telling me all I needed to know. I'd do it as soon as we got Shea settled into his apartment. I mentally kicked myself for not asking sooner. I *was* supposed to be taking care of her.

Focusing my attention back to the fae, I grinned at their reaction. They were still holding hands but staring at Yuki and I like we were monsters. "I was kidding! She's not going to eat you!"

"Just a nibble?"

"Yuki."

"Sorry. Couldn't resist."

Candace shook her head and realized she was still holding Shea's hand, letting go and wiping her palm off on her jacket. I wasn't sure if Shea had sweaty palms or she just didn't like touching the dark elf. I hoped it was the sweat.

"Come on. Let's get your stuff moved in."

Shea nodded and stood, sorting through the boxes. "All of my things are here, by the door. The rest belongs to Miranda."

"Why didn't you use magic trunks? You could have just rented a car instead of a moving truck."

"I have many volatile items that do not take kindly to being magically compressed into five-dimensional spaces. I had planned on walking everything into my apartment, but that woman insisted on a...road trip...I believe she called it. Had I not been worried about the sheer amount of power I'd have expended shadow walking, I would never, ever, have agreed."

31

"I'd wondered. I just figured it was because Miranda can be so damn pushy. Ten bucks says I have to forcibly remove her from my place within a week."

Candace sighed and slumped to the ground.

"It won't be that bad, sweetie."

"I see how she talks about *you*, the high priestess of our coven, and I get upset. If she talks that way about me…"

"I won't let her."

She looked up at me, blinking back tears. She stood back up and walked over to hug me around my stomach. "Thank you."

Shea was watching our exchange, curiously. When he noticed me looking at him, he began stacking boxes by the door.

"Take a break, Shea. Go open your apartment so we can start moving the boxes while you sort."

He stopped and nodded, jumping nimbly down from the truck. "It's right here on the first floor."

"Yay. No stairs."

He led us toward the stair well, heading for the first door on the right behind it. He whispered something to the lock, and it clicked and opened with a rush of warm air. Another whisper and dim lights illuminated the already furnished apartment.

I'd expected a modern look to his apartment and furniture, but nearly everything was ancient and made solely from wood. Cushions had been spread around for comfort, not décor. It was positively medieval, and I was in love.

"Your apartment is awesome!"

He bowed. "Thank you."

"How is your furniture here already?"

"I shadow walked what I could."

"You dragged all this here by yourself?"

"Furniture, I could magick."

"Ahh. I see. Well, let's get the rest of your stuff unloaded."

He nodded and led the way back outside. I almost slipped on the walkway. Building maintenance had salted everything, but I happened to find the spot they missed. If it weren't for Yuki, I probably would have tasted the walkway.

"Thanks."

"What I'm here for."

"Keep me from busting my ass?"

"Yep."

I chuckled as we walked back to the truck.

It didn't take us long to get the boxes inside. Between Yuki, Candace, and I, we made short work of it. Less than a quarter of the moving truck was filled with Shea's boxes. The rest were Miranda's. I fervently hoped they didn't split the cost of the truck evenly. I found it amusing he'd been roped into driving with her, but if she took advantage of another member of our coven… I'd be less than happy. I had no plans of prying, but if Shea complained, I would take action.

"All right. That was easy."

"I thank all of you for your help," Shea said with a little bow as he locked up his apartment. He was going to drive the truck back to my house and shadow walk home. I was almost jealous of his ability. I'd save a ton on gas, not that I had to worry about it, but still.

We made it halfway down the walkway when I noticed the arrow protruding from my chest, the feathers twined around the shaft fluttered in the light cold breeze. Focusing on the vibrant white color, the rest of my vision started to fade to black until they were the only things I could see. My heartbeat, wooshing through my ears, the only thing I could hear.

Except for Candace's sweet scream.

Even filled with terror, it reverberated musically off the buildings around us, driving my tunneled vision out a little and giving me a little more focus.

I wanted to feel the softness of those feathers before I left. I reached out to run my fingers along their edge, until my survival instinct kicked in. Grabbing the shaft instead, I yanked the arrow from my chest.

Blood splattered on the walkway beneath me as the barbed hook of the tip ripped the wound open a little wider. Dropping the arrow, I fell to my knees after it. I couldn't breathe. The pain blossoming in my chest drove all the air from my lungs. My heartbeat picked up speed. I could hear it clearly and focused solely on that and the small patch of walkway I could see. Feet shuffled all around me as hands tried to lift me from the ground. Shrugging them off, I concentrated on trying to draw in a breath. If I could just do that, the pain in my head would fade and I could think again.

Slowly, the icy shards slid past my throat, inflating my chest. I was doing it, the cold air hurting as much as it helped. My heartbeat slowed and became more normal as I exhaled and inhaled again, repeating it over and over until the world around me shifted back into focus.

"She's still alive! Candace, can you heal her?" Yuki's voice held an edge of panic that hurt my heart. More than the arrow had. I lifted my left hand off the frozen ground and touched my chest, feeling the warm blood saturating my shirt and the hole in the fabric. Pressing further, I searched for a wound that was no longer there.

The arrow hadn't killed me, and I'd healed, thanks to having a vampire familiar.

"Let me guess, wooden stakes don't kill vampires," I managed to croak out through my still raw throat.

"What? No?"

I got a foot underneath me, and lifted myself up off the ground, still swaying and dizzy. "That fucking hurt."

"How are you still alive?"

Turning my head, I cocked an eyebrow at the vampire still steadying me.

"Oh. Well that's good." She nodded emphatically.

"Where's Dar?"

"He took off after the elf."

"Elf?" Shea and Candace asked simultaneously.

"Go," I told Yuki. "Bring him back."

"The elf?"

I shook my head. "Dar."

She made a grim face, but nodded, taking off in the direction he went with inhuman speed. The gust of wind that washed over me was enough to give me shivers.

"Help me to the car."

"Are you going to be okay?"

"Yeah. I'm mostly fine, just drained."

Doubt crossed Shea's face, but he didn't utter a word. He lifted my arm and slid underneath it, using his shoulders as a crutch. By the time he got me to the vehicle, I was practically panting. Getting shot with an arrow takes a lot out of a girl.

Instead of putting me in the driver's seat, he eased me gently into the passenger's side and tilted the seat back, fussing over me. He even put my seatbelt on.

He was squinting in the late afternoon sunlight, but his eyes were as beautiful as the rest of him, caramel colored but glinting like amber. "You have pretty eyes."

He blinked in surprise. "Thank you, Lady."

"If you don't start calling me Dot, I'm going to start calling you Sheamus."

"But that is not my name…"

"And Lady isn't mine."

He nodded, the curve of a soft smile touching the corner of his lip. "You are very beautiful, too."

"My eyes?"

"Your everything."

Blame it on the blood loss, or at least that's what I was going to tell myself, but I blushed. "Says the gorgeous hunk of fae tucking me in."

"I am far from a hunk. More like piece. A smidgeon?"

He was referring to his smaller stature, I knew. While most of the men in my life were near, or over, six-feet. Shea was an inch or two shorter than me. He was still gorgeous, but fun-sized.

Next time he calls me Lady, I'm calling him Snickers.

"If you were any bigger, the world wouldn't be able to handle that much hotness."

He gasped in surprise. "You are too kind."

"No. I'm kind of a bitch. Just ask Chief."

"You're only that way when he aggravates you. I noticed. Otherwise, you are kind, caring, and fierce. I admire you quite a lot. So unlike your mother."

"Wow. That's the nicest thing anybody has ever said to me."

"That you are kind and caring?"

"No. That I'm unlike my mother."

He shook his head, unable to tell if I was joking, but gently laughing anyway.

I reached up, the overwhelming urge to touch his skin almost painful. Sighing contentedly when my fingers brushed his cheek, I passed out.

Chapter 3

The taste of blood in my mouth and overwhelming heat woke me up. I pushed Yuki's arm away and tried to crawl out from under the dog covering most of me.

"What happened? Ew. Get me something to wash that down."

"Are you saying I don't taste good?"

I shot her a dirty look. She'd been hanging around with Josie too much. "I just don't like the taste of blood. Period."

"Oh. *So* many more jokes, so little time," she said and snickered.

"That's disgusting."

"That's what she said."

"Oh, my goddess. Will you *stop*." I stared at her in disbelief. She really *was* hanging out with Jimmy too much.

Yuki chuckled and got up off the bed. "Feel better?"

"Yeah. Dar get off me. You're hot."

Thank you.

I kind of wanted to scream. "What happened?"

"We brought you home. Shea drove. He went back for the moving truck. Jimmy called and he is on his way to pick you up for dinner, so we juiced you back to full health."

"What? Why? I could have canceled dinner."

"And break the hearts of your boyfriends?"

"Huh?"

"They have something planned tonight. We don't know what, but Dar overheard them talking about it earlier."

"Oh. Well help me up so I can get changed."

"And showered. Unless you want to go smelling like a blood bath."

"Uh. No. Shower. Help me to the shower. Wait! The elf! What happened?"

Dar growled. *He got away.*

In a way, I was glad. While it would have been nice to have had a solution to my extermination problem, I didn't want them doing it on their own. If anything ever happened to them, I'd feel horrible. I wouldn't die like they would if I kicked the bucket, but I'd feel like shit about it.

I grabbed her hand and she hoisted me to my feet. I was still a little wobbly, but that might have just been the after effects of drinking vampire blood. She ushered me into the bathroom and helped me get out of my shirt. She let me do my leggings by myself but held me upright. I was grateful. When I stood up, the room spun a little.

"Woah."

"It will wear off."

I reached into the shower and turned it on, letting the hot water get a little warmer before getting in. Yuki lifted off her shirt next to me.

"Uh. Whatcha doin?"

"Taking a shower?"

"With me?"

"Do you want Dar to do it?"

"I'll be fine."

"On wet tile?"

"Yuki…"

"I'm going to *help* you. When I say that I am not in the least attracted to you, or anybody for that matter, I mean it."

She bent over and pushed her pants down to her feet.

I gave a little gasp when she stood back up. "See? Just a flat-chested girl that's going to keep you on your feet."

She wasn't kidding. She was definitely smaller than an A cup, but anything larger would have been too much for her slight frame. However, there was nothing boyish about her figure. Her hips, thighs, and stomach were perfect. I found myself a little envious of her figure. "You're beautiful."

"Um. Thanks?"

Shaking my head, I got in the shower. I'd just washed my hair that morning, so I squirted a bit of body wash on my loofa and scrubbed the dried blood off me. True to her word, Yuki's hands hovered by my elbows, ready to catch me if I fell.

"You and Josie never showered together?"

"Yeah, but we've been friends for almost a hundred years."

"But she's sexually attracted to you."

"Yeah. But I'm not attracted to her and she knows that."

"But you don't feel weird getting naked in front of her?"

"Nope."

"You get naked in front of your whole coven regularly, so I can see that. Why were you hesitant about getting in the shower with me?"

"Because… I don't know. Interesting things happen when I get in showers with other people."

"But not Josie."

I sighed. Unable to explain it. "Josie is like a perverted little sister. She might say she's attracted to me, but if push came to shove, she would never try anything. Don't feel bad. I wouldn't shower with Candace, either."

"But you sleep naked with her?"

"Are you just being a pest, or are you really curious?"

"Just trying to understand. Bathing in Japan is… It's a lot different. Here, hand me your sponge thing."

I handed it to her over my shoulder, expecting her to wash herself. I gasped as she started scrubbing my back with it.

"I understand. Now that I've showered with you, I would never have a problem with it. It was just a shock."

She slowly worked her way down my back and stopped above my butt. "Americans are weird."

"Oh, shut up. You're American, too."

"But I was born and raised over there. We moved when I was in my thirties."

That came as a shock. "How old are you?"

"I was born just after the end of World War II. I'll be seventy-four my next birthday."

"Woah."

"You thought I was younger?"

"Yeah. But time is different for us, so not too shocked."

"Rinse."

I turned around, facing her and let the water rinse the soap from my back, holding my hair out of the way. "Thanks, Yuke."

"For?"

"Everything."

"*Hai.*"

"I think that might have been the first time I ever heard you speak Japanese."

"Meh. The only people around me who understand are my mother and George. Even my father doesn't."

"I didn't think he looked very Japanese."

"With the name Abernathy? Try Scots."

"He doesn't look Scottish, either."

"He looks like himself. He's *very* old. Even older than your mother, I think. I don't know for sure."

"You going to get clean?"

"I am. I was just helping you."

I reached over and shut the water off. She held out her hand to help me out of the shower, but I shook my head and smiled. "I'm fine now. Thanks."

I opened the door and stepped out, nearly screaming. Jimmy was standing in the bathroom door, arms crossed, eyebrow cocked, and a very perverted look on his face.

"Uhhh…"

Yuki did squeak when she stepped out, hiding behind me.

"That's hot," he said and turned around, leaving the two of us standing there.

"Great." I sighed.

"You worried he's going to get the wrong idea?"

"No. I'm worried how much this is going to drive his teenage-boy libido into hyperdrive. If I'm walking funny tomorrow, you know why."

She giggled behind me.

"Laugh it up. He saw you naked."

"Yes, but between the steak and the cutting board, where do you think he was looking."

I rounded on her and flashed her a stern look. "No."

"No?"

"No."

"No what?"

"No. You don't get to do that, Yukina Abernathy. Ever." I reached out and cupped her cheek. "You may not be interested in sex, but don't think for one minute that you are not beautiful in every way. I mean that."

"I see that."

"Huh?"

"When you touched me, I could feel your sincerity." She was blushing, but she broke my damn heart when the tear rolled down her cheek. I didn't care if we were both naked. I wrapped her in my arms and hugged her. We stayed that way for a few moments until she tapped my shoulder.

"I'm okay now."

"Good." I let go and grabbed a couple of towels out of the linen closet. I was going to need to mop the floor, but it had been worth it.

"Go get dressed. I'll clean up in here."

"Yeah. I need to get out there before Candace spills the beans about the elf."

"Dar and I told them not to say anything, per your request."

"Really? I figured passing out would have given you guys free reign to tattle on me."

"Standing orders. We tried."

"Sweet."

"I'm kidding. We probably could have told them, but we chose not to."

"Why?"

"Because *you* are our master, whether you like the title or not. We might not agree with your logic, or lack thereof, but we will do as you ask." She bowed her head.

"I'll tell them. Eventually."

"That would be wise. He'll try again."

"Well, he's going to have to try harder. Since arrows don't work."

"Yeah, but if he gets close enough with a sword to take your head and heart…"

"I'm done for?"

She nodded. "Fire, too. But, you're still a witch. I'm sure strangulation, drowning, and other fun things like that would do the job."

"Well, that sucks."

"Poison might work."

"You can stop now."

"Crushing. Stay away from Zambonis and steamrollers."

"Okay, Yuki." I left her there, drying herself off, and headed into my bedroom.

"Don't go skydiving, either. Or tall buildings…"

I went in my closet and shut the door.

∞ ∞ ∞

"Where are we going?" I asked Jimmy for the tenth time.

"It's a surprise."

"But… I hate surprises."

"I don't. Like walking in on your girlfriend taking a shower with another woman? That was *awesome*."

"And…here we go."

"What?"

"Was waiting to see how long it took you to bring that up. I told you. I was a little dizzy and she was making sure I didn't slip on the tile."

"Uh, huh."

"I swear!"

"Don't gotta explain to me."

"You're right. I don't."

"Ouch."

"Sorry." I sighed and looked around, trying to guess where we were heading, but he had made three left turns, just to go right. He was circling around to keep me disoriented. I didn't know the town well enough to guess. If it wasn't on Main, I probably hadn't seen it.

"So, how come you were dizzy?"

"I don't know. Probably just hungry. Hurry up."

43

"You're not…" He looked down at my belly.

"What? Hell *no.* You know witches can't get preggers unless they want to."

"Do you?"

"What?"

"Want to get pregnant."

"Do you?"

"Want you to be pregnant?"

"No. Want to die. Shut the ever-loving hell up. I'm *not* having a baby anytime this century."

Dar chuckled from the back seat.

I looked over my shoulders and gave him a withering stare. He put his head back down on the back seat, and I continued staring until he gave me an apologetic doggy look.

"So, back to Yuki. Is the reason you brought Dar along because you don't feel comfortable around her after taking advantage of her in the shower?"

"I'm going to kill you. Keep it up, Mr. Jokerman."

"What? I'm just asking."

"No. You're fantasizing. Big difference."

"Yep. I was. Probably will be tonight, too. Definitely tomorrow morning."

"Good. Then you'll have something to occupy yourself while you're sleeping alone."

"Are you mad?"

"Are you still breathing? If I *were* mad, that would be the first indication."

"*Touché.*"

Jamming my elbow on the door, I used my arm to prop my head up. I loved Jimmy's crazy ass. But, sometimes, he could be a bit much.

"*Hypothetically…*"

"Choose your next words very carefully, Jimbo."

"I was just going to say, suppose you came over to *my* house and I'm nowhere to be found. You hear the shower running and you decide to surprise the love of your life. You pad quietly into the bathroom and find Dennis washing *my* back. Would you believe me if I told you he was there to help me not fall because I was dizzy?"

I nearly gasped at the shiver of pleasure that ran through me picturing *that* scene in my head. There was no way in hell I was going to tell him that, though. "Oh, no way. You guys were totally doing it. And you liked it."

"No way. It hurts at first."

"What?"

"What?"

"Jiiimmy…"

"I'm kidding. Don't worry. If I ever have sex with my best friend, I'll tell you. I expect you to do the same."

"There's something very wrong with you. But you have a deal. I want videos though or it didn't happen."

"Same." He reached over and we shook on it. I couldn't get the goofy ass smile off my face.

I groaned as we pulled into Bunyan's parking lot.

"Surprise!"

"Really? You had to take the covert way to take me to Bunyan's? I don't know if you thought about this, but the idea of putting meat in my mouth right now isn't exactly a good idea."

"Well, that's boring."

I slapped him in the arm. "No innuendo. What happened the last time I ate steak?"

"You ate two of them. Messily."

"Yes. Do you think I want to do that in the middle of a restaurant?"

Dar chuckled again in the back seat.

I ignored him.

"Hadn't thought about that. But, we're here. And it's not the where, it's the who."

"What is?"

"Your surprise."

"I know. It's Chief."

He pointed out the windshield.

Chief was standing outside by the door, next to another guy of slightly smaller stature. A man with shoulder-length, wavy brown hair, chiseled jaw, and stunning good looks. A man who had ditched me forty years ago to move to another country with his mother…

"Derek?"

"Surprise!" Jimmy chuckled and pulled into a parking spot.

There was no way in hell I was getting out of the truck. "No!"

"You're not hungry?"

My stomach growled. "James Whateveryourmiddlenameis Duncan. There is no fucking way I'm going to go into a *steak* house with the three of you. You saw what I was like! You saw how Derek looked at me when he found out I had two boyfriends. What the hell do you think is going to happen if I start munching moo-moo like a deranged sociopath, cuddled in between the two of you?"

"First of all, Dean. Second of all, there will be three of us."

"Dean what?"

"My middle name. It's Dean."

"Like James Dean?"

"Not like, is."

"I liked your mother. How could she do that to you?"

"I asked her that, myself."

"But what about the sociopathic bovine feeding frenzy?"

"I'm sure you'll be *way* too nervous to slip into a frenzied state. In fact, I bet Chief twenty bucks that you would hardly be able to form sentences. Come on. This should be fun!"

"You keep using that word. I don't think it means what you think it means."

Chapter 4

"Wine for the lady."

Chelsea set my glass of wine down on the table in front of me. The freshly-washed glass immediately left a wet ring on the paper tablecloth. I stared at it in utter fascination, not wanting to look up at Chief and Derek sitting next to each other on the other side of the booth. I could feel Chief's grin from across the table. That damnable little quirky smirk of his. I loved it, but not under the hellish pressures of what the two of them were putting me through.

That was what bothered me the most. Chief thought he was just being a darn swell guy! Taking me out with the ex-boyfriend he had taken an immediate dislike to, to bury the hatchet. Show me he was a bigger man than that.

Fucking boy scout.

And Jimmy…he was just along for the show. He *knew* this was going to blow sky-high and he was solely there for entertainment value. I'd take it out on him later.

Fucking shit disturber.

"Are you ready to order or do you need a few minutes?"

"Chicken."

"Pardon me?"

"Do you have…chicken?" The smell of steak in the air was slowly driving me insane. I wanted an eighty-ounce porter house, medium raw with a side of au jus as my

49

beverage selection. But, I was going to eat frickin' chicken and drink wine. My safe word was pineapples. All I had to do was say it and Jimmy would whisk me from the restaurant, bound and gagged if needed. I made sure he understood that last part. *If needed.*

"Um. Yes. The Montreal Chicken is quite popular."

With the fucking herbivores. "What's that?"

"Chicken."

"I know that. What kind of chicken?"

"Well, it's boneless chicken breast topped with shredded Montreal smoked meat, cheese curds, and gravy."

"Give me a steak."

"You don't want the chicken?"

Chelsea was going to fucking die.

"She'll have the prime rib, king cut, rare. No veggies or potato. Hurry," Jimmy ordered for me.

I nodded, emphatically.

"What would you gentlemen like?"

"I'll have the T-bone. Baked sweet potato and asparagus. Medium on the steak and another beer."

"Sure thing, Chief." She giggled. They were seriously going to be one person short on their waitstaff in about thirty-eight seconds.

"I'll be havin' tha smoked brisket, baked potato. Do ya have any other green vegetables other than tha asparagoos?"

Chelsea stared at Derek. She shook her head. "I'm sorry. What did you say?"

"Smoked brisket."

"Smoked brisket," she repeated, finally remembering to write that part down. She was lost in his eyes and was being warmed from within by his silky voice. I knew. I'd been there.

"Po-ta-to."

"Butter and sour cream or loaded?" she asked with a sultry chuckle. If she didn't stop, she'd be asking with a bloody gurgle.

"Just booter."

"Aye. I mean *yes*. Sorry. Your accent is just like…wow."

My head dropped to the table. My forehead banging against it hard enough to jostle my wineglass.

"Are you okay?"

"She's had a little too much to drink."

"Aye, she does that quite offen."

"Shut up, Derek," I said with my forehead pressed against the coolness of the paper-covered table.

"Just bring me anythin'."

"I'll have the same as Chief," Jimmy said with an over-amused voice.

"Okay! I'll get your orders in right away."

"Thanks, Chelz," Chief answered her, practically pushing her toward the kitchen.

"What jus happed? Dot, are ya okay?"

"Fine. Just leave me here to die."

"Pineapples?"

I could hear the worry in Jimmy's voice. I raised my hand above me and shook my hand. Chelsea, of the grating voice and flirty ass, was gone. Maybe I could make it through dinner.

"What da pineapples have ta do wit anythin'?"

"I'll be right back." I lifted my head from the table. "You *two*, explain to him what is going on and why taking me to a steak restaurant was a horrible idea. That way if I start gnawing on the wood table, he'll know why."

Leaving them sitting there and staring at each other was the wisest decision I'd made all week.

I slipped outside without my coat, wanting nothing more than to cool down a little. I felt like I was burning up

51

from the inside out, and it had little to do with Derek's voice.

I blinked as the truck door opened across the lot and a very naked Dar stepped out. Without so much as a glance around him, he shifted back into shepherd form and trotted across the way.

You okay?

"Yeah. I just needed to get some air. The smell of meat was killing me."

I feared this would happen. I've been back for only a day and the changes are coming upon you again.

"Well, it seems to be limited to red meat. Honestly, the thought of chicken kind of turned my stomach."

You want to hunt, and a piece of undercooked meat is as close as you can get. If you feel any other…desires. Let me know at once.

"Yes, sir."

I intended no disrespect. I worry.

I scratched his head, just above his eyes. He pressed his face into my hand, enjoying the sensation. "I know, Dar."

The door opened behind me and my boys and Derek stood there, looking at me sheepishly and holding four takeout containers and my coat.

"Sorry, Dot. I didn't think." Chief gave me a sad smile.

"Sorry, Dot. I didna know."

"Sorry, Dot. I'm just me," Jimmy gave me a contrite smile.

"Wait. How the hell did you get the food so fast?"

"My friend is working tonight. We changed our orders to four prime ribs and potatoes. He carved it himself and put it together when I told him you weren't feeling well," Chief explained.

"Aww. That was nice of him. Did you tell him to fire Chelsea?"

"*No*," he said with a little chuckle of disbelief, thinking I was joking.

I let it go.

"Well, you two follow us."

I blinked at Chief.

"Okay," Jimmy answered him and led us back to the truck, not even giving me a chance to ask where we were going.

"Um. Where are we going?" I asked once we were in the truck.

"Chief's."

"Huh?"

"Bill's. The man with the brown shirt that says police on it. You know the guy with the really big—"

"Jimmy."

"Nightstick?"

He probably *heard* me roll my eyes. "I've never seen his place. You been there?"

"Couple of times."

Instead of asking, I went with the flow. Luckily Chief had taken all the food with him so I wasn't trapped in a moving vehicle with beef-scented Dot-nip.

We turned on Main and headed in the opposite direction from my house. Chief caught the greenlight at Maple and made it through, but it turned yellow just before we would have been close enough to actually make it.

"Shit."

"It's okay. I can't smell it anymore. I can wait to eat now."

"It bothers you that much?"

"It doesn't *bother* me, it drives me insane. I get this surge of carnal urges…"

"Carnal urges?"

"Not those kind. The rip flesh with my face kind."

"That's much less fun."

"Not when you're eating."

"True."

Somebody stepped out into the crosswalk and started across the street. They were bundled against the cold in a long leather cloak that seemed pretty far out of place in Cedar Falls. He looked like an escapee from a renaissance faire. I almost chuckled until I put two and two together…

"Gun it!"

"What?"

He didn't draw a bow this time, finally understanding the futility of it. Instead he pulled his glowing hands out of his pockets and brought them down in a flaming arc toward the hood of the truck.

Jimmy slapped it into reverse and stomped on the gas at the same time. I reached over and put my hand on his arm, the words of a stoneskin spell on my lips.

The engine whined as the gas flowed into the engine and the transmission caught, whining as it slipped into gear. The tires didn't spin, but chirped as we surged backward. The tip of the elf's finger grazed the front of the truck, leaving a glowing scorch mark.

"What the fuck is that?"

"Elven assassin."

"Are you kidding me?"

He was doing about thirty-five, backward down Main Street by looking in the rearview mirror. I couldn't even back out of my driveway without turning my head around. I was officially impressed.

His hand reached up and grabbed the gear shift. "Hang on," he said and jerked the wheel. As we spun in an arc in the middle of the street, he put it back in drive and gunned it. This time the wheels did spin as we slung sideways, finally catching and thrusting us forward, in the opposite direction of Chief's and the murderous elf.

"How do you know it was an elven assassin?"

Now you're in trouble.

Shut up, dog.

Unfortunately, he was right. I *was* in trouble.

"I'm only going to do this once. Go to Chief's. I'll explain there."

∞ ∞ ∞

"What? Why?" Chief didn't know if he wanted to be angry or confused. He went with the latter option...first.

"Don't ask me."

"How do you know?"

"Well, this isn't the first time." I sighed, leaned back and took a swig of my beer. *Cue the outrage in three...two...one and go!*

He used his right hand to rub his face before pushing his chair up and walking out of the kitchen. Jimmy and Derek sat at the kitchenette table with me. Jimmy was sipping at his beer and picking at his food. Derek was happily shoveling meat and potatoes in his mouth, and I was afraid to open my container until I got the news out.

Chief walked back in the kitchen. "How many times?"

"For?"

"How many times has this elf tried to kill you."

"Once or twice."

"Which is it."

"Twice."

"And we're just hearing about this now?"

"Twice before tonight."

"So three?"

"Yeah."

He left the room again, hands on his hips. His heavy footfalls echoed through the quaint little two-bedroom house. His house had been a total surprise. I'd expected deer heads, beer cans, and a hunting lodge motif. His deceased wife must have decorated the place. There were doilies *everywhere*. The couch even had a hand knitted afghan draped across the back of it. It was cute...in an eighty-year-old, grandmotherish sort of way. I felt bad for cringing, though.

But there were the pictures of them together. It was hard to be jealous of a dead ex-wife, but I managed to do it, spectacularly. I caught myself snarling at a framed eight-by-ten of her on the fireplace mantel. She didn't have to be so damn gorgeous.

"Is he angry?"

"Yes, Derek... He's pissed."

"Why did'n ya tell im?"

"Because he gets like this."

"Damned if ye do, damned if ye don't?"

"Something like that."

The bootsteps were heading back our way. I took another sip of beer and shot Jimmy a tired look. He was angry, too, but would *never* say anything in front of anybody else. He'd wait until we were alone and then logically list his reasons for being disappointed. I wasn't sure which was worse.

"How are you still alive? I've seen the movies. Elves don't miss."

"Well... He did. Except the one time."

Chief strode forward. "What?"

"He got me, Chief. He got me real good."

"Dot, I swear upon my life, you are one joke away from me shooting you, myself."

I opened the container. Maybe the novelty of them watching me eat would deflect some of the hostility I was sensing. "When I was helping Shea move. When we finished, I was walking back to the car and...he was waiting across the way."

56

Chief took two more steps and closed the lid to my takeout container. "No food. Talk."

"But I'm *hungry*."

He sighed and I thought he was going to capitulate, until he picked up the Styrofoam container and put it on the kitchen counter behind him. "Where?"

"In the apartment complex."

"No. I mean, where did he hit you?" He snarled in frustration.

"In the chest. With an arrow."

Not caring who was around, he reached down and unbuttoned my shirt. Luckily, I'd worn my pretty bra. He leaned forward, looking for the wound. Surprisingly, he reached out and ran his finger over the faint white lines where I'd ripped the arrow out.

He shifted his eyes up to mine and his mouth dropped open. "He got you in the fucking heart?"

"Just a little."

"A little?"

"What can I say? I'm a quick healer."

He backed up a step, still bent over, putting his hands on his knees and staring at me incredulously. "How?"

"Guess he was a good shot."

"That's not what I fucking meant, and you know it."

"Vampire healing."

"Even a vampire wouldn't have survived that."

"It turns out, they would. I got a rundown from Yuki. Apparently, you have to cut off their head *and* cut out their heart. She didn't advise me to get run over and squished, or eat poison, though. She wasn't sure how that would affect me."

Dar chuckled from beneath me.

Chief glowered down at my dog. "You knew about this?"

57

Dar sighed. He got up off the floor and went straight from canine to blue demon. Derek choked on his steak when he saw the naked, horned man standing in front of him. I turned my head. Dar was…rather handsome. And at eye level.

Jimmy was wiggling his eyebrows at me.

I sighed and turned to look at Derek. At least he had clothes on and wasn't a pervert.

"Yes. I was the one who stopped the first arrow."

"But not the second."

"No. She was ahead of me and the elf fletched his arrows with owl feathers. I did not hear it coming. I am sorry." He bowed.

Don't bow. You have nothing to apologize for, I told him.

I failed you.

I'm still breathing. The other team is bound to get a lucky shot in once in a while. Plus, it made him change tactics, which is a good thing. Arrows hurt.

"It's not your fault. It's hers. She should have told us!"

"Why?" *Everyone's* attention shifted to Derek who had asked the question around a mouthful of steak.

"Because she was in danger! She's always doing shit like this. Shouldering everything by herself, never asking for help, always putting herself in harm's way. Do you have any idea how frustrating that is?"

He nodded. "As a matter of fact, I do, Chiefy." He finished chewing his morsel, setting his fork and knife down on the table. "But, do ye think it's any less frustratin' fer her?" He paused to push his chair back, grabbed his beer bottle and hopped up on the counter, perching and taking a long swig. We were in for a speech and I was curious as to what he was going to say.

"Comfy?" Chief cocked an eyebrow.

"Aye. Where was I? Oh, yes. There's one thing ya need to be knowin' about our precious Dorothea. She doesn't give a shit about yer sensibilities. That's not how she was raised. Blame her ma, blame her nan, but she was taught to be more than self-sufficient. She was taught to handle her own damned problems. So, unless ye want ta piss her off, my suggestion would be to stop *tryin'* ta coddle her."

I clapped.

It was totally inappropriate, but damn if his speech didn't totally remind me of why I fell in love with Derek in the first place. He didn't worship me. He didn't see me as some sort of princess that needed a royal guard. He saw me as a witch and saw me as an equal.

I stopped clapping when I saw Chief's face.

Derek handed me my container of food.

"I don't coddle her!"

Even Jimmy laughed.

"Do I?"

I nodded, practically ripping the lid off. "Most of the time I find it charming. But, when shit gets sour, you have a tendency of being overbearing and kind of dickish."

He sat down with a hard *thump*.

"Don't feel bad, Bill. I get cranky when she gets hurt, too," Jimmy said and patted my leg.

"I'm sorry," Chief said, quietly.

I looked up in confusion, making sure it was Chief who had said it. "Wha?"

"I said I'm sorry. For being overbearingly dickish."

"Well, you do have an abundance of dick," Jimmy said and chortled.

I punched his thigh. "You're oversharing again, sweetie."

"Oops."

Derek blinked in confusion, settled his eyes on Chief and smirked. "Well, now. That's settled. Shall we let Dot eat in peace?"

Nervously cutting a piece off my rib, I popped it in my mouth. I wanted to cry because it tasted like the wing of an angel, but I didn't tear into it like a ravenous she-beast. I smiled and chewed happily.

Jimmy looked disappointed. If I were being honest with myself, Chief did, too.

Perverts.

Chapter 5

"You coming in?"

"Do you want company or are you tired? You did almost die twice today. That takes a lot out of a witch."

"I ate. I'm fine."

"Okay." Jimmy put his truck into park and shut off the engine.

"Thanks for a wonderful evening."

"Yeah. That was fun, huh?"

We laughed and got out of the truck. "Not what you were expecting?"

"Nope," he answered.

"Well, I'm sure your expectations had something to do with three naked men pleasuring me senseless." I put my key in the lock and turned it, trying to hurry because my eyelashes were freezing. By the time the door opened, I was shivering. I let Jimmy and Dar in and shut the door, throwing the lock back on and casting a little bit of a sealing spell. It wasn't for the cold, it was for any unwanted elven guests. Kicking off my shoes, I stood by the door and let the magic flow from me into the house, kicking up the defenses and wards. Safe was better than sorry.

"Expecting a thermonuclear attack?"

"What?"

"I'm no mega-witch like you. I have trouble even *seeing* energy flows. But, it feels like you just sealed us inside NORAD." He was looking up at the ceiling with a glazed look in his eyes. "Lady bless, Dot. That's a hell of a shield."

I shrugged. "Chief's got me all paranoid. It would be my luck, the minute he decides to let me be, that I would get attacked and end up on the pointy end of an elven sword."

"Good call."

"Yeah. If I died, I'd never hear the end of it."

"You can knock *that* off, *Mrs.* Jokerman."

"That better not be a marriage proposal."

"Nope. Don't worry. When, and if, I do, it will be *spectacular.* Lots of surprise, probably a flash-mob or two. Music. And baby platypuses."

"Baby platypuses?"

"They're fucking adorable. You won't be able to say no, inundated by their cuteness. You'll be begging me to marry *you*."

"You're evil."

"Only on Thursdays."

I laughed and slid my jacket off, tossing it on the hook by the door. Jimmy hadn't gotten his off yet, but I hugged him anyway, wrapping my arms through it and around him, pressing my face against his chest.

"Love you," he whispered and kissed the top of my head.

I grinned and rubbed my face against him more. "Love you, too. Even on Thursdays."

I felt his chuckle in his chest.

"Oh. It's the love birds." Josie was standing by the kitchen, arms crossed and tapping her foot. She looked like she had run a marathon. Through a pack of hyenas, wearing pork chop leg warmers. Not that she was tore up, just emotionally exhausted.

"You okay?"

"*No*," she hissed and quietly stamped her foot.

"Oh, sweetie." I let go of Jimmy and practically ran over to her, hugging her tightly. "Mom?"

She nodded against me, sniffling.

"Where is she?"

"She finally drank enough wine to pass out. Yuki picked her up and threw her in her room. You're out of wine, by the way."

"That's okay. It was for a good cause."

"We need to find her a place. In Albuquerque. *Before* she wakes up and can find her way back here."

"I'm sorry. I tried to get her to stay at a hotel. Was it that bad?"

"She won't shut up. Ever."

At least I knew where Josie got it from. "That sounds horrible."

"Don't joke. It wouldn't have been if every other sentence out of her mouth wasn't a criticism. Candace isn't talking to me, my mother hates me almost as much as she hates you, and I'm out of chocolate!"

Jimmy laughed, coughed, and ran when he saw her face.

"Why isn't Candace talking to you?"

"I don't know! She's been acting weird ever since Mom and I got back from dinner. She says polite things, but it's like she's hiding something. Like somebody got shot or something."

If there was one thing I hated about my best friend, it was her intuitiveness. Okay, there were a lot of things that I hated about my best friend but that was the most inconvenient of them. Sometimes. "Yeah. I did."

"And then– Wait. What?"

"I got shot."

"By?"

"An elf."

"With?"

63

"An arrow."

"Why?"

"Don't know."

She stepped back, trying to tell if I was joking. I nodded my head. "Really?"

"Yes. I also instructed your girlfriend not to say anything, I didn't want people to worry."

"And you're okay?"

"Superhuman healing ability."

She sighed in relief, grinned, and practically skipped back to her room. "Night!"

"Night, Jose."

She's such a simple girl.

I looked down at Dar and nodded.

"Uh, Dot?"

"Yeah?" I looked over at Jimmy standing in my bedroom doorway.

"There's um…somebody sleeping in *your* bed. Looks like Purplylocks."

"Shit. Sorry, papa bear. Forgot she was going to be staying in my bed."

He wiggled his eyebrows again.

"Come on. You can sleep here but no threesomes."

"Aw, man. I took one for the team with Jason."

"I didn't see him putting his dick in *you.* So, technically, I took *two* for the team. Top that."

"You win."

"Always." I grinned at him and walked into my room. Yuki was passed out on top of my comforter. I smiled at her. She was wearing a simple white T-shirt that stopped just above her belly button and a pair of plain white cotton panties. Both of them nearly matched the color of her skin. She was simply adorable.

Jimmy thought so, too. He was openly staring, next to me. I smacked him in the back of the head. "Get a good look, perv?"

"You wouldn't blame me if you knew the amount of Japanese, school girl porn I've watched."

I gave him a disgusted look.

"What? They weren't really school girls, just women dressed like them."

"Yeah. I kind of figured *that*. The look was for sharing. I don't want to know what kind of porn you watch."

"Sure, you don't."

He was right. I kind of did. But, I didn't need him sneaking peeks at my familiar all night. Or getting any ideas. I went into my closet and got a light blanket, draping it over her.

"Spoilsport."

"Pervert."

"At least we're both aware of our shortcomings."

I pulled off my jeans and my shirt, tossing them in the hamper. My pretty bra took its place of honor atop my dresser. The panties I was wearing to bed. Lifting the cover, I slid into the middle, facing Yuki. I wanted to be spooned and coddled in a non-dickish way. "Kill the light."

"Yes, Lady."

The room plunged into darkness and I don't know why I bothered. I could still see clearly. Sighing, I closed my eyes.

"What's the matter?"

"Seeing in the dark has its advantages, but not when you're ready for bed."

"Huh. I can see that. You can see just like in daylight?"

"Yep."

"How many fingers am I holding up?"

I looked over my shoulder. He was making obscene gestures with his hands. One finger slowly sliding into the hole he'd made with the fingers of his other hand.

"You're holding up *I want to sleep alone on the couch* many."

"Damn. That's pretty cool."

"Sleeping alone on the couch?"

"No. That you can see in the dark."

I rolled back over.

"Hey, Dot. How many am I holding up now?"

I looked back over my shoulder. He was holding one, but it wasn't a finger. He had pushed down the front of his underwear and was stroking himself about a foot from my face.

"Your mother dropped you as a child. Repeatedly."

He chuckled and slid into the bed behind me. I smiled as he slid one arm under me and pulled me back against his chest with the other. I snuggled in for the night.

"Hey, Dot," he whispered into my ear.

"Yeah?"

"You asleep?"

"Yeah."

"Is Yuki still asleep?"

I opened my eyes. Yuki might have gained the ability to walk in sunlight and adopted a more human-like sleeping schedule, but she was still dead to the world. "Yeah," I whispered back.

His arm lifted off me for a moment as he leaned back. When it flopped back over me, something long and hard was pressing into my ass.

I shook my head, but still smiled, knowing he wouldn't be able to see it.

"Gosh. What is that?"

"Little Jimmy."

"No. Don't ever call it that. There's nothing little about it."

"Well I'd feel funny calling him *big* Jim."

"Yeah. That doesn't work, either."

"How about… The knob goblin?"

"Hell no."

"Sir Lancelot?"

"Over used."

"Jigglestick?"

"I'll laugh every time you say it."

"Shakespear?"

"You're not a poet."

"Beef Jerkme?"

"Too dry."

"I know! Let's just call it *yours*."

"Ooh. *That* I like," I whispered and grinned. Reaching between us, I slid my panties down over my butt and pushed back against him. "Quietly."

"Hey. You're the screamer, not me. I just grunt a little bit."

The game was on.

I let him take his time, slowly teasing me open with the tip. He used his hips to move himself back and forth, the sensation sending little ripples of pleasure through me. His head parted my flesh, dipping inside for just a moment before grazing my rapidly hardening spot above. My legs involuntarily parted for a moment.

His lips found the sensitive spot behind my ear and he dragged them across it, tickling the fine hair there. Turning my head, lost in the sensation, his arm slid under the comforter and gripped my breast.

"Jimmy."

"Yes, Dot?"

"Tease them."

"Yes, Dot."

He let go and his thumb and middle finger gently pinched my nipple. When his index finger grazed the tip, I nearly lost it. Turning my face into my pillow, I mewled as quietly as possible. His fingers were sending pleasure racing through my body as I curled my hips and bucked against him.

"Oh. You like that."

"Just a tad," I managed to say.

"I love learning new things like that about you. I love *you*."

"Love you, too."

His hand left my chest and slid down over my stomach. "Lift your leg for a moment."

"Why?"

"Gasp. After all this time, you still don't trust me?"

I rolled my eyes and did it.

"Good girl," he whispered in my ear before licking the edge from lobe to tip. It was almost as pleasurable as him teasing my nipple.

His hand slid over my hair and cupped me, his middle finger dipping inside. I fought very hard not to push my legs together as he started sliding in and out of me. My breathing became more rapid until he pulled his finger out.

"Just wanted a little honey, honey." He pushed himself forward and used his fingers to slip inside me with his hardness. One knee in the air, he spread my wetness all around, using his cock to tease me as he slowly pushed it back and forth. When he had collected enough, he pushed my leg back down.

I thought he wanted to taste me, but I was wrong. He brought the tips of his fingers back to my chest and spread my wetness gently over my nipple, using it to make little circles. The sensation was overwhelming. I opened my mouth and hissed in pleasure.

"Fuuuck," I whispered.

"Okay."

He pushed against me, driving himself inside me. I felt every inch of him as he slid deeper. He was throbbing and hot, and I was addicted. Hopelessly and wondrously addicted to my Jimmy.

He didn't pound into me. He held me and made love to me, not wanting to wake up our guest. His lips danced across my neck as he teased my breast and used slow, long strokes to drive me to the edge.

"Are you going to come for me?"

I nodded, not able to do anything else.

"Climb on top of me. I want to be kissing you when you do."

He pulled back a little and I rolled over, facing him and sliding my leg over him. As gently as I could, I worked my hips over him and used my arms to lift myself off the bed and on top of him. I reached down between us and guided him back into me, lowering myself until he was back where he belonged.

My hips began rocking, the motion moving him inside me. He reached up and grazed both my nipples with the back of his fingers before sliding them between them, gently pinching. The breath I'd been holding escaped in a soft moan.

"Kiss me," he whispered.

I leaned over and my lips met his. I started breathing again until his tongue met mine. My hips, which had been holding a subtle rhythm began bucking sporadically as I couldn't control myself any more.

His hands slid down my back, cupping my ass and pulling me into him even harder. My betraying body was tipped over the edge as I came, fighting for breath in his kiss. He moaned as he emptied himself inside me. I collapsed on top of him and curled into his neck.

"Woah."

"Woah," he echoed.

"Woah," Yuki said beside us.

I couldn't, or wouldn't, look over at her. I could feel her pleasure and happiness wash over me in a wave over our bond.

"Night, Yuke," Jimmy said with a chuckle.

"Night, Shakespear."

I groaned in embarrassment.

Chapter 6

My wards and shields flared and burst in a shower of sparks. The pain of having them ripped away woke me in a cry of agony. Lifting myself off Jimmy's chest, I blinked as I tried to fight through the haze of pain.

Jimmy's sleeping, smiling face came into focus. I shook him, and when he didn't wake up, I gently slapped his face repeatedly, trying to wake him. It wasn't working.

I flopped off him and looked at my vampire. She had rolled over and was facing the wall, head on the mattress and pillow clutched tightly in her arms. I reached over and shook her, too. "Yuki!"

There was no response. Something was terribly, horribly wrong. I pulled up my panties, slipped on my T-shirt, and crept from my room, spells at the ready.

There was no movement in the house, and I could barely make out the sounds of traffic and birds from outside. Light filtered through the front window, dimly illuminating the inside with a soft glow. It was after dawn, but not quite early enough to be called morning. That didn't happen until just before lunch.

Padding across the house, I slipped into Josie's room. She and Candace were cuddled under their fluffy pink comforter. I shook them both and practically shouted their names. Neither of them woke up either. Even a spell to wake them didn't work.

The lock on my front door clicked and I froze.

Fuck.

When the door opened, I finally forced my body to move, silently stepping toward the door.

Peeking around the corner, I narrowed my eyes at the elf standing in the middle of my foyer, grateful for the great room layout of my house. But, if I could see him, he could see me. I pulled back a little and listened for him to move.

The floor creaked beneath him by my bedroom door. Taking the chance, I crept from the hall by the bedroom over to the kitchen, putting my back against the wall next to the entrance.

I turned my head, trying to get a look at the bedroom. Not seeing him, I peeked around the other side of the wall and gasped when the tip of the blade touched my throat.

"Do not move."

"Wouldn't think of it."

"As bright as you are difficult to kill." He pushed the tip of the blade, driving me back against the wall. Any more and I would have been breathing through my neck.

He was absolutely beautiful, even more so than Shea. The tips of his pointed ears were much longer, too. They pushed up through his waist-length blond hair that they just couldn't quite capture correctly in the movies. His eyes were green, but instead of a normal, round pupil, they were slit like a cat's. He wasn't the first elf I'd seen, but he might be the last if I didn't come up with a plan.

"Why are you trying to kill me?"

He studied my face, tilting his head as he did. "I hit you in the heart. I am sure. Why did you not die?"

"My friends healed me."

His eyes narrowed and the blade pricked the skin on my neck. "How? There is no way to heal the dead and it should have been instantaneous."

The feeling that the less he knew about me, the better I would be, permeated every cell in my body.

"Tell you what. Let's play let's make a deal. You tell me why you want me dead, and I'll tell you why I'm not."

His eyes flashed down to the wound, or where the wound *should* have been, and back to my face. My shirt was low-cut, but not that low.

The tip of the dagger moved from my throat to just under my chin faster than I could follow. He lifted my head, forcing me to stare at the ceiling. I gasped when his fingers pulled down my collar and traced my skin where he'd put the hole in my heart.

He stopped and his hand clasped my throat, pulling the blade away at the same time. I looked back down at him to find he had raised an eyebrow in confusion.

"You can no longer go unchecked in this realm. The hellmouth you summoned nearly destroyed our elfhame. Our king's dying command was to stop you."

Oh.

"Well, that wasn't me. I just closed it."

He scoffed and the dagger flashed, digging into my shoulder. I didn't give him the satisfaction of screaming. Gritting my teeth, I gave him a hateful stare.

"I'm telling you. It wasn't me, and it was an accident to begin with. If you don't believe me, just fucking kill me."

"I plan to." He drew the tip of the blade from my flesh and brought it to his face. His eyes moved from mine to the blade and his tongue darted out, tasting my blood. His lip curled and he spat. He was cleaning my floors when we were done. "You're not even a witch."

"Wait, what?"

His eyes narrowed. "You do not even know."

"Know what?"

"You are going to die not knowing," he said as his lip curled in a sneer. I felt the gathering of his power and felt

73

the murder of his intent. My hand was halfway to his chest when he froze.

"You will not harm my daughter."

Half expecting to see my mother behind him, I gasped when a very glowing Candace floated in the air, eyes blazing with fire.

The hand around my throat pulled away and the elf kneeled, bowing his head. Witches worshipped the Lady. Elves followed the Lord, and not the Christian one. They were the children of the sun and prayed to the god of the hunt, the horned one. But, just like us, they acknowledged the consort of their god and would *never* invoke their wrath.

I joined him on the floor.

"Rise, Daughter."

I did, but kept my head bowed. It was uncomfortable staring at her, anyway. When I became High Priestess of the Coven of the First Moon, she had used my body to speak to the coven and give us a name. Since then, she had repeatedly channeled herself through Candace. There was no question about the girl's purity of character.

"*You*," she said to the elf. "It is as she said. The portal to Gehenna was not created by her, and she went through great lengths to close it. You would slay your savior?"

"No, my Lady."

"Tell Prince Renlynn what I have said, and that Dorothea is not to be accosted, anymore. Do you understand?"

"Aye, my Lady."

"If he needs to hear the words from my consort, that could be arranged…"

The elf's eyes flashed in fear. The Lord of the Hunt was just that. If he paid a visitation, death and feast were to follow. I didn't envy him for riling her ire, or for the invocation of his name. "That will not be necessary, Lady. I shall relay the message and the intent."

"Wise, child of the sun."

The elf bowed his head again.

She left him kneeling on the ground. "Daughter. You will go with him."

"I…what?"

"You will travel to the elfhame and assure them of your innocence. I send you for another purpose, and you will know it when it arises."

"Yes, my Lady."

"Jaeren, I am entrusting my daughter's safety to your hands. Do not disappoint me. Again."

I swear I heard him whimper.

"As penance for your attempted assassination, after you have delivered the news to your new king…you will serve my daughter for the period of one century. Do you acknowledge this?"

"Aye, my Lady." That's what he said, but I'm sure that's not what he was thinking.

"Fear not, Daughter. You will be back by the next moon. Take this girl with you." She motioned at the body she was occupying. "Take the shadow walker as well."

"My familiars?"

"You have little choice. They would perish by the time you returned."

I nodded. That was my fear, and why I asked.

"But no more. It would be considered impolite."

"Yes, my Lady."

She floated over to me, smiled, and kissed me on my forehead once again. I winced as the Lady's mark flared. Pain made my eyes water and I fought the urge to rub them.

"I am sorry."

"For what, my Lady?"

"For causing you pain. And for many other things."

I rubbed the spot on my forehead, wondering if it were visible again. "Thank you, my Lady."

She nodded and the light radiating from Candace ebbed as she slowly lowered to the ground. When the white fire faded from her eyes, Candace blinked. She took one look at the elf starting to stand and holding the knife and kicked him in the face, putting herself between us and backing us away.

"It's okay, Candace. He's a friend. Now."

She looked up at me and gasped, spinning and dropping to the ground in front of me.

"What are you doing? Stand up, sweetie."

She did and just stood there staring at me, reverently.

"What?"

"The mark."

"Yeah?"

"It's glowing."

My fingers shot to back to the place she kissed me. "Hopefully not for long. That's going to be a bitch to conceal."

"If it doesn't, you should not conceal the mark of the goddess."

"Well, I can't exactly walk around town with it, either."

She sighed.

Dar jumped over the back of the couch and growled, bearing down on Jaeren.

"Dar, no!"

He skidded to a stop, ass sliding across the hardwood floor and front paws splayed out in front of him.

He's not attacking? Dar was utterly confused.

He already did. Long story.

We slept through it?

"Everybody was asleep. Was that some kind of spell?"

Jaeren looked up at me from the floor. "May I stand?"

"Yes."

He lifted himself off his knee and replaced the wicked looking, curved dagger back into the sheath behind him. "No. 'Twas the venom of the dream asp."

"I got bit. By a snake?"

"Aye."

"A snake. There was a snake in my house. You let a snake go in my fucking house?" I didn't like snakes.

"Aye?"

I punched him in the face. "That's for the snake and shooting me with your little bow."

Candace's kick had left his nose a little bloody. My punch busted open his lip and my knuckles. I shook my hand to get through the pain and stopped, watching the flesh on my hand knit itself back together. So did Jaeren. He was a little more shocked than me.

"That's why you did not die."

"Yep. Vampire familiar. Makes me bloody hard to kill. See what I did there? *Bloody* hard to kill?"

He didn't appreciate my humor. "That is not possible, even for a–" He choked on his last word and fell to the ground, out cold.

"What the hell is going on? Is that the elf?" Jimmy rubbed his face groggily as he walked over to us.

"Yeah."

Jimmy kicked him. Hard. In the side. I almost felt bad for letting him, but I wanted the elf to wake up. He pulled back to do it again, but I stopped him.

"Don't. He's my bodyguard."

"Oh. What? Say that last part again?"

"Come, little children, I'll tell you a tale," I said and headed for the coffee. It was too early to be un-caffeinated.

"Dot, what the hell is going on?" Jimmy was getting impatient and I'd just made it to the coffee maker. Candace slipped in front of me and worked her magic. I was officially giving her the title of pod-barista. She had my mug brewing and three more set to go by the time it made the final squirty noise in my cup.

She swiped it out of the machine and slid it across the counter into my waiting hand. If my wallet wasn't in my bedroom, I would have pulled out a dollar bill and given it to her. I took a sip, set it back down, and said, "Be right back. I need more clothes."

"Start your story. I'll get you some pants." Yuki zipped into my room and was back before I started.

"You're gonna wear grooves in my floor."

"And you can magically repair them." She handed me my plain gray sweats. The ones I usually saved for laundry day.

"You have a point. Continue zipping," I said drolly and slipped into their fuzzy warmth.

"It's actually called swifting."

"Like the mop thingy?"

"No, that's swiffing."

"Hence the name. Otherwise it would be a swifter."

"Are you two done?"

"One who swifts," I finished and turned to Jimmy. "Now. So back to the elf."

"Maybe you should take some Adderall first."

"You telling me I have ADHD?"

"Wouldn't think of it."

I shook my head and continued with my story. The fun of tormenting him, lost. "Speaking of the devil," I said and chuckled softly as Jaerun walked up behind Jimmy, confusedly rubbing his side with one hand and his head with the other. "Welcome back, sleeping beauty."

"What happened?"

"You tell me. One minute, you were telling me something, and the next, you were lying on my floor."

"That's right. I was telling you that you are–" He collapsed on the floor again. I sighed and bent down, lifting his eyelid and checking his pupils. They were completely dilated.

"What the hell is wrong with him?"

"He let something called a dream asp loose in the house? Maybe it's biting him?" I mused to myself. I got up and backed away. Not wanting to get within a mile of the damn thing. Candace hopped up on the counter.

"I think you have a dream ass." Jimmy rubbed my butt.

"Asp. Snake. Little fangy things."

"Like Yuki?"

"With scales."

Yuki crouched low and circled the elf. "I don't see anything. Maybe it's in his clothes."

"Strip him," I said jokingly.

She leaned forward and started undoing his buttons. I debated letting her, when I sighed and told her to stop. "I was kidding."

"Oh."

"You just wanted to see the elf naked," Jimmy said with a chuckle.

"Maybe."

The elf sat back up. "Again?"

I nodded. "That snake thingy isn't loose, is it?"

"No. I released it Underhill when I had no further use for it."

"Odd. You aren't sick, are you?"

"I do not understand. With disease?"

"No. Like a fever and coughing?"

"Wasting disease?"

"Never mind. Why do you keep passing out?"

"I do not know. It seems to happen when I try to tell you…that…you are a–"

This time he hit his head when he collapsed.

"You're a what?" Jimmy blinked in confusion.

"I don't know. He tasted my blood and mentioned that I wasn't a witch. Do elves get sick? What about psychological disorders?"

"He tasted your blood?"

"Oh, shit."

"You didn't familiarize him, did you? You need to come with a warning label."

"You really want me to walk around with a 'Do not lick' label?"

"Um. No."

I thought about it, but I was pretty sure I hadn't. At least I hadn't been able to hear his thoughts. That was usually the first clue. Pretty sure. "I'll tell him to do something stupid when he wakes up."

"In the meantime, continue with your story."

"Well, he released the snake in the house, and it knocked us all out. Danny Elfman, over here, crashed through my wards and shields and the pain woke me up."

"That is not possible, but I wondered how you had awoken," Jaeren said and sat back up. He hoisted himself up off the floor using the kitchen counter.

"Welcome back for the third time…"

"I am not well."

"You mean you're sick."

"No. I am not well. Elves do not get sick." He put air quotes around the sick part. Somebody had been watching human television.

"Why do you keep taking naps on my floor?"

"I do not know." He was getting angry.

"Bark like a dog."

"What?"

"Bark like a dog."

"I will do no such thing!"

"Well, he's not my familiar."

80

"That is ludicrous. An elf cannot be tamed by a witch."

"That's what they said about vampires," Yuki said testily.

"Demons, too. Right, Dar?"

Woof.

"Well, I am no familiar."

"We established that. Just trying to figure out why you keep rebooting."

"Rebooting?"

"Never mind. You keep passing out every time you try to say what I am!" I turned around and grabbed a pad and pen from by the phone. "Write it down."

He took the pen and drew a line on the paper. He started writing a word in elvish and got two strokes in before he crumpled like a sack of rice. He hit his face against the counter before falling to the floor.

"That's gonna leave a mark," Jimmy said with a wince.

"Not that he doesn't deserve it, but what the hell is going on?"

"The goddess is preventing him from telling you," Candace answered.

"Dot?"

I turned to Jimmy. "What?"

"What's that on your forehead?"

"It's still there? Why are you just noticing it now?"

"Well, you were pantless up until a few minutes ago… Plus, it's not very noticeable."

"Good. That means it's fading. And what, you didn't notice because I was standing here in my underwear? You're such a man."

"Thank you."

"Not exactly a compliment. Okay. Long story, short. He showed up, tried to kill me, the goddess took over Candace, and told us to go to faerie land."

"Is that in New Jersey?"

"No. It's apparently right here. The hellmouth caused all kinds of hell there, and the king is dead. Fearing for the safety of their realm, he put out a hit on me before he croaked."

"Elves do not croak," Jaeren said and picked himself up off the floor.

"Figure of speech. Morning, sunshine…"

He nodded, rubbing his forehead. "It would appear that–"

"The goddess doesn't want me to know whatever it is you're trying to tell me. Yeah. We figured that part out."

He nodded, giving me a half-disgusted look. "There are more pressing matters to deal with. Believe what you think you know."

"Well, I'm not fae blooded if that's where you're going with this."

He held up his hand. "I do not wish to play a guessing game. Your secret is safe with me and from you. I will not risk further injury."

"Awww. But I was having fun."

"Dorothea…we are stuck together for the next century… Could we maintain a modicum of civility? And dignity."

"Yeah. Bashing your face on my counter top isn't very dignified."

"Neither is baiting me."

I held my hand up and covered Jimmy's mouth. "No!"

The elf glowered at me.

"Not going to shoot me, stab me, or sick snakes on me?" I stared at the elf.

"That would fall outside the parameters of keeping you safe. So, you have my word."

"Fine. Coffee?"

Jimmy pulled my hand away from his mouth. "Hundred years?"

"Yeah. While you were sleeping, I got another bodyguard."

"He said baiting," Jimmy said with a boyish chuckle.

Chapter 7

"Mom, you're going to have to move into the motel. It's not like we can have an elf check in…"

"But…"

"I'm sorry, Miranda, but Josie's right. Things are happening *way* too fast. Any more supernatural rumors and we'll be facing lynch mobs."

"I understand, but…"

"Mom. I'm sorry." You could hear it in her voice. She wasn't. Not even a little.

"Will you listen to me for a minute?"

We both shut up and stared at her expectantly.

"*As* I was trying to say… Your assistant was very helpful. I gave him the name of the delightful apartment complex that Shea moved into and he not only found me a vacant unit but also secured it for me. I was planning on moving this evening."

Shea gonna be pissed. "That's wonderful! They're very cute apartments."

"They are. I saw pictures on Jason's computer. That boy is adorable! Josie. You should totally marry him."

"Um… Candace, Mom."

"Well, it's not like you can marry a woman. And have children."

"Mom…" Josie pinched the bridge of her nose.

"I'm not saying you have to be strictly dickly, dear, but every now and again, a nice hot throbbing–"

"Mom. If you finish that sentence, it will be six months before I can talk to you again."

"Cockatrice," she finished with a little embellishment, unable to let it go.

"Besides, Mom. Jason is Dot's boyfriend."

I spit my coffee. That was more information than Miranda needed.

She turned her attention from Josie to me. I gave a little nod as I wiped off the kitchen counter.

"More and more like your mother, every day."

Them's fightin words, bitch. "I keep watching for signs like that in Josie, but she seems pretty level headed. Most of the time."

"Well, there's still hope for *my* daughter."

"She made me promise to put her out of my misery before that happened."

Josie hopped between us, our playful banter turning deadly. "Well, let's go check out your new place!"

"We will, dearie. Just waiting for the boy to bring my key and contract."

I owed Jason a raise. Maybe some oral administrations. Maybe I could buy him a house, or a car. He was a total lifesaver. Seriously, I was about to kill Miranda and deal with Josie not talking to me. I was pretty sure it would only be like a week before she got over it. Lifting my right hand, I let energy flow between my fingers, watching them crackle.

Miranda was saved by the doorbell.

I used it as excuse to put a room full of furniture between us. Undoing the deadbolt, I pulled it open without bothering to check who was outside. It could have been the grim reaper and it would have been better than who was *inside*. Spectacularly enough, it was the man of the hour. My new favorite person. My savior.

"Hey, handsome."

"Hi, Dot." Jason grinned and held up a shiny new key on a ring.

"That is the answer to all my prayers."

"I figured."

He went to hand me the key, but I stepped out of the way. "Come on in."

"Okay, but I have to run back to the trailer and change. I have class tonight."

"Fuck."

"What?"

"I still haven't fixed your hole."

"Um…"

"The one in the trailer."

"Whew."

I slapped his arm. "I'll have Jimmy fix the other one."

"Dot!"

I gave him an evil chuckle. "Let me get changed. I'll follow you home and fix your hole."

"Still talking about the one in the trailer, right? Dot? Dot?"

Ignoring him, I went to my room to throw on a sweater.

Dar padded up behind me. *Which of us would you like to take with you?*

"Well, danger over. Elf good. You can all stay home if you want. Just doing a bit of trailer repair."

That's not happening, but I do not see the need for all of us to go, either. I shall. The others may stay or go as they please.

"So. You're alpha male?"

Pardon?

"Alpha male. Leader of the pack."

Yuki defers to me in strategy. The elf cannot hear me. I shall simply pass on my thoughts to be translated through the vampire. The elf shall really be with you for a century?

"Unfortunately. One does not go against the wishes of the goddess."

That is wise.

He left as quietly as he came, and I followed him out of my bedroom. "Ready?"

Jason nodded.

"I'll be back later," I shouted to whoever was listening. Josie could help her mother move. I was kind of done dealing with her. Candace was holed up in her bedroom. I debated rescuing her, but she could stay home and get some peace while Josie dealt with the old bat.

"I'm staying here."

I nodded at Yuki. "Everything okay?"

"Yeah. The elf insists on going and Dar is going to watch him. I'll keep Candace company."

I narrowed my eyes.

"What?"

"I was just worried about her and then you said you were going to keep her company. You're not mind reading me, right?"

She laughed and shook her head. "She and the mother don't exactly get along. I was worried about her, too."

"Oh, how the mighty have fallen."

"What?"

"Just remember how jealous you would get whenever she got too close to me. Now you're all worried about her."

"We've gotten a lot closer. Ever since I gave Josie my blood to save her life…she's been kind of clingy."

"Ahh. Yeah. Well, you're kind of awesome," I said and reached out, ruffling her purple spikes.

She blushed and headed toward Candace's room.

Grabbing my keys, Jason and I headed toward the door. Dar ran out as soon as I opened it and Jaeren followed behind us.

Guess he really is coming. Joy.

"Where are we going?"

"I need to fix something at my friend's home. You're welcome to stay here. I won't be gone long."

"Nay. Tis the Lady's wish that I protect you. While the thought does not bring me pleasure, attracting her ire for failure to meet her wishes sounds much less appealing."

"Suit yourself." The three of us got in my car while Jason jiggled his door handle a dozen times before it finally opened. I half-expected the door to fall off in his hand, too. "That boy really needs a new car."

Do not buy him one. I practically heard Dar roll his eyes.

Why?

Because not everybody likes to have everything handed to them. He is working and you are paying him. Let him grow on his own. He'll appreciate that more than the gift.

Fine. And thanks for the advice.

Bessie started with a bang and a puff of smoke. When he backed out of my too small driveway, I slid out after him and followed him to his trailer.

"He lives in that?"

"Yeah. A lot of humans do. They appreciate the solitude."

"I shall guard outside."

I chuckled as I rolled to a stop beside Jason. "You coming in, Dar?"

I shall keep an eye on the pointy eared one.

"Have fun. I shouldn't be long."

The smell of the inside of his trailer was a lot different. It wasn't musty, but it smelled like outside. And it was freaking cold, even with the heater on. "I can't believe you were living here like this. It's a refrigerator in here."

"I haven't. I've been staying at Farrell's like you told me to."

"Oh. I just assumed you ignored me like everyone else does."

"Not a fan of hypothermia."

"Good boy."

He headed for his bedroom. I squatted by the hole and pulled the plastic tarp off. Debating setting fire to the whole structure and forcing him to move, I sighed and put my hands on the linoleum tiles around the gaping wound. Dropping Chief through the floor had been a quick end to an argument, but guilt still nagged at me for destroying Jason's floor. I should have fixed it days ago.

I poured a little bit of power into the structure beneath me and whispered, "*A bheith mar a bhí tú.*" Tile and wood flew up into the trailer from the ground below, righting themselves as the framework mended beneath it. The tiles went from dingey gray to brilliant white. The wood paneling in the kitchen brightened, as did the cabinets, appliances, and ceiling. I tried to let the power go, but it was steadily increasing. "What the fuck?"

Finally, it snapped back, knocking me on my ass on the new floor.

Jason came running out of the room. "What did you do?"

"Poured a little too much power into it."

"Um. Dot?"

"Yeah?"

"The bed made itself."

"You're welcome." I got up from the floor, a little afraid. I'd used the same spell a thousand times, even on my own house. Usually, I had to guide the whole process, picturing in my mind what it should look like. This time, I just told to trailer to become what it was, and it practically sucked the magic out of me. Everything inside looked brand new. Old in style, but out-of-the box in appearance.

"Dot?"

"What?"

"Even the holes are gone from my T-shirt…"

I looked over at him. He was standing in the middle of the doorway, shirtless and holding a plain white shirt up and staring at it in awe.

"Weird." My attention deficit disorder went into hyperdrive, staring at him shirtless.

"Even the ketchup stain is gone…"

"I'm sorry."

He lowered his arms and looked over at me, smiling. "Could you do that to Bessie?"

Groaning internally, I nodded. "I can try."

He grinned and put the shirt on. Damn it.

"You should probably take that off. It might still have some residual magics and those have been determined to cause cancer in laboratory animals in the State of California."

"Huh?"

"Just a joke."

"Oh. You just want to see me topless again."

I nodded and gave him a shy smile. "I could uh…return the favor…"

"Wouldn't you be cold? It's not exactly warm in here."

"Yet."

He chuckled softly, pulling the shirt back off and tossing it on the bed behind him. I didn't know why. It was only going to get in the way, again.

I started walking toward him, but he met me in the kitchen, his lips pressing gently to mine. The boy seriously needed to learn to read the mood. Gentle kisses were for movies and dinner. Not for horny witches begging to touch your bare chest. Sliding my hands up his back, I pulled him to me and showed him how I wanted to be kissed.

He groaned into the kiss, making it a hundred times sweeter.

"You drive me insane," he whispered softly.

"Like padded-wall insane or the hot kind?"

"The hot kind. Whenever I'm around you, I want you. Want to touch you. Feel you. Taste you."

A shiver of happy ran down my back. I pulled away and started to lift my sweater off, but he stopped my hands.

"Can I?"

"Oh, yes you can. Please."

His lips curved up and he slid his fingers under the hem, lightly grazing my stomach, just above my pants. It was like he turned the faucet on and left it on. I wanted him that much. We were alone. The one and only time we had fooled around, Jimmy had been there. Now it was our time.

He lifted my sweater and leaned down. His tongue tickled my stomach and as he lifted the heavy material, he trailed wet kisses over every inch of me he exposed. My knees were getting weaker by the inch.

"Hurry."

"No."

"Please."

"Shhh. We have time."

I braced myself, no stranger to being teased, just not expecting it to come from Jason. It should be me teasing *him*. Seducing him. When his lips found my breasts, I stopped caring.

He sucked me in, licked me as he held me with his lips. Pleasure travelled down from my nipple to my already wet pussy. I moaned his name.

He let go and pulled my sweater off the rest of the way, setting it on the counter beside me and pulling me to his chest. The heat between us grew and the chill air around us went unnoticed. While his hands fumbled with the button on my jeans, I reached down and stroked him through his, teasing him and enjoying the feeling of him hardening in my hand.

With a happy sigh, he finally got them undone and began working them down over my hips. I stepped back and pushed them down in a rush, stepping out of them and kicking them behind me. I will never forget the look of pure lust on his face as he drank me in with his eyes. Kid on Christmas, puppy with a new toy, call it what you want, but there was no mistake that he wanted me.

"Your turn."

He undid his belt and jeans, but took his time with his zipper, still trying to maintain his illusion of teasing me. Maybe it was working, I wasn't sure. I couldn't take my eyes off him as I waited for his show to end. I dropped to my knees in front of him and yanked them open. He sprang free and I took him in my hand, pulling him forward.

Pants around his ankles, I devoured him, groaning as his soft flesh filled my mouth. I enjoyed it almost as much as he did, his throbbing sending waves of desire through me. His pleasure became everything to me.

"Dot…"

I looked up at him, pulling him slowly out of my mouth and smiling. "What?" I managed to ask with the tip still against my lip.

"You're going to make me blow."

"That's the whole idea."

"But I want to fuck you."

"You're young. It shouldn't be hard for you to get it back up, right?" I gave him a seductive wink and took him back into my mouth, pulling at him with my tongue.

He groaned again and put his hands back against the counter. It was all the warning I had when I felt his torrent of release flood my mouth. I pulled back, letting each rope land against my tongue. When he finally finished, I stood. Luckily the sink was beside him. He chuckled when I deposited it into the shiny, stainless-steel basin.

"Not a swallower, huh?"

"Not even a fan of the taste. Just didn't want to get your new floor all dirty."

He chuckled and pulled me close, leaning in and kissing my neck instead of my lips. Guess he wasn't a fan of the taste, either. "That was amazing. *You* were amazing."

"Well, consider *that* a thank you for getting that woman out of my house so quickly."

"Oh. Was that what that was?"

"Yep."

"Well, I guess I should say thank you for thanking me. A you're welcome, if you will." He grinned as he reached down and put his hands around my waist.

I squealed when he lifted me up off the ground and set me on the counter behind me. "What are you doing?"

"I'm a little hungry. All I have is chips, but I'm craving something sweet." He lowered himself to the floor. The angle was kind of awkward and his countertops were freezing, but I let him lean in and kiss me, his tongue dancing across my clit. My head rolled back against the cabinet as another moan escaped me.

He gently eased my legs apart and worked his tongue across my opening. Waves of pleasure rolled through me and it wasn't long before I felt the first stirrings of my orgasm.

"So good," I managed to blurt.

"You taste so sweet."

"You talk so sweet. Get back to work. I'm almost there."

He chuckled and slipped a finger inside me, moving his tongue back up and letting it circle my hardness.

"Yesss."

"Come for me," he paused to say and added a second finger to the first, increasing the speed of his strokes.

94

I could feel myself tightening around his fingers as my pussy began contracting. Even the entrance below it started to quake as my hips started pushing forward, trying to drive his fingers in farther.

"Jaaason…"

I came. My head shot forward, and my eyes scrunched as every nerve ending in my body was lit on fire from within. Gasping for breath, I rocked into it, hitting my head behind me more than once. He didn't relent, either. He sucked my clit into his mouth with a loud slurp, pressing his tongue against me and curling the tip around it. I started to see spots behind my eyelids. I let out a string of mewling noises and he chuckled into me, enjoying the overload of pleasure he was inflicting on me.

I finally reached down and pushed him away, unable to take another moment.

"Where the fuck you learn to do that…"

"Internet."

I coughed out a laugh. "Well. Next time you're watching the source material, let me know. You can practice while you watch."

"That sounds like fun."

"Doesn't it?"

He stood up and his cock was hard again. Stepping forward, he wanted to take me right there on the counter.

"Oh, hell no. This is hurting my ass, I don't need you driving me into the cabinets, too. Go sit on the couch."

"I'm sorry. You should have said something."

"Oh, don't worry. I didn't feel a thing until you stopped."

Always the gentleman, he offered me his hand. I took it and slid off the counter. Yes, I meant slid. Like a waterslide. I was lucky I didn't land on my ass on the floor. He was going to need a towel when we were done.

He pulled me with him, turning and plopping down on the middle cushion. Without a word, I pushed his knees together and turned around, slowly lowering myself onto his lap. "Scoot forward and lean back."

He gently touched my butt and I lifted off him, letting him shift further between my legs. His cock was pointing straight at me, exactly where I wanted. Reaching down, I took him in my hand, pumping him a few times as I slowly lowered myself onto him while holding myself open with my other hand.

He slid right in and I closed my eyes, smiling at the sensation of him filling me. "You feel perfect inside me."

"You feel perfect in my lap."

"Aww." I leaned back against him and kissed the side of his face as his arms wrapped around me, each hand taking a breast and squeezing gently. I convulsed around him, massaging him with my wet tunnel.

"The things you do to me…"

"Are you complaining?" I turned my head.

"No. I didn't think they were possible. It shouldn't feel this good. *Nothing* should feel this good."

"You're going to make me come again just from your words."

"I love you," he whispered in my ear.

I probably would have come if I wasn't so shocked. "What?"

"Was that not okay?" He sounded so nervous my heart stopped beating for a moment.

"Just unexpected."

"Dot, I loved you from the moment you told me I was worth it. How could I not? Not only did you save me from that hell they call a factory, you gave me a job, you're always there pushing me to be better than I was… If it weren't for you–"

"Stop! That part's not okay. Even if I had never rolled into town, you would have been just fine. You have a good head on your shoulders. Might have taken you a while but you still would have gotten there *without* me."

"Maybe. But I might not have ever found the drive to do it. So, thank you for that. And thank you for making the journey worth taking."

"You sweet-talking son of a snake. I swear the men in my life take Shakespeare lessons behind my back."

"Only because we don't want to sound like idiots when we talk to you."

"See?"

"But, I'm sorry I blurted that out, if that's not something you wanted to hear."

"Jason?"

"Yes?"

"Make love to me. Because, yes. I love you, too."

He kissed my neck and I craned my head, wanting his lips on mine. I started grinding my hips against him, undulating to feel him move inside me. Still kissing me and holding a breast, his hand snaked its way down my belly and cupped me. A moment later, he used his whole hand to rub me from where he pierced me, to just above my patch of red hair. I whimpered at the sensation and the movement in my hips became erratic, trying to get every ounce of pleasure from him.

He pulled back a little and gave me the happiest smile I'd ever seen. "I'm going to come again."

"Do it. I want you inside me."

He spread his fingers, pulling me open and letting my clit slide between his fingers as he rubbed. My head fell back completely against his shoulder. His other hand squeezed my breast almost to the point of discomfort, it was perfect.

"Are you close?"

All I could do was nod.

He started shifting his hips back and forth, adding fuel to my fire. Curling his hand, the tips of his fingers found my nub and applied pressure, sliding from side to side. It was more than enough to finish me off.

It started in my toes, curling them up against the cold floor as I rocked on top of him, short spasms as my orgasm worked its way up and up into my brain. Gasp after gasp flew from my mouth as his fingers stopped dancing and he buried his face in my neck, shuddering with an animalistic grunt as he came.

"Fuuuuck," I shouted as everything else faded from my vision.

Everything except for Chief walking through the front door and shouting, "Jason! You home? Dot?" His voice trailed off as he took in the scene on the couch. His eyes widened until the whites were bigger than the blue. "Shit! Sorry!" He turned around and walked back outside.

I couldn't help it. I started laughing.

"I'm a fucking dead man."

Chapter 8

Thanks for the heads up Chief was here.

Was I supposed to?

It would have been nice!

What were you– Never mind. My apologies. Next time hang a sock on the door.

You're a funny puppy. Yes, you are.

Don't get pissy with me because you got caught with your pants down.

Har har.

I smiled. For a dog, he did have a tremendous sense of humor. But then again, he wasn't really a dog. For a demon, he had a tremendous sense of humor.

I pulled my sweater down and opened the front door. Chief was standing there talking to Jaeren. I was surprised he didn't have a gun pointed at him, pretty sure I hadn't told him he was now on Team Dot.

"You can come in now."

He looked over his shoulder and nodded. "Nice…uh…talking with you."

"Sorry about that," I whispered when he got close enough.

"Don't worry about it. I didn't think to knock. It was actually my fault."

I didn't even make a sarcastic comment. "Yeah, well. I'm sure that's not something you wanted to see."

He stopped in the door, leaned over, and gave me a kiss. "I *always* want to see you naked. Jason, not so much, but beggars can't be choosers."

I chuckled.

"Now where's that asshole, brother-in-law of mine? I'm gonna kill him," he shouted toward the closed bedroom door before silently belly chuckling. Chief had a *huge* sadistic side. I stared at him in shock.

"First words out of his mouth were, 'I'm a fucking dead man.'"

"That's awesome."

"No, it's not. It's mean!"

"But, funny."

"That's true, too. Go tell him you're not mad before he jumps out the window or something."

"Jason. I'm kidding! You can come out now."

"No, you're not," came his muffled response from behind the door.

"See what you did?" I turned in Jason's direction. "He's not kidding, Jay. Come out."

"You promise?"

"I promise." I swatted Chief as he unholstered his weapon.

"Come on! It will be *classic.*"

"No!"

"Fuddy duddy."

"That means a lot, coming from you."

"Ouch."

"Just kidding. You're a lot of fun. Sometimes."

"Double ouch."

"Quit picking on my Jason."

He chuckled. "Fine."

The door clicked and creaked open. "You're not going to shoot me?"

"Maybe."

"Chief! He's not, Jason. He's just teasing you."

He sighed and opened the door. "Sorry, Bill."

"Don't be. She's right. I'm just teasing your dumb ass. I've known for a while."

"Really?"

"Really really."

"You're not mad?"

"Nope. I'm actually happier about her and you than that pervert she hangs around with."

"Josie?" I couldn't help it. I had to.

"No. The one with the dick."

"Josie?" I was on a roll!

Chief and Jason both snorted. Then looked thoughtful.

"Anyway. What brings you out to the middle of nowhere, and how did you know not to shoot the elf?"

"Jimmy gave me a heads up on the phone. Well, I came to see Jason, actually." He turned to Jason. "You wanna grab a beer and hang out?"

"Tomorrow? I have class tonight."

"Oh. Yeah. That sounds good. Class?"

"Business management class."

He looked from Jason to me. I nodded and smiled.

"That's fantastic! I want to see your report card, though."

"Yes, Dad."

"No. That's kind of creepy," I said, wide-eyed.

Chief even made a disgusted face and nodded. "Yeah. What she said." He looked over at me and said, "As for the elf, I ran into Jimmy downtown."

"Ahh. Sorry, I forgot to call you."

"You sounded busy. No worries."

"Yeah. Now I have to plan a trip Underhill."

"Under who?"

"Hill. Faerie. Where the elves live."

"Oh. Need a Chief?"

"No. The Lady was very adamant about who gets to go with me."

"Yeah. Jimmy mentioned that, too. I don't think I'll ever get used to that."

"Try talking to her in person… It's rather unsettling."

"Nope. That's what our high priestess is for. I'll arrest the bad guys, you talk to the gods."

"Gee, thanks."

"No sweat."

"Speaking of which, I need to go see Shea. He…um. He's on the list."

"Of potential boyfriends?" He grinned.

"No. Trip to Faerie." I rolled my eyes. He was getting as bad as Jimmy.

"Aww. Shucks."

"Shucks? You just want to see him naked."

"Man's gotta be sure."

"Of?"

"That he's a man. I swear he's a woman."

"He's fae and feminine. Hell, look at Jaeren. Put some makeup on him and he'd be beautiful."

"He's too tall."

"I have some foundation and eyeliner in the car…"

"You can stop now."

"I will if you will."

"Deal," he said and held out his hand to shake on it. As soon as I took it, he pulled me in for a kiss. I didn't mind at all, throwing my arms around him. When I pulled away, I stared into his beautiful blue eyes and smiled. "You switched aftershaves."

"Bout time you noticed."

"Just took me a minute to process it. I should have noticed when you walked in the trailer and my eyes didn't water."

"Do you like it?"

"I do. It's very masculine. Just like you."

"Rawr," he said jokingly.

"I hate to interrupt… But I need to get going. Wash the sheets before you leave," Jason said with a chuckle and headed for the door.

I blushed. Okay, my head almost exploded, but I shook it off and stepped back from Chief. "No kiss?"

He sighed and rolled his eyes. "If I gotta. But you were just kissing Dad."

"I swear to gods, one more Dad joke and I'm going to barf on your shoes."

"Yeah. That is kinda gross. I'll stop. But tell him to quit acting like it sometimes," he said with a wink and kissed me fervently, right in front of a very defensive looking Chief.

"Okay, this stepped into the realm of surreal. I'm headed out, too," Chief said.

I grabbed his arm and Jason's, taking the one step to the door before we had to let go to fit out the door and down the step. It was awesome while it lasted though.

"Bye, honey. Honies."

"Bye, Dot." Chief said and headed for his Jeep.

Jason grabbed my hand and walked me to my car. As I passed by Bessie, I trailed a finger over the hood and whispered, "*A bheith mar a bhí tú,*" under my breath.

"I'll see you tomorrow?"

"Sure. Come by the house in the morning before heading to the store. I don't know when we're leaving for Faerie, but I'll let you know when I figure it out."

"Can I bring you coffee? Wake you up with a kiss?"

"Holy fuck, that sounds perfect. I'm keeping you."

"Forever?"

"Forever."

"Then my plan worked. Who knew all it would take is a little coffee?"

"It wasn't the coffee. It's all the sweetener you just poured into it."

"But you hate sugar in your coffee."

"But I like sweet things *with* my coffee."

"You gonna eat me?"

"That's your job," I said with a wink.

I'm going to throw up in your back seat if you keep it up. Dar made a mental gagging noise.

Come on, Dar. This. This sweet shit right here is the reason for living.

Hmmph. Meat.

That, too.

"That's two jobs I absolutely love."

"You love your job?"

"Helping you full time? Who the hell wouldn't?"

"Just about everybody else on the planet."

"I think that might be the most untrue statement anybody in history has ever made. Most of us would fight each other to help you."

"That's because I do sexy things for you."

He frowned. "No. *That* was the most untrue statement. Even if we weren't dating and doing sexy things, I would still have said the same damn thing. You…you're very special. We see it. You need to start, too."

And just like that, I cried. The smooth talking, sweet little shit reduced me to tears. "Damn it."

"Dot!"

"Shush. Not another word. Get to class."

"Are you happy or mad?"

"Are you serious? You just said the sweetest thing to me and made me happy. Joyful tears."

"Oh, whew. Thought I went too far."

"When you're being sweet, there's no such thing."

"I'll keep that in mind."

I nodded and let him kiss me goodbye.

"See you tomorrow."

"Be careful."

"Love you."

"Love you, too."

He turned around and saw his brand new 1967 fire engine red Buick LeSabre. "Holy shit!"

I chuckled softly to myself and got in my car. He could thank me later.

Hehehe.

I started the engine and backed up enough to turn around, laughing at the poor kid on his knees, paying homage to his vehicle.

You're too nice to that boy.

He deserved it.

Oh? Did he work extra hard making you feel lovely?

Yes, he did.

Insert prostitute joke here.

Go ahead if you want to walk home.

"Next time you wish to drag me along so you may mate, please advise me to stay home."

I took my eyes off the road and looked at Jaeren. He was staring intently at the road ahead of us, not wanting to make eye contact. That's not how I rolled. "Well, it wasn't planned."

"I could hear every word and sound."

Ew. I loved an audience, but the thought of him listening…didn't work for me. Not even a little. He was too much of a prick. "Not my fault. You should have gone for a jog or something."

"I could not leave you alone. What if ill had befallen you?"

"Like getting impaled on something? Cuz that kinda happened, anyway."

His reaction made it totally worth it. "Are all humans this vulgar?"

"First of all…not human. Second of all…no. I'm kind of special."

"Humanity might still have a chance."

Dar snickered from the back seat.

"Shut up, elf."

We rode in silence. I debated turning the radio on but decided to take the opportunity to press him for some information. "When are we going to Faerie?"

He opened his mouth to speak but made no sound. I didn't think anything of it until he grabbed his throat.

"What's wrong with you?"

He couldn't even make a wheezing sound. He was panicking and slapping the dashboard. "What the hell is wrong. Are you choking? Answer me!"

"I cannot speak!"

"Uh…pretty sure you just did."

"Strange. For a moment, no words or sounds would leave my mouth."

"Strange, but wonderful."

He shot me a dirty look.

You told him to shut up and then answer you.

What?"

You told him to shut up. He couldn't speak. You asked him what was wrong and commanded him to answer you. He may not be a familiar, but he can't ignore your commands, apparently.

That's not true. I told him to bark like a dog and he didn't. That proved he wasn't a familiar.

You told him to bark like a dog. Remember, Dot, magic is one third intent. You might have told him to, but did you really want him to?

Well, I wanted to find out if he was a familiar. He wasn't.

You didn't want him as a familiar. You never intended for him to bark.

106

Well fuuuck.

He may not be a familiar, but he cannot ignore a command that you mean. This is not a good thing?

Maybe.

Try again. Focus your intent. You wish to hear him woof.

"Hey, Jaeren. Bark like a dog."

"I will not play your games, Woof. What did you just do?"

"You said I'm not a witch. Tell me what I am."

He narrowed his eyes and pursed his lips. He started panicking again when he said, "You're a–" At least the seatbelt stopped him from banging his head against my dashboard.

"It's a good thing," I answered Dar.

Do not taste his blood. Just in case.

Good idea.

On a whim, I turned the car and headed toward Shea's. I didn't have his number, but now would be a good time to talk to him. I'd mentioned the trip to Candace and she reluctantly agreed, only when she found out the goddess herself had put her on the guest list. I hoped Shea's reaction would be a little better.

We're not going home?

"In a bit. I want to talk to Shea about the upcoming trip."

Dar morphed into a human in my back seat. I tried not to think about his naked ass on my leather. Not that there was anything wrong with his ass, it was quite lovely. And blue. I just didn't really want naked buttocks leaving ass prints. Or ball prints.

He stretched and smiled at me in the mirror. "That's better."

"Why don't you shift more if it's more comfortable."

107

"Because it would make others uncomfortable. Sometimes I do at night while everyone is asleep. I raid your refrigerator and have a few beers."

"Help yourself."

"I did not think you would mind."

"Not at all. And forget everybody else. You do what's comfortable for you. You might want to put some clothes on, though."

"They do not shift with me. It is why I always appear naked. Even in Gehenna, nudity is the norm. We do not need clothing to protect us from the elements."

"This is upstate New York. You' might need some clothes to protect you from shrinkage."

"Gehenna is warm. Some might even say hot. But the cold does not bother me, either."

"Hell never freezes over?"

"Rarely. Only when the Cubs make it to the World Series."

"Huh?"

"Baseball joke. I should have known you were not a fan."

"No. No sports at all. Guys in sports uniforms, yes."

"You have quite the…drive."

"Must run in the family."

"Yes. After meeting the other two members, I must agree."

"So, you're comfortable in this form around me, but not other people?"

"Yes. Mostly."

"Why?"

"Because, you are my master and have accepted me in whatever form I have worn. For that, I thank you."

"Don't mention it."

"I won't."

"Good." I chuckled.

Chapter 9

I knocked softly on the door and glanced back at my car. Jaeren was giving me dirty looks through my windshield, not appreciating my joke, at all. We needed to work on his humor if I was going to be forced to spend a hundred years with him. I was amazed he could walk with the three-foot-stick he had up his ass.

The door cracked open behind me. I turned around and saw Shea peeking out at me.

"Lady?" He opened the door and I gasped. He was wearing a gray sweatshirt hoodie. It was the first time I had ever seen him without his heavy black cloak.

"Hey, Shea. Have a minute?"

He nodded and stepped aside, letting me in. "I was just pouring some wine, care for a glass?"

"Sure."

Once he closed the door, he pulled his hood back and I noticed how dim the lighting was in his apartment. My eyes adjusted and I could make out every detail. If I didn't have vampiric vision, I wasn't so sure I could have. It was that dark.

Instead of lamps, large pillar candles illuminated the living room, casting flickering shadows on the walls. It felt more like a den than a living room. I liked it.

"Smells good in here. Lavender?"

"Yes. The scent calms me."

"You don't seem like the uptight kind."

"Usually, I am not. But moving and being in a new place brings stresses of its own."

"Well, I might have some more to add to that."

He paused, having just finished pouring the two glasses of wine. He added more to both of them with a little sigh and set the bottle down on the counter. The bottle was unlike anything I had ever seen. "How much more?"

"Like quest level."

"You have a quest for me?"

"No. I have a quest. It was recommended that you accompany me."

He walked over and handed me a glass. I took a sniff, and the sweetness and heady scent of alcohol nearly made my eyes water. I took a tentative sip.

"Woah."

"Tis potent."

"What is it? Moonshine?"

"Elderberry wine."

"It's good."

"I do not recommend more than one glass if you wish to operate your motor vehicle."

"I'll keep that in mind. I wonder if Dar knows how to drive. I doubt the elf can."

"Elf?"

"Yeah. He's the reason I am here."

"Is this the same one who put an arrow through you?"

"Yep."

"He is in your car?"

"Yep."

Faster than my eyes could follow, he had set his wine down and had a wicked looking curved dagger in his hand.

"Woah! Hold on. He's on our side now."

Not quite believing me, he flittered over the furniture to the front window and peeked out through the curtain. Only when he saw the elf sitting calmly in my front seat, not a threat, did the dagger return to its sheath. I always thought of Shea as a humble little librarian. Quickly, I reevaluated my thoughts on him. He moved like darkness and seemed as deadly as a serpent.

Assassin. That was my new opinion of him. I raised my eyebrows in appreciation.

He turned back around, and the humble, meek appearance returned. "My apologies."

"Don't. That was impressive."

"When I saw you fall... Let's just say, had I not been so worried about you, I would have removed the threat, then and there."

I blinked in surprise. There was definitely more to Shea than I *ever* imagined. "You were worried about me?"

He blushed and reached for his hood. Wanting to hide.

"Don't." I didn't want him to. I enjoyed seeing his delicate features, and it was much easier to see how he was feeling with his face exposed.

"The light..."

"Bullshit. It's darker than Miranda's heart in here."

He laughed. I wasn't sure if I'd ever heard it before. It was as cute and warming as Candace's. Taking my wine, I sat down on his couch without so much as an invitation.

"Sit. I'll start at the beginning."

He nodded, picking his wine back up and joining me, sitting on the chair closest to me. "Please."

"The elf is now my bodyguard."

"How?" He scooted forward.

"Well, even an elf can't ignore a command from the goddess..."

His impossibly large eyes got even larger. They were absolutely beautiful, just like the rest of him. Not my fault, I was a sucker for eyes. "Perhaps you *should* start at the beginning?"

"Right." I shook my head trying to get the image of his eyes out of mine. "So. Yeah. The elf showed up at my house. He let a dream asp knock everybody out and broke through my wards and shields to come finish me off."

"A dream asp?"

"Yep."

"It must not have bitten you."

"I'm pretty sure it did. It was the pain of having my wards and shields torn down that snapped me out of it."

"That is not how their venom works. You do not wake up until it wears off. Had he used his knife to remove your skin, you would not have woken."

"Huh. Maybe I didn't get bit. Or my healing healed me."

He seemed unconvinced, but he motioned me to continue.

"Anyway, I snuck up on him, but he saw me coming. He had me pinned to the wall on the point of his dagger, but the Lady…possessed…Candace. She stopped him from killing me."

"The Lady… She inhabited your fae friend? She appeared before you?"

"Yeah. I wish I could say it was the first time. She even took over my body when I became high priestess."

"You've had…multiple visitations?"

"Yes?"

"You have been visited. By a god."

"Yes."

He was awestruck. "This is…"

"Weird. I know."

His face said it was something other than weird. But I let it go. Not the point of my story.

"Truly blessed…" He was still staring at me in awe.

"Anyway," I continued. "She made the elf get down on his knees. She told me I needed to travel tohill and visit his

112

elfhame and that I would know why, when I saw it. She also told me to take my familiars, Candace, and…you."

"What?"

"You."

"Why?"

"I don't know."

"She specifically said my name."

"Unless there is another shadow walking, fae-blooded witch in our coven, pretty sure she meant you."

He sighed, draining half the contents of his glass in one swallow. Not that I blamed him. If it were me, I would have finished it and asked for seconds.

"I am…in shock."

"I see that. You gonna be okay?"

He nodded.

"You gonna go with me?"

He nodded again. "It would appear I have little choice."

"You and me both."

"Is that it?"

"No. She told Jaeren, that's the elf, to tell his king that I didn't have anything to do with the ruin of their elfhame. Oh. And he has to be my bodyguard for the next hundred years."

He downed the last of his wine, got up and poured another. When he looked at me, I held up my hand. I still had a motor vehicle to operate.

"This is… this is unusual."

"Tell me about it."

"I mean, I've always known that you were special…" He sat back down.

"Wait. What?"

"I've…" He seemed to realize he had said more than he wanted to.

Thank you, elderberry wine… "What do you mean?"

"Nothing."

"Doesn't sound like nothing. I'm just sayin'."

"I've… I just noticed that you were a little different. There was always something special about you that I could not explain. Nor could I even quantify your differences. It was just a feeling."

"Aww. That's sweet."

He blushed again and I saw the war in his eyes. He *really* wanted to pull that hood back up. I could always resort to slapping his hands. Negative reinforcement. Positive worked better, though.

"Don't pull up your hood. Don't even think about it. I've known you for how long? Let me enjoy seeing you."

"You… You enjoy looking at me? I don't disgust you?"

"Why would you?"

"I'm descended from the unseleighe sidhe. You heard Candace."

"Yeah. I'd probably care but the seleighe sidhe in my car is kind of an asshole, too."

He broke out in a smile. It dazzled me.

What the hell is wrong with me?

"Thank you for seeing me as me, and not what I am."

"My pleasure."

"What is?"

"Seeing you."

I didn't think it was possible for him to blush any more than he already had. If I didn't get out of there soon, I was pretty sure he was going to stroke.

"Thank you," he said, earnestly.

"Why?"

"Why what?"

I was no longer in control of my mouth. *Thank you, elderberry wine.* "Why did you move here, Shea?"

"Your mother…"

114

"I don't think she had anything to do with it at all. What's the real reason. Don't ask me how I know, but I will be able to tell if you lie to me."

That scared him a little. He took another gulp of wine. "You."

"Me?" That wasn't the answer I was expecting.

"Yes."

"Why?"

"Because I am fascinated by you."

Woah. "Fascinated like a science experiment kind of fascination, or fascinated like you like me kind?"

He didn't want to answer. I saw him struggling with it in his head. The poor bastard was breaking out in a cold sweat, but he was too afraid to answer.

"Shea. Do you find me attractive? Is that why you followed me?" I spelled it out for him to make it easier on him. He could nod or shake. It was up to him.

I gasped when he nodded. He wasn't lying, I knew.

I needed to get the hell out of there. Not because I wasn't attracted to him, but because I *was* attracted to him. A lot. I mean, anybody with functioning eyeballs would be. Hell, I think even Chief had the hots for him, not that he would ever admit it.

"Shea…"

He held up his hand. "I know. I am not worthy."

Oh, no he fucking didn't.

My weakness…

My heart…

He pulled the trump card. The wounded puppy dog ploy. I was doomed. Doomed I say. I had no recourse, no defense, no coherent thoughts. I fought the urge to hug him and cuddle him, pet him and quite possibly lick him…

I opened my mouth to tell him how wrong he was from the safety of not being close enough to touch him. "Come here," came out instead. I swear. It was like I had a

Siamese twin living inside my mouth. One that took over vital functions at exactly the wrong time.

He looked like he wanted to run away. I just couldn't let that happen. I couldn't. Nope.

"Come here," I said again, gently.

He drank the rest of his wine and stood, slowly inching his way closer to me. I set my empty glass down on the table and pulled him down next to me.

"You are more than worthy. It's me who isn't."

Nooo! Why am I doing the whole it's not you it's me thing!

What the fuck, Dot?

Shut up, me! You already have three boyfriends!

But look at him! And he's sweet. And apparently a fucking shadow ninja…

I really needed to schedule a therapy appointment. I was long overdue.

He sighed. Fully expecting me to pin this on me. Pretty sure every guy did. Two phrases they absolutely feared more than anything else in this world. "It's not you, it's me," and "I'm pregnant."

"That's not what I'm trying to say. I'm saying I already have three boyfriends."

"You are high priestess. That is normal."

"Not for me it isn't. I've had a lot of difficulty coming to terms with it."

He blinked up at me with those amazing eyes. "Why?"

"Because I've only ever had one serious relationship. It didn't end well and because of that… Let's just say I wasn't exactly eager to jump back into another one. And another one after that. And another. Jeez, what the hell is wrong with me."

"You find me attractive?"

"Woah. Hell yeah."

"Truly?"

116

I nodded. Vigorously, I might add. Very emphatically at the least.

"Do you wish to get to know me? Spend time with me?"

Guarded, I nodded. I did. If for no other reason than to let him know he was worth it.

"Could we?"

"Could we, what?"

"Spend time together. Get to know each other?"

"Absolutely."

"I would be more than satisfied with that. I thought moving here might have been a wasted effort on my part. That thought did not fill me with joy."

"Why didn't you say something sooner?"

"Confidence. More, my lack of it."

"You really don't see it, do you?"

"See what, my Lady?"

"How freaking beautiful you are?"

"What is on the outside is not at all important. It is my insides that worry me. My blood is dark, unlike your friend, Candace. I walk in the shadows. I often go unnoticed. When you live your life eluding those around you, when the time comes you want to step into the light, you are either blinded by it or burned by it."

"Not if you find someone to hold the umbrella. Or rub sunscreen on you." I must have had a glazed look in my eye.

He chuckled softly. "You are picturing that, now. Are you not?"

"Oh yeah." I grinned at him.

"You have never seen me without my cloak before. I could have the skin of a toad or a hidden third arm."

I wiggled my eyebrows at his second choice of words. "Do you?"

"What?"

"Have the skin of a toad. The arm I could live with."

"Nay."

"Show me. Show me what you look like, Shea."

"Pardon?"

"I'm not asking you to strip naked. Just take of your sweatshirt."

I'd thought he looked nervous before, now he looked like he was going to cry.

"You don't have to!" I held up my hands. "I was just curious. Chief totally wants to see you naked, though." I winked at him.

"I was happy when you asked. You are the first."

"To ask you to take you shirt off?"

"Yes."

"Boy, if I had a dollar…"

"For what?"

"Nothing. If you don't mind…please take your sweatshirt off for me."

He nodded, standing in a fluid motion with a grace I had *zero* chance of ever matching. Not even if I studied Kungfu for a thousand years. Unfortunately, there was a severe lack of a drumroll or stripper music as he grabbed the bottom of his sweatshirt and lifted it up over his head. If he wore a shirt beneath it, it came off with it, too. I gasped as his stomach came into view.

He wasn't ripped, but there wasn't an ounce of fat on him, anywhere. His stomach was prettier than mine. I was jealous and more than a little turned on. It was also the only exposed part of him free of tattoos. I blinked in surprise.

Sides, chest, and arms were all covered in elvish runes with a delicate swirl pattern connecting groups of them. None of them were more than a pencil line thick. The entirety of it didn't diminish him in any way, it even enhanced his beauty. The runes and the swirls followed the

118

taut lines of his muscles. I wanted to run my fingers over them. Seriously. I really did. Maybe even my tongue.

"Not what you were expecting?"

"The tattoos? No. I'm actually kind of shocked."

"They are a part of me. They're not tattoos."

"Wait. You were born with them?"

"As far as I know, yes. Or they were magically implanted on me. They grew as I did. Sometimes they change."

"Can you read them?"

"They are the reason I became a sage. I wanted to learn their secrets."

"Did you?"

"No. It is not any language I have ever been able to decipher. As far as I know, they are just more patterns."

"I thought they were elvish."

"As did I."

I leaned closer to his chest. To study them for purely scientific reasons. He smelled fucking good. Like warm amber. I shuddered as I reached up and ran my finger over them. They illuminated with an eerie blue light, wherever I touched. "Cool."

He stepped back and gasped in shock.

"What?"

"They have never done *that* before."

"You're kidding."

"No." He rubbed his arm, nothing happening.

I reached over and he held it out for me. Wherever my fingers touched, the runes and patterns briefly glowed. "That is really cool. I wonder why."

"I know even less about them now than I ever have."

"Sorry."

"Don't be. I find it fascinating, as well."

"Well, don't stay up too late, playing with yourself."

"Lady… I–"

"I'm kidding! But, Jeez. Don't ever be embarrassed about that. Everybody does it."

"Everybody?"

"Everybody."

He chuckled. "I know. I have read much on the subject."

"And done lots of homework, too. I'm sure."

He nodded and gave a little blush.

"So. I have to ask. Do they go all the way down, too?"

He shook his head. " No. My stomach, neck, and posterior are free. My legs and the tops of my feet, yes. Obviously not my face or hands.

"Hips?"

"Yes."

"Thighs?"

"Yes."

"Your um…"

"No."

"Damn. A glowing willy would have been interesting."

"Lady…"

"If you don't start calling me Dot, I'm going to make you prove the rest of the tattoos to me."

"Do you want to see?"

Yes!

"Not tonight. I do not trust myself to have you standing in front of me naked. I'm being honest. Yep. Definitely, bad Dots."

He chuckled and flashed me with that brilliant smile. "I like that."

"Bad Dots?"

"That, too. But that you don't trust yourself around me. It makes me happy."

"You cute, little shit."

His smile got bigger and he pulled the sweatshirt back over himself, alleviating my temptation. That scored him more points with me than getting naked when I asked him to.

"So. What are you doing tomorrow?"

"I have no plans."

"Want to go on a date?"

"Where would you like to go, Dot?"

"Thought we might make a trip to Faerie. Wanna come with me?"

"I would absolutely adore spending time with you. Even if it is to another realm."

"Sweet. I'll pick you up tomorrow afternoon."

"I shall be waiting."

I stood up and put my hands on his shoulders. Leaning over, I gently caressed his lips with mine. "Thank you for the wine. And the lovely evening."

"The pleasure was all mine."

For now.

Chapter 10

"Want to grab some dinner?"

I clutched the towel a little tighter around me. Jimmy's timing had been impeccable. I'd *just* gotten out of the shower when my phone rang on the bathroom sink. "I'd love to. Where?"

"Was thinking about something a little romantic."

"No steak or Italian."

"How about seafood?"

"Really? They have that here?"

He chuckled and even through the phone it gave me a little shiver. I loved his laugh. It made me happy.

"Well, it's Red Lobster, that close enough?"

"Works for me. I didn't even know there was one in town."

"There isn't. We're going to have to drive."

"Awww, man."

"I'll drive."

"Okay. But you can drive my car."

"Deal."

"See you shortly."

"Us," he answered, and the phone clicked dead.

Staring at it for a moment, I briefly wondered what I had gotten myself into before setting it back down on the counter. I needed to get dry and dressed.

Dar?

Yes, Lady?

I'm going out for dinner. Let Yuki know. I'll tell Sir Galla Nad.

Was that an attempt at a testicle joke?

Yes.

Feeble, and yet still amusing.

Thank you?

By the time our conversation was over, I was dressed and had my towel wrapped around my head. Since I wasn't driving, I figured a nice glass of wine before dinner sounded kind of awesome.

The elf was on my couch watching TV with an astonished look on his face. I poured my glass of wine and sat on the love seat. "I'm going out for dinner."

"I shall make myself presentable."

"While I appreciate the thought, this is a romantic evening. I would advise staying here."

"Oh. Another one?"

I do believe the elf just called me a slut…

"Yeah. You know us human types. Fuck like bunnies."

"I see that. While the fae appreciate making love in all its forms–"

"It's like painting a living room?" Nana's description on their technique popped out of my mouth before I could stop myself. Damn Siamese twin, again.

"Pardon?"

"I just meant that it should only be done with care and thoroughly. But not too often."

"Precisely. *Yes*. It is much like painting a living area."

I was crying on the inside. Barely being able to contain my laughter, I took a sip of my wine.

Bwahahahahahaha. I got him to admit it!

"Well, anyway. You have the night off. Enjoy your documentary on crayon making."

"They are extraordinary! I would love to have some. To think of the ease of wich art could be created…"

"Um, yeah. I'll pick some up for you."

"Truly?"

"Sure." Now I felt bad for picking on him. Maybe he wasn't such a bad guy.

"I shall be eternally in your debt. Though, it saddens me to be indebted to one such as yourself."

"It saddens me to see you sad, when silent would be so much better."

He harrumphed. "I meant no offense."

"Still talking."

"You wish me to be silent?"

"Tell me what I am, Jaeren."

Things were much quieter after that. Thankfully he wasn't leaning forward when his face turned red and he passed out. Hopefully I would be sitting in a restaurant, eating skrimps, before he woke up.

Mmmm. Skrimp. Garlic skrimp. Coconut skrimp. Skrimp scampi… Eat all the skrimps!

I closed my eyes and leaned back against the soft cushions of my love seat, sipping my wine. It was a dry white and I fervently wished it was elderberry instead. That stuff was magical.

So was the fae serving it.

My thoughts drifted to Shea. Shirtless Shea.

Garlic Shea. Coconut Shea. Shea scampi…

Woah.

I was disappointed in myself. For not checking out the rest of his tattoos. That thought caused my breathing to pick up a little. I fanned myself and took another sip of wine. I smiled as my hand, already in my lap, began tracing patterns over my thigh. I looked around the kitchen and saw I was utterly alone. Yuki had gone to eat. I'd made a call to her dear old dad and set it up for her, or any of my people, to make withdraws. Yuki was so happy, she even gave me a hug. Josie and Candace were out. Dar was nowhere to be seen…

My finger moved on its own down *between* my thighs. As my vision danced with glowing tattoos and tapered ears, I began breathing even heavier as I touched myself.

"Woof!"

Dar was sitting up on the floor next to me, staring at my face over the arm of the love seat. All the heat that had been warming me from within cooled as it traveled up and settled in my cheeks.

I'm going into my room to go die now.

Sorry to disturb you…

Yeah. This shall never be discussed.

As you wish.

I thought you were outside.

Obviously.

I wasn't…

Yes, you were. In front of a passed-out elf, no less.

I wasn't thinking about him, though.

I'm sure.

Alrighty then. Good talk.

He just let out a doggy chuckle as I slinked into my room. I closed the door and leaned back against it. I liked my room and since I would no longer be able to face the damned dog in my living room ever again, I should probably get used to staring at the four walls.

The doorbell wrecked that plan.

I pulled the towel off my hair and whispered the canting of my drying spell as I ran my fingers through it. I still needed to brush it, but at least it didn't look like I had just gotten out of the shower or busted masturbating.

I power walked from my bedroom to the front door, ignoring the still chuckling dog.

Better I caught you than those two.

126

Pulling the door open, I smiled at Jimmy and panicked when my eyes flicked to Derek standing behind him...

"Hey...guys. Come on in. I'm almost ready."

"Hi, baby." Jimmy kissed me as he walked in.

"Hi, Angel," Derek said and leaned in with a goofy grin. I pushed him back.

"Nice try."

"Damn it all ta hell. Thought I had ya with that one."

"Not even close. And I'm not your angel. Not anymore."

"Ouch. Right in tha feels."

"Should I be worried that you two are hanging out together?" I cocked an eyebrow at Jimmy. He was horrible at looking innocent.

"Of course...not."

I wanted to swat him for the pause. "Let me go throw on some shoes and brush my hair."

"Okay. We'll occupy ourselves in the living room."

"Don't hurt the elf."

By the time I looked over my shoulder, he was already poking him in the face. I chuckled and grabbed my shoes, slipping them on and running the brush through my hair as quick as the tangles would let me.

When I was back in the living room, the elf was awake. I briefly wondered where else Jimmy had poked him. "I'll be back later, Jaeren."

"A word?"

I sighed. "Wait for me in the car, kids."

"Come on, Derek. Momma and Daddy are having a fight."

"Aye."

I waited until they left through the front door with Dar. Apparently, he was going with us. "Yes?"

"I apologize."

"What?"

"I am sorry. I consistently say the wrong thing and anger you. I am having a difficult time accepting my role and taking it out on you. Some of it was unintentional. Would you please bear with me and not cause me to lose consciousness again? I find it rather disturbing."

"Fine. No more snark from you and no more roofie phrases from me."

"Roofie?"

"Long story. I'm sorry, too. Have fun and I will get you some crayons if I see any."

His face brightened a little. He was rather attractive when he wasn't being a complete asshole. "Thank you."

"See you later."

"Have a good evening, Lady."

Damn it. Now I feel guilty.

Pulling on my jacket and grabbing my keys, I headed out the door. All three of them were standing by my car, waiting patiently. "He confess his love?" Jimmy asked after I closed the door.

I nearly panicked, visions of Shea dancing in my head. The visions were dancing, not the Shea's. But then he was holding on to a stripper pole…

What the fuck?

"Ho? I mean who?" I shook my head to clear it.

Jimmy cocked an eyebrow at me and tilted his head a little. "Or did you profess yours?"

"Whaaaat? To the elf? Are you kidding me? *No*."

He turned and looked at Derek, who shrugged and looked like he wanted to run. I didn't blame him. I kind of did, too. "Anyway. I'm starving. Let's eat!" I tossed Jimmy the keys and headed for the passenger side door.

I slid into the car and Derek got in the back with Dar.

"I know he's your familiar, but do ye go everywhere with him?"

"With as many times as I've been shot, blowed up, bitten, stabbed, and magicked, he and my vampire have sworn to never leave me alone again. You're lucky I got the elf to stay home."

"Ya. He seems like a bit o' a stick in the mud."

"You have no idea. The other end of the stick is in his ass."

Jimmy started the car and we were on our way to dinner. Thankfully. My stomach was chewing on my backbone. I gave a brief, silent plea that I didn't react to seafood like I did meat.

I wouldn't worry. I can hardly even stand the smell.

Let's just hope you don't inherit my desire for skrimp.

What's a skrimp?

Shrimp. Shellfish.

I would not worry. He made a gagging noise in the back seat.

"You okay, doggy?"

I could feel Dar's piercing glare.

"So. What's the special occasion?" Jimmy took his eyes off the road for a moment to see if I was talking to him. I was. I wanted to know what he was up to.

"Nothing. Just trying to get to know Derek a bit more. He's really fun."

"Thank ya. Not so bad, yerself."

Oh, goddess. They were bonding.

"So. How was your day?"

I glanced at him in panic. Having no intention of withholding any information about my morning with Jimmy and my evening with Shea… I wasn't exactly keen on discussing it in front of my ex-boyfriend. Who left me. Good thing I wasn't bitter anymore.

"You don't want me to tell you right now."

"Oh, now I do."

"No."

"Please?"

"Nope."

"If it's about the chief, I don't mind, Dot."

I'm not so sure about that. "It's okay."

"Don't make me turn this car around."

"Fine. I was riding Jason on his couch and Chief walked in. Happy?" I added testily.

"Well, a little more detail would have been nice. My junk barely flinched."

"I'll make your junk flinch."

"Ouch."

"You have no idea…"

Derek leaned forward, putting his head closer to us. "Is Jason another boyfriend?"

"Yeah."

"So, you have three of em now?"

He wasn't angry, and didn't sound disgusted, either. Which was refreshing. He was merely curious. "Yes."

"Never woulda thought I'd see somthin' like this happen. You were so…reserved in our youth."

"She still is. It took her longer than I thought for her to come to terms with it. She wanted to take things slow, but all of us wanted her so bad, we kind of egged her on." Jimmy smiled at Derek in the mirror.

"Aye. I can see that. I still do na understand how ya don't get jealous of each other. Step on each other's toes. Or dicks."

"Simple. It turns me on. I love the thought of Dot being with other people. Chief loves her but doesn't want to get married or live together. And Jason…probably just thinks he's the luckiest sonofabitch in the world."

That made me smile. It was probably true. "Yeah. Chief and I would both probably end up arrested for attempted murder if we lived together. We're too much alike."

"And do ya love him?"

"Yes. Jason, too."

"Sorry. I not pryin'. Just tryin' ta understand. If I ask too many questions, tell me ta shut me mouth."

"Don't worry. I will."

He chuckled. "Just the three?"

I hesitated a moment too soon. Jimmy caught my pause. His head turned completely toward me with a curious expression on his face. "Yes."

"What aren't you telling me?"

I sighed. "I'm finding myself extraordinarily attracted to somebody…"

Derek seemed to swell in the back seat. With pride. Not lust. "Who?" He asked, thinking he already knew the answer.

"Not you," I said honestly. When he came back over Thanksgiving and I saw him at my door, I was. I practically drooled while watching him eat. But when I saw how afraid both Chief *and* Jimmy were, it made me stop and think. I thought about the hurt and betrayal I felt after he left. He never even tried to contact me once while he was in Ireland. Not once. I hadn't heard shit from him in forty years. That kind of pissed me off and I wasn't the little lovestruck witch he left behind.

I turned my head and gave him a steady glare. Even thinking about it just made me angry. He gave me a sad smile and a knowing nod.

"Who?" Jimmy asked, again.

I turned my head back and said, "Shea."

"Woah."

"Librarian Shea?" Derek asked incredulously.

"Trap Shea?" Jimmy sounded intrigued.

"Trap?" I was trying to make the connection but failing miserably.

"It's a trap!" He sighed when I didn't get the joke. "A trap is a man so feminine and beautiful that you receive a surprise when you see him naked."

"Oh. He's definitely a trap," I said as the car jostled as we entered the Red Lobster parking lot. Jimmy almost hit three parked cars in shock.

"You saw him naked?" He pulled into the closest open spot. At least they weren't busy.

"What? No. Only half naked. I asked him to take his shirt off."

"So, ya aren't sure if the lad has a package?"

"Oh. No. I just meant I got a surprise when he took his shirt off."

"He has tits?" Jimmy sounded like he was about to shoot a load in his pants.

"What? What is wrong with you people? He has tattoos, not tits. He's covered in them and they glow when I touch them."

"You touched his tattoos?"

"Yeah. It was really cool. They almost looked digital when my fingers slid over them."

Jimmy groaned and shut the car off, they were both staring at me with open mouths.

"She moves fast, Jimmy."

"Aye, Derek," he answered, mimicking his accent perfectly.

"I'm starting ta see the attractiveness of her touching another man, though."

"Aye."

I was shifting, uncomfortably, under their stares. "Come on. Let's eat. Roll the window down for Dar."

He turned the key back on and rolled the window down before shutting it off again.

"Be a good boy and I'll bring you a doggy bag!"
Bite me.

132

I shut the car door, heading toward the entrance while the boys adjusted themselves. It only took a few moments, and I was glad I hadn't mentioned the kiss. Yet.

"Hi, welcome to Red Lobster! Just you tonight?"

"No. Two more are on their way in."

On cue, they opened the door and walked in. Little Suzy, if I read her name tag right, lost all sensibility and stared hungrily.

Mine.

"A table in the back if you have one."

She blinked and looked back to me. I almost heard the ripping noise as her hungry gaze was torn from my man flesh. "Sorry! Yes. Right away."

She grabbed a handful of menus and led the way. What bothered me more than her staring was the jealousy that flared inside me. I was getting used to it, but this time I wasn't sure if it was for Jimmy, Derek, or both of them. I sighed and followed her after palming a pack of kiddy crayons for the elf. I'd buy him a big pack next trip to the store. He could make pretty things with four colors for now.

We were seated in a corner booth. Shockingly, I ended up in the middle and the two of them were a little closer than necessary. I mean, they both smelled good and I didn't mind if we weren't going to be eating. They hadn't seen me devour skrimp. I didn't want to take out an eye with a stray shell. I spread my elbows and they took the hint, looking a little embarrassed.

Our waitress, a cute little blonde with short cropped hair, thankfully seemed to be more interested in me than the guys. She efficiently took our drink order and left while the guys looked at the menu.

"Did anything else happen?"

"Where?"

"At Shea's."

133

"I might have kissed him when I left. Softly. Oh, and I agreed to go on a date with him when we get back from Faerie."

"Did ye say Faerie?"

"Yes?"

"Why?"

"Elven assassin. Goddess commanded me to go. Long story. Jimmy fill him in."

He nodded, not looking up from the menu.

"Ye are so different from so long ago."

I looked over at him, a little in shock. "That was forty years ago. Of course, I am."

"Am I?"

"I don't know. You haven't left yet." I laughed and slapped my knee.

"Ouch."

"Tell me you didn't deserve that."

"Aye. I did. I should have kept in contact with ya. I figgered I was makin' things easier on ya."

"You didn't. But thanks for trying."

He nodded and focused back on the menu.

Our waitress brought our drinks. "What can I get you folks to eat?" I tore into my strawberry daiquiri as fast as I could without freezing my brain. I hated frozen drinks, but it sounded yummy. And had dark rum on top.

"Ultimate shrimp feast."

"Same."

"Same."

"Have it out to you shortly."

I grabbed a biscuit, ripped it in half and shoved both in my mouth. That way, I had an excuse not to answer anymore of Derek's questions. Maybe I could chew slowly enough that the food would be out before I finished. My plan worked until I started choking on the biscuit. It literally tried to end my life. Sure, I'd tried to kill it first, but it was one of those garlic cheese thingies. They deserved to die. Nothing should be that delicious and live.

Derek started pounding my back, Jimmy got ready to do the Heimlich, and I grabbed my drink. I poked a hole with the straw through the wad of buttery, garlicky wad of drywall paste it had transubstantiated into in my mouth and started sucking as hard as I could. The liquid, thankfully, started to dissolve it and I swallowed it down like a spider sucking out the innards of a fly.

I suddenly wasn't very hungry anymore.

"Well, this is fun," I managed to croak out through my raspy, biscuit scraped vocal chords.

"Watchin' ya eat...tis interestin' ta be sure."

Chapter 11

My belly looked like I was heavy with child. Thankfully it was just a food baby. I'd devoured my ultimate shrimp feast, and part of Jimmy's. If I were more comfortable with Derek, I might have stolen more of his, too. After all that, there was the brownie with ice cream. The waitress even brought three spoons like I was going to share it. She was cute, but stupid.

I groaned in the passenger seat of my SUV, wanting nothing more than to get home, strip naked, and curl up in my nice warm bed. My groans elicited a couple of chuckles from Jimmy and Derek. Dar ignored me. I walked back to the car without a steak for him. In penance, I texted Josie to order him something from somewhere. No shellfish.

"Dot?"

"Yes, Derek?"

"I missed ya."

Sighing, I looked over my shoulder at him and gave him a nod. I wouldn't admit it to him, but I did miss him, too.

"Do ye think–"

"No."

Jimmy blinked in surprise but kept his eyes on the road.

"Yer not even going to hear me question?"

"Does it involve you and me?"

"Aye."

"No."

He sighed again, heavily. "Might I be askin' why?"

"Do you really want to have this conversation? Here? Now?'

"Aye."

"Because."

"Because?"

"Yes. Because, Derek. Because you left. Which I'm sure I would have gotten over and forgiven you for. You were moving with your mother. Starting over in a new country. I get that. But you left. I loved you and you went away. Fine. But you didn't write. You didn't call. You didn't tell me if you were alive, doing okay, happy, sad, rich, poor. *Nothing.* You didn't just leave, you walked out of my life. You were the very first person I ever fell in love with, and your actions told me I meant shit to you, so *no.*"

"But…"

"There is no buts. You're back and you want me back. No."

"Aye. I do. But I understand. I tried to spare ya, but in truth I was sparin' meself."

"Yes. You were."

"Can I be yer friend? Can ya forgive me that much?"

I wiped the tears that had sprung from my eyes and were rolling down my cheeks. It had to have been an allergic reaction to the shellfish. I was going to write corporate about posting about food allergies on all their menus. "Friends?"

"Aye."

"Yes. We can be friends."

"Thank ya."

Jimmy reached over and rubbed my knee in a totally understanding and sympathetic gesture. I think he was afraid of me. Probably because he smelled the burning plastic. I looked down and saw I had a death grip on the arm rest of my brand-new car. It had melted in my grip.

"What's that godsawful smell?"

Jimmy looked over and saw the door. "Probably just some electrical tape on the wires in the engine. New cars often have that problem. It gets too close to the block because it wasn't harnessed right and poof, burnt rubber."

I reached down and put my hand over his to say thank you.

"Don't melt me," he whispered softly and gave me a wink.

"Oh, so you're allowed to melt my heart, but I can't melt your hand?"

He turned his hand over and gave mine a little squeeze.

"So. Ya wanna play baseball tomorrow?" Derek asked from the backseat.

"What?"

"Play baseball. That's what friends do isn't it?"

"Not when one of the friends hates sports. We can go shopping or have our nails done on Tuesday, though."

"Tuesday it is."

I chuckled as we pulled up into my driveway.

Derek opened the back door and Dar shot out of it like a streak of black lightning, stopping in the middle of the front lawn and raising his hackles.

Stay in the car.

What is it?

Danger, obviously. Let me concentrate.

"Back out of the driveway. Slowly."

"What?"

"Derek, close the door."

He did what I said without arguing. He did have some *redeeming* qualities.

Yuki. You home?

Yes?

Dar's outside. Says there's danger. The rest of us are in the car.

Are the wards up?

With all my preaching to the coven about maintaining shields… When the elf attacked, I never got around to putting them back up.

Oops. No.

I heard her mental sigh as the front door was pulled open in a rush. She strode out first, with Jaeren close on her heels. They formed a small semicircle with Dar and scanned each direction. The elf pulled out a blade from nothing. By nothing, I mean thin air. One second it wasn't there, the next it was, shining brightly from within. I wanted a magic sword.

"Should we let them handle it and leave?" Jimmy moved his hand to the gear shift.

"I'll pretend I didn't hear you ask that."

"You're going to go out there aren't you."

"Bet your ass I am," I said and pulled the handle on the door.

Jimmy started to do the same, but I stopped him. "This is the part where you and Derek leave."

"You don't want us to help?"

"I want you to protect yourself. And my car."

"I'm not leaving you."

"Yes. You are. Go, or no nookie for two months."

"I'll be around the corner."

"Good boy."

I shut the door and walked over to my protectors, taking position between all of them. "Do you see anything?"

No. But I can smell them.

Yuki?

Same. They smell like Jaeren, but spicier.

Maybe they had tacos for dinner?

"They're unseleighe," Jaeren said.

"What?"

"Dark elves."

"I know what the hell they are, why the hell are they *here?*"

"I do not know," he answered honestly.

Green light rocketed at us from the roof of the house across the street. I threw up a hastily erected shield and it exploded in green fireworks.

"Are they using roman candles?"

"Elf-shot. That was a test shot to gauge our defenses."

"What is elf-shot?"

"Not something you want to get hit with. Or touched by."

"Got it. Elf-shot bad. Hear that guys?"

Quit teasing him. Dar still sounded amused.

But it's so easy...

The sky lit up and turned green. No less than ten arrows, flaming like they had been lit with phosphorous, hurled at us. No shield was going to stop them, either.

I dropped to the ground and sang to the earth, slamming my hands against it and pouring as much power as I had behind it. Rough jagged pillars of sandstone shot out from my front yard in a staggered circle. Most of the arrows exploded in brilliant showers of green, one got through. It was about to hit Jaeren when Yuki spun and plucked it out of the air.

"My thanks."

"No problem."

We were in the middle of an earthen cylinder. We could still see out between the columns, but them shooting us from afar was no longer a worry.

"What do we do now?" Yuki was on edge, wanting something to slice with her claws.

Dar settled on the ground, sitting. *We wait.*

"For what?" The frustration dripped from Yuki's question.

"To see if they retreat or attack," I answered for Dar.

"There are too many of them to seek them out." Jaeren sighed.

"What are they doing here in the first place?" I moved closer to the pillars.

"Probably looking for me," Jaeren said with a sad sigh.

The rest of us turned and looked at him. "Why?"

"To barter with. They would, no doubt, love to have a royal hostage."

"Oh. That makes sense. Would you care to elaborate on that a little, you pointy eared monkey?" My anger flared. I spun on him, both hands on my hips.

"I planned on telling you."

"When?"

"When we reached my elfhame."

"Oh, by the way, Dot. I'm king?"

"I am not. I am my father's second son. I am merely a prince."

"Oh. Is that all."

"Yes, I am afraid."

Sarcasm eluded him. He hurt my head. I turned to the others. "Do you hear or see anything? Smell?"

"No. I think they left. You should dump the earth walls before the neighbors call code enforcement," Yuki said appreciatively.

Do not yet.

"I must say. I am impressed by your earth magic." Jaeren ran his hand over one of the columns.

"Me, too. First time I've ever done anything like that. Holes are a lot easier than walls."

"I just pray you have not done further damage to my kingdom."

Oops.

"I doubt it," I said after thinking about it. "They're only about twenty feet tall. The hellmouth went all the way to hell."

Gehenna.

Shut up. Hell sounds way more impressive.

We'd been standing there for five minutes. There was no sign of attack.

Want me to scout it out?

I looked down at Yuki and nodded. "First sign of pointy ears and you hightail it out of there."

"Yes, Lady."

She slipped between the columns of earth and I heard the wind blast from her taking off in the direction the arrows had come from. She was back a moment later.

"Um. One of them is standing across the street. Unarmed."

"That's *my* cue. Keep Princey safe."

She nodded and I slipped out from the pillars, Dar right behind me. As soon as we were clear, he shifted into his hellhound form. Guess he wouldn't have fit going through.

"Where are the rest of your people?"

"I have sent them away. We were at an impasse, so I would propose an end to the stalemate."

"What stalemate? You attacked us and I defended. I still have plenty of power left."

Don't tease the bad guy, Dar chided.

You're no fun sometimes.

"We wish you no harm."

"Care to explain the exploding arrows?"

"They were merely an attempt to separate you from your guardians."

"Me?" That was kind of a shock. Apparently, Jaeren wasn't as hot of a commodity as he thought. I couldn't *wait* to rub it in his face. If I lived.

"Unless there is another red-haired high priestess with unusual familiars who closed the portal to Gehenna that I should be aware of…"

We'd finally gotten close enough to talk at normal volume levels and for me to see him clearly. My vampiric vision only worked in dark conditions. The streetlights above us rendered it rather…useless. "Why are you looking for me?"

"We, the Unseleighe Court of Willowmere, wish to retain you."

I was expecting a monster. Tales of the unseleighe sidhe were passed down from time immemorial. When Ireland was just an island of tribes, living in tents, and drinking lots and lots. They were supposed to be fearsome creatures of the night. The one standing before me looked like an…elf. His skin was a little paler than Jaeren's, and he was dressed entirely in black leather. He was kind of hot. "Restrain me? Sounds kinky."

He said retain, dolt.

I know he did. I'm playing dumb.

Choose the role for which you need little practice. Very wise.

The headlights of a car turned onto my street, illuminating all of us in a flare of halogen. I backed out of the road, not wanting to get run over. The bad elf stayed on his side of the street. I was expecting the car to screech to a halt to figure out what the hell was going on in my front yard, not pull into my driveway. The three of us watched him get out of his car, walk up to the front door with a white plastic bag, and ring the doorbell.

Josie answered it, slapped some cash in his hand and took the bag. The driver, without so much as a head scratch, got back in his car, backed out, and drove away.

What just happened?

I believe your roommate ordered takeout.

Oh. That must be your dinner.

He sniffed the air. *Chinese?*

I don't know. Whatever Josie ordered.

Could you hurry this up? I'm hungry.

My apologies, my canine friend.

"I glamoured the humans mind so he would not see your little construct or us."

"Thanks… What is your name?"

"Delron."

"That's it? No Delron the Black? Delron the Merciless?"

"Just…Delron."

"Alright. Well my familiar is very hungry. Could we speed this up a bit? What is it exactly you want to retain me for?"

"Marriage."

"Um, excuse me?"

"Our Queen wishes to pass on. She is ancient to the eldest of us but refuses to pass the crown to the prince unless he is wed and with heir. Our court…is not what it once was. There is little place for elves in this world and our attempts at coaxing brides from other courts has met with utter failure. We even petitioned the elves of Elfhame Autumn Glade for a bride. They turned us down and killed all but one of our diplomatic entourage. The treacherous bastards."

"They sound like a big bag of dicks."

He blinked in confusion. "Yes. They are."

"Unfortunately, Delron. I am already in a committed relationship. Several of them. Marriage, at this time, is not an option for me. I'm sorry."

"Would you at least pay us a visit and hear the proposal formally?"

"It would be a waste of time and you just tried to shoot me…"

"The shots were meant for your underlings. The archers faced pain of death if you were hurt in any way."

"That's some incentive not to miss."

"We find that to be very true."

"Look, Delron. I was already commanded by the goddess to go to Faerie. I was leaving tomorrow. Let me check out this elfhame like she–" His face went from pale to translucent. "Are you okay?"

"The goddess? You have spoken with her?"

"Yes?"

He bowed. Not like a Yuki bow, either. Like, dropped to the ground on one knee and lowered his face to the ground kind of bow. I didn't know it was possible. The elf was pretty limber…

"So. As I was saying. I have to go to the elfhame tomorrow. How about we talk after that?"

He reached behind him and pulled out an arrow. Dar immediately started growling. "I merely wish to give you this. Will you accept it?"

I nodded.

He crossed the street and held it out in front of him, handing it to me across both of his open palms. "What am I supposed to do with it?"

"When you wish to speak to me, launch the arrow into the air. I will come."

"You will? That's a pretty exciting arrow." I chuckled. "Does it vibrate?"

"Vibrate? No. It will send a song for my ears to hear." He didn't get my joke. Shocker.

"Oh. Cool. Well, okay then. Have a good night."

"You as well, Lady." He bowed again and jogged away.

Hey, Dar?

Yes?

That was fucking weird, right?

Very much so.

Okay. Just checking. I'm starting to be a bad judge of what's weird anymore.

I live to serve.

Could you run around the corner and bark at Jimmy to bring my car back?

I will have the vampire do it. I doubt your boyfriend would understand the implications of my bark. He would probably think Timmy was stuck in a well.

You really need to quit watching so much television.

I refuse to watch soap operas. And your remote wasn't exactly made for doggy paws.

You can watch television in your humanoid appearance. Want me to get you some clothes?

If you would. And you are out of beer.

Chapter 12

"I'm sorry. If I'd known how strongly you felt, I wouldn't have invited him."

I gave Jimmy a small smile. "I know. Don't worry about it. Honestly, when he came back, I was so excited to see him. But the longer I had to think about it, the angrier I got. I meant what I said. I don't trust him, not anymore."

"I know. Now."

"You're a good boy."

He barked.

I wish I had my phone to take a picture of the look Dar shot him. I nearly spit my coffee. Setting it down, I wandered over to the fridge. I hadn't eaten since dinner, and I wanted some toast. With copious amounts of Nutella. I hated toast, but it was hard to pick Nutella up and eat it. Especially in public. And Josie called me an addict the last time she had caught me with the jar and a spoon.

"Want some toast?"

He groggily wiped his face and sipped his coffee. He'd spent the night and with as much power as I'd thrown into the earth erecting the wall, I'd pretty much passed after the dark elf left. I'm surprised he wasn't cranky from lack of nubbins.

"Tell you what. How about instead of toast, I'll make you crepes?"

"You can do that?"

"I can."

"Here?"

"Yes."

I can put Nutella on those! "Sure. I'll try them."

"So you say, but your face says you just had a little O."

"O?"

"Gasm."

"Oh."

"Gasm."

"Yes. I get it."

"Ask me nicely…" He was grinning from ear to ear.

"For an orgasm?"

"No. You never need to beg for those. For the crepes you desperately want."

"What? I mean… I'll eat 'em if you cook 'em, but I'm not a super huge fan."

"Oh. Well, then you might as well eat toast."

"Don't get me wrong. I have Nutella. I could probably pour some on a bumper and eat it. But I'm not a fan of toast. Crepes might be a *little* better."

"I could probably be persuaded…"

"Never mind. I'll make toast."

"What?'

"I was going to try your crepes. But, if you're gonna make me work for it..."

"All I wanted was a kiss and a please. Sheesh."

I looked at him dubiously. "And where did you want me to kiss you?"

He started rooting around in my cupboards, pulling down flour, sugar, and vanilla. "Right here in the kitchen."

"Uh huh." I snuck up behind him and grabbed two handfuls of ass. "Gonna tell me the truth?"

"You can't handle the truth."

I chuckled. "Oh. I don't think there's *anything* I can't handle." I squeezed his boxer-covered buttocks.

"You better knock that off if you want to eat."

150

"*Pléisiúr*," I whispered, letting the trickle of power flow through my hands, directly into his glutei maximi.

I had to practically support his weight until he got a firm grip on the counter. Luckily, the flour was sealed tightly. "Dot!"

"Yes, Jimmy?" I chuckled softly, waiting for him to give in.

"Don't."

"Don't what, Jimmy?"

"Stop. I'm almost…there!"

I amped up the power and he shuddered and fell to the kitchen floor, quivering and smiling up at me. "There is something wrong with you!" I couldn't help but laugh.

"That was *awesome*!" He was smiling up at me, which was quite the picture in his T-shirt and boxers. Especially, since he was sticking out of the front of them, straight, hard, and proud.

"Put that away."

"But I didn't finish…"

"You can finish after you feed me."

"I knew you wanted me for my crepes."

I turned around and saw Candace standing there, staring curiously at the front of Jimmy's underpants. "Sorry, Candace," I said and laughed. "Jimmy's making breakfast, want some?"

"Not if he's using that."

"Nah. It's not very good for beating eggs." I stepped in front of him, cutting off her view. No need to scar the poor girl.

She shook her head and smiled up at me. "What is he making?"

"Crepes."

"Yes, please!"

"See? She appreciates my cooking."

"She hasn't tried it yet."

151

"Fine. You ladies sit and I shall be your chef for the morning."

"Coffee, Candace?"

Instead of answering, she grabbed my mug and a clean one and started making us both a cup. I should have known she wouldn't let me do it. I grabbed my mug out of the machine and drained it before setting it back down.

"Can't waste the magic bean juice."

"Is that what you two were doing in the kitchen?"

I blinked at her. In surprise. She made a sexual innuendo charged joke. "Uh…"

Her smile faded and she looked at me guiltily. "Lady, I–"

"Don't! That was funny and awesome and totally unexpected!"

I held up my hand for a high-five.

She just stared at it.

"So close and yet, so far." I grabbed her wrist and slapped her hand against mine. I realized something. "What are you doing up so early?"

"I was having difficulty sleeping."

"Josie snoring?" I grabbed my now full mug from the machine.

"No. I am nervous about our journey."

"I know. I am, too. But, when the lady demands…"

"I know."

"I wish I could go with you guys."

I looked at Jimmy dumping measured cups of flour into my blender. I guess it really did serve another purpose other than supplying Josie with Margaritas. When I bought it, she listed all the things that we could do with it, but to date…that had been its sole role.

"Maybe next time."

"I just wanted to see your reaction around all the hot guy elves."

"Yeah. Due to recent events in my life, the odds of me ever bedding an elf have gone from slim to none." *Half-elves, maybe.*

"What about marrying the dark elf king?'

I was sorry I'd told him about it. "Shut up."

He laughed and hit frappe on the blender. The mixture spun and I fought the urge to plug my ears. I understood their purpose was to liquify anything put inside of them, but I just wished they could do it with a more pleasant sound.

Maybe I should start selling magical blenders. I bet people with hangovers would appreciate that for making breakfast smoothies. Nice and quiet.

"When are we leaving?" Candace asked as soon as the blending stopped.

"Well, we'll ask his heinous when he wakes up. I'll text Shea to be ready."

"Want me to?"

"You have Shea's number?"

"Yes. We have been talking."

Growl. "You have?"

"Yes."

"About?"

Her lips curved in an ironic smile. "Lady... You are jealous?"

"Whaaat? No."

"That means 'yes' in Ancient Dorothean," Jimmy said from the kitchen, ignoring the blender full of batter in his hand and watching our exchange. "She totally is!"

"Nuh uh."

"Fear not, Lady. We were discussing our fae heritage. My heart belongs to the woman in the other room."

"I know. I wasn't jealous."

"She was."

"Shut up, Chef."

He chuckled as he set the blender down by the stove and searched for a pan.

"Cabinet next to the stove."

"Thanks."

Candace got up and padded softly into her bedroom, returning with her pink cellphone in her hand. She finished typing as she sat back down at the table, flashing me another smile. "I told him."

"Thanks, Candace. And sorry for the jelly monster."

She got back up and walked around the table, hugging me tightly. "I do not like men," she whispered in my ear.

"I know," I whispered back and giggled. "You were staring pretty intently at Jimmy's man-whisk, though."

She blushed. "It's been a long time since I have seen one. Unpleasant memories were flooding back, and I was trying to face them."

Open mouth insert foot up to calf. I'm a fucking idiot. Yes, I am.

"Candace…"

She interrupted me with a hand over my mouth. "Not your fault."

I nodded and she pulled her hand from my mouth. "Sorry, still."

She sat back down and picked up her mug, pausing when her phone vibrated. She held it out for me to read.

Be there shortly.

"Well, it's a little early, but at least we'll all be here."

The shadow on the wall behind Candace darkened and a hand appeared, followed by a cloaked Shea.

"Just in time for breakfast."

He blinked and looked around, orienting himself. "Greetings, Lady."

"Hey, Shea." That was more fun to say than it sounded. "Hungry?"

"No. But you have my thanks."

"Do you even eat?" Jimmy flipped a crepe and rolled it on the long thin spatula before transferring it to a plate.

"The shadows provide me with all the sustenance I require."

That stopped Jimmy. He stood there in front of the counter and stared at Shea. "No freaking way…"

"I jest. I ate a plate of fruit and cheese when I woke."

Jimmy narrowed his eyes, and Shea and Candace both started laughing, Shea's just a little deeper but still cute. Jimmy finally got over it and deposited a plate of crepes in front of me. Candace got up and got the jug of Nutella and a knife for me.

"You're going to drown my flavorful and delicate crepes with what looks like baby sh–"

"Don't finish that sentence."

"–owers are fun. Want to have one when you finish eating, baby?"

"Nice attempt at a save."

"I thought so. How many crepes, Candace?"

"One is enough. Thank you, Jimmy."

I took a bite without hazelnut spread and groaned. "Give her two."

She opened her mouth to protest but I held up my hand. "You'll thank me later."

She sighed and stuck her finger in the Nutella before popping it in her mouth. "Mmm."

"Hey. Get a spoon, we know where that finger's been," Jimmy said and wiggled his eyebrows.

Candace's face turned sixty-shades of red.

"I do not understand," Shea said confusedly.

"Well, you see, Shea… When a girl loves another girl, quite often–"

"Don't finish that sentence, either." I paused from spreading Nutella to glare at Jimmy over my shoulder.

"Oh," Shea said with a blush, not quite the same shades as Candace's.

I was going to drown in cuteness.

I tore into my perfected meal. "Oh, my goddess."

Jimmy grinned. "Good?"

"Fanfuckingtastic. Holy shit. You're hired."

"Jason works for you. If I did, too, how much work do you think would actually get done?"

"Who cares?"

"I like that answer."

"It was the only answer."

By the time he brought Candace's crepes, I was finished and wanting more. I handed him my plate and he cocked an eyebrow at me. "And you wanted toast," he said with a throaty chuckle.

"No. I was going to suffer through toast, thank you for teaching me the errors of my ways."

"You're welcome." He leaned in and gave me a kiss. "Wow. You taste better than the crepes."

"Sweet talker."

"Sweet lips."

"Sweet ass."

"Sweeter ass."

Kill me or send me back to Gehenna. Dar whined.

Behind Jimmy, Dar was sitting on the couch and staring at us over the arm. "You're just jealous, Darling. Hungry?"

Yes.

"Instead of me, could you whip up a batch for Dar? No Nutella, though. Chocolate is bad for doggies."

Jimmy smiled and headed back to the kitchen. Dar jumped off the arm of the couch and followed him.

Smiling, I turned back to the table and saw the curious look Shea was giving me. It reminded me of Dar staring at crepes. "What?"

He shook his head and hid behind his cowl a little more. I hadn't noticed, but he'd been lifting his head, exposing more of his face than usual, since he entered my breakfast nook. "Sorry."

"What for?"

"Staring."

"Is not a crime. Stare away. I kind of like it."

Even hiding his face, I could see the smile that plastered itself on his lips. "Thank you."

"If I give you some sunglasses, will you take that cloak off?"

"The light goes around the edges."

Candace stood up and pulled the curtains over the window, lowering the sunny levels of the room. She even ran over to the sliding glass door and closed the blinds.

"Thank you."

It was dark enough for him to be a little more comfortable. He pulled the hood back and stood, letting the cloak fall behind him and deftly catching it with his hands. He folded it in half and placed it over the back of the chair.

He was dressed for Faerie in a rough spun tunic style shirt and leather pants. Leather freaking pants. He looked…incredible. Incredibly edible. I wanted a nibble. I let out a sigh that was audible. "You look nice."

"Thank you, Lady."

"It wouldn't kill you to call me Dot."

"It may, for such a beautiful name cast from my unworthy lips might be the actual death of me."

Oh, fuck me. He's fighting dirty.

"Say it."

"You wish me to perish?"

"I wish to hear my name from your lips."

He leaned toward me, but not close enough. I cursed the small table between us. "Yes, *Dot*." He made my name a breath of need. I shivered involuntarily.

157

"I think she liked it." Candace was happily forking small pieces of crepe into her mouth and watching the exchange like a tennis match on television. She smiled and licked a stray bit of Nutella from her fork.

"Oh, I did."

Shea leaned back, a small worried look on his face as he cast nervous looks at Jimmy, happily cooking and giving Dar a play by play of his cooking methods.

"Don't worry about that one. He's happy as long as he gets to watch. Or I tell him about it later."

"If it were a chance to merely stand by you, I would brave an audience of a thousand."

"Did you google 'how-to pick-up chicks' before you came over? Cuz I'm going to be honest, it's working."

He smiled and blushed again.

The fork fell from Candace's hand and a glazed look filled her eyes just before they started to glow with a golden light.

Shit.

At least she didn't start floating in my kitchen. "Greetings, Daughter."

Putting my hands together, I bowed respectfully. "My Lady."

"Be at ease." She reached down and cut a piece of crepe off and popped it into Candace's mouth. "Wonderful! Gently seasoned with the love that one has in his heart for you." She pointed at an incredulous Jimmy, holding the pan and spatula in each hand, not knowing what to do.

Shea backed his seat up, stood and bowed, not daring to meet her eyes.

"We're leaving for Faerie, today," I told her. In case she didn't know. I knew she probably knew, being a god and all, I just wanted to make *sure* she knew.

The goddess nodded. "I know of your plans. You did not think of an integral point before leaving."

158

"I did? I mean, I didn't?" I felt like an idiot.

"Nay. You are bound to all of those who will travel with you, save this one." She reached over and stroked Shea's cheek.

Surprisingly enough, the jelly monster didn't rear its ugly head. Hard to get jealous of a goddess, though. Especially when she can smite thee and all that.

"You wish me to bind myself to him?"

"Nay. You should bind him to the coven before you go."

Oh. That's much less fun.

"But, it's daylight..." I didn't think the ritual would work with the sun up. That is the Lord's territory.

"And the moon is still in the sky."

"Oh." I nodded appreciatively. Even the sun and the moon shared the sky at times. "It will be done, Lady."

"Dot?"

The light had faded from Candace's eyes and she was staring at us, bewildered. "Welcome back, Candace."

∞ ∞ ∞

"You sure about this, Dot?" Chief glared at me over the makeshift altar I'd pieced together in my back yard. He, Jason, and Dwight were the only other members of the Coven I'd been able to round up on such short notice.

"About what?"

"First, performing the ritual without the entire coven."

"No choice. You tell the Lady no."

"Good point."

"Second point?"

"You. Blood. Bindings. You trying to make another familiar out of a witch?"

"Pshah!"

"I'm serious."

159

"Can't be done."

"You said that about vampires and demons, too."

"I'm serious. Witches are the binders, not the bindees. Is that a word? We'll just go with bound."

"Okay. I've said my piece. Now when something goes horribly wrong, you can't blame me."

"Probably will, anyway."

"I don't doubt it. But at least I can throw an I told you so out there. Everybody heard my objections, right?" He looked around my back yard. Every head was shaking. "Traitors!" At least he chuckled in the face of mutiny.

"Shea? You ready?"

"What did he mean?" He was staring at me, worriedly.

"Don't worry. He thinks I'm going to turn you into my familiar."

"Oh. That might not be so bad…"

Chief blinked and stared at him, openmouthed. "You quite sure about that, Shea?"

"Positively certain." He looked back up at me. "Would I be allowed to curl up in your lap?"

That image sent happy little thoughts to all the wrong places. Well, technically they were the right places, just at the wrong time.

With a thought and a word, I ignited the circle around us, a shield flaring over my property and hiding us from the prying eyes and ears of my neighbors. The neighbors who had yet to introduce themselves. Not that I blamed them. I full on realized I was the creepy crazy neighbor to be avoided. For now. But come Halloween… I'd have all the kids lined up for my planned haunted house. That and the king sized candy bars I gave out every year. I guess I couldn't complain about the neighbors too much. I hadn't introduced myself yet, either. I'd have to bake them some fruitcakes for Christmas. That would earn me some brownie points. I'd make them brownies, but I didn't need to score anymore fruitcake points with them. I'd already blown up the neighborhood once.

Jimmy ignited the fire in the hastily erected firepit in the middle of my frost encrusted lawn. The air around us began to warm and another spell took the last bite of chill from the air. It was the best we could do without a bonfire.

I took off my cloak and set it next to the altar. Everyone else shuffled out of pants and shirts. One of Jason's first jobs had been to order cloaks for the entire coven as a gift from me for Yule. They still hadn't showed up and I was starting to panic.

"Greetings, Coven of the First Moon."

"Greetings, Lady."

"We are gathered today to bring new blood into our fold. What say thee?"

"Aye," they all said in unison, voicing no objections.

"Shea Donovan, step forth."

He stepped from the circle and stood before me. I smiled at him and grabbed the scian from the altar. He held out his hand and I gently grasped his wrist. The plan was to bind him to me as I was bound to the coven. This was an abbreviated rite, hence Chief's worry. I knew in my heart nothing was going to happen. I hoped. Okay, maybe I was a *little* worried, but I wasn't going to tell the pompous boy scout that. But it was better to find out now, than when I had to bind other individual members of the coven. It was hard to get all of us together on short notice. People had lives. Even witches.

"It is time. Do you, Shea, wish to be forever more, bound to the Coven of the First Moon? Do you accept me as your high priestess, severing all binding ties laid down before?"

"I do."

I gently sliced across his palm, letting his dark blood flow freely into the copper bowl between us.

"I, as your high priestess, gladly welcome you. May we always be your home."

I sliced my own hand and tilted my hand over the bowl. Nothing fell in. Turning my hand back over, I saw the wound had already closed.

Well, this is awkward.

I tried it again, the shallow cut healing almost as fast as the blade passing through it.

Shit.

I braced myself, driving the blade *through* the palm of my hand, and nearly crying out as the pain traveled up my arm.

Son of a bitch.

Everyone around us surged forward, thinking I had lost my mind. Maybe I had, but the freaking blood was finally flowing. I just had to hold the tip of the dagger over the bowl. My blood dribbled into his. When enough had fallen, I pulled the knife from my hand and stared at the wound, angrily, until it closed.

I wiggled my fingers to make sure everything still worked. Shea was staring at me in awe. Ignoring the feeling in my chest, I swirled the tip of the dagger in the bowl of blood.

"As our blood mingles may the ties that bind be freely embraced."

I picked up the bowl and brought it to Shea's lips. His eyes had been mostly closed as he squinted painfully in the sunlight. I wished we could have waited until sundown, but thought it best not to put off what you were commanded to do. As soon as the blood touched his lips, his eyes opened all the way and he gave a little gasp.

Here goes nothing.

"As you have taken us into you, so shall we drink from you." I grimaced as the rapidly cooling magical mojito hit my tongue, the already coppery taste magnified by the copper vessel.

His name wasn't Shea Donovan. That was the name he gave himself as he stepped off the boat from Ireland over a hundred and fifty years ago. His *true* name was Shelandriel Veth. He wasn't just fae blooded, he was half elf. Half dark elf to be exact, and it was from his father that he inherited his shadow walking ability. He came from a family of assassins. His mother was a witch. When she saw he had been born with the runes covering his body, she feared for him and ran before the father could take note. They weren't originally from Ireland, they were from France. She'd gone to Ireland to hide. Unfortunately, that is where his father found them. His mother sacrificed herself to give Shea the time he needed to escape and flee to the New World. In one last great explosion, she made sure the father would never be able to chase his child again.

The rest of his history flashed before my eyes until it wound down to the latter years. He happened upon Mother's coven out of sheer luck and immediately fell in love with Ashville. He was quite content to spend his days reading books and became the town librarian, having inherited his mother's love of the written word.

Until the day he saw me.

I wasn't even twenty the first time I caught his eye. For years, he watched me from the shadows, never quite building up the nerve to talk to the bubbly youth with fiery hair and a temper to match her mother's. How he desperately wanted to, until the day I met Derek. I was gone, a casualty of his hesitation.

He was jealous of Derek, of course, but he couldn't be angry, not when he saw how happy I was whenever he was around. Maybe it had been for the best. There was no way a woman as beautiful as me could ever love a half-elven mongrel.

163

He was there when Derek broke my heart. He just happened upon the scene and he had reached out a hand to strangle him with shadows. They slowly reached for his neck until I said something. When he pulled his hand back, he pulled the shadows back, too. Thankful he had been unable to do something so heinous, he could only imagine what Derek's death would have done to me.

He resumed his role as my watcher. My keeper. At least twenty times flashed before me of him popping from the shadows, keeping me from harm. The daughter of a high priestess was always the target of those who wanted something in exchange. He kept me safe, from monsters, elves, and even the vampires once. His role became well known to, and encouraged by, my mother. But she made him swear to never abuse his station at my side. A trade he couldn't have been happier making because that is all he *ever* wanted. To be there for me, and for me to be happy and safe.

Shea's face came back into focus. As did the rest of the coven standing over me, lying on the cold grass, naked under the morning sun.

"Are you okay, my Lady?"

"Yeah. Help me up. Quickly. My ass is frozen."

Shea backed up, edging the rest of them away from me a bit. He reached down and offered me his hands. Taking them, I lifted as he pulled. When I got back to my feet, I instantly regretted leaving the stable ground.

"I told you so!"

I shot Chief a withering glare.

"What? I did."

"Shea. Help me inside, would you?"

"Yes, my Lady."

Chapter 13

He kicked my bedroom door closed behind us, not wanting to let go of me with his hands. I'd barely made it inside without falling over on top of him, but after spending ten minutes in his head, I was pretty sure he wouldn't have minded that *too* much.

"Think something at me."

"What?"

"Do it. Think of a string of numbers and say them over and over again."

"Okay," he said without hesitation. I could almost feel him reciting the digits, but I couldn't *hear* him. Whatever had happened, I hadn't made him my familiar. Thank the Lady.

"You can stop now."

He stepped closer when we reached my bed, letting me hang on him as he pulled back the cover before gingerly lowering me into the warm softness. "Why the numbers?"

"Well, when your blood hit my lips, something weird happened. Just wanted to make sure Chief wasn't right and I'd made a familiar out of a witch."

"I cannot hear you, either. I believe I am safe."

"And yet, so disappointed…" I smiled at him.

"You can tell?"

He was standing next to me. Which I wouldn't have minded so much if he was wearing pants. Or a shirt. Maybe even underwear. It was a little hard to look him in the eye when his beautiful, yes even his penis was beautiful, cock was staring at me, too.

He might have been a fae, and demure of stature, but there wasn't a damn petite thing about his package. It was strange seeing a guy without tan lines, too. He had none, whatsoever.

Guess there aren't many tanning opportunities in the shade.

"Sit," I said and patted the bed next to me.

Usually, when you tell a naked person to sit down, they look for a towel or something to park their ass on. He didn't hesitate at all, sitting by my hip and turning his leg. Thankfully it had the effect of covering him up. Mostly. Conversation was going to be a bit easier.

"Did anything happen when you drank *my* blood?"

"Yes," he answered, nodding slightly.

"What?"

"I could feel the ties of your mother's coven wither away as the ties reformed here. For a brief moment, I knew where everyone was." He closed his eyes. "I can still feel them if I concentrate on them. Your friend Dennis is at the firehouse. The rest are a warm presence in your kitchen. There are even faint glows of the ones I have not yet met."

"That's awesome."

"Is this how you feel all the time?"

"No. That's a new one on me."

"Then how did you know I felt different?"

"Probably because I got knocked on my ass."

"What happened when you drank?"

"Oh. I don't know, Shelandriel Veth. You tell me."

He gasped and slid backward, falling off the edge of the bed with a small *thump*. I almost started laughing until his head popped back up over the side of the bed and he stared at me in horror. "You know my name?"

"I know more than that. I know *everything.*"

"Everything?"

"Every little thing. Your life flashed before my eyes. Which is also a new one on me."

"You saw everything?"

"I'll reiterate. Every. Thing."

"You know?"

"I know."

"I am sorry, Lady. I shall leave at once." He got up off the floor and dizziness be damned, I shot up on my hands and knees and grabbed his arm.

"Don't you move a fucking inch, Shea."

He hung his head and stared at the floor.

However, he didn't budge. So, I pulled him back to my chest and lay my chin on his shoulder, wrapping my arms around him. Every emotion he had over the past seventy years, every feeling he kept bottled up inside of him. Every touch he longed to take, every chance he passed by, and every hope he ever had for something more, welled up once more inside of me. My heart was broken and exuberant at the same time. Broken for him, and happy for not missing any more time with him. If it took me the rest of my life, I would make it up to him.

"You're very foolish, you know," I said softly in his ear.

"How so?"

"That you never took the chance."

"On what?"

"Me." I kissed his neck and then the tip of his ear, smiling as he shuddered.

He slowly turned around, his lips brushing mine. "I wanted to. So very much."

"I know. I felt it as I saw it."

He nodded. "Where does that bring us to?"

"I'd like to say my bedroom," I said and waved my hand around us. "But…"

167

He nodded, fully accepting whatever I said next, before I said it. "I understand."

"No. You don't. But," I continued, "it's kind of funny. I mean, I cared about you before the rite. A *lot*. Especially after sharing wine and conversation with you. I wanted to get to know you better, but now… Now, I know everything about you. Literally everything. Now, that makes it so much more. I want you."

"I've always wanted you."

"I know." I pulled him that last fraction-of-an-inch closer and kissed him. As my lips mashed against his with a burning need, I wanted to run my hands all over his body, but I didn't. Instead, I pushed him back. "With that said," I chuckled briefly at the bewildered, happy look on his dazed face, "I am also in several other relationships. I'm not going to do anything else."

"You're not?" His bewildered look morphed into outright confusion.

"No. Not until I've had a chance to speak to the others about this. That wouldn't be fair to them."

He smiled and nodded, relief plainly etched upon his face. "I have waited this long, a few days more should be nothing. I just hope they say yes."

"I was just hoping you didn't mind me having more boyfriends than just you?"

"Of course not!" He seemed indignant. Which came as a little bit more of a surprise.

I just shook my head and fought the urge to rub my eyes. While their acceptance of other lovers was often a happy surprise, just *once* I wanted one of them to say, "Fuck that! I want you all to myself." After they said that, I could tell them no and tease the hell out of them until they can't stand it anymore and agree to be with me anyway. Just *once*.

I guess I shouldn't look the gift horse in the ass.

"Are you all right?" Shea was staring at me, a concerned look replacing the indignant one.

"In the head? No. Happy? Yes. Still shaky? Yes."

"Do you need anything?"

"Maybe a couple of Advil and some caffeine." I sat back down to slide off the bed, but his hands quickly braced my shoulders, leaning me back onto the mattress.

"I shall get them for you. Rest."

He moved silently across my bedroom floor, grabbing the handle and pulling the door open. Chief, Jimmy, and Jason nearly fell into the room.

"We were…uh…just um. We were making sure you were okay. No uh…lasting effects. What happened?" Chief rubbed his neck, realized what he was doing, and shoved his hand in his pocket, the other one already on his hip.

Shea seized the opportunity to skirt around them to fetch my coffee and headache removal pills. I just happened to catch Jimmy's glance as he watched the gracefully moving naked Shea. He caught me looking at him looking at Shea. He gave me a little smile and wiggled his eyebrows.

I rolled my eyes.

"What? Asking you why you passed out isn't too much to ask for is it?"

"I wasn't rolling my eyes at you, Chief. The pervert next to you."

"What?" Jimmy tried to sound innocent. It was like watching Josie try to open a new jar of pickles. Entertaining, but it just wasn't going to happen. "I was just making sure he was a guy."

"Glad you got an answer to the big question." I sighed and looked at Chief. "Never mind. To answer your question, I'm fine. I think. The good news is I don't have another familiar."

169

"That's twice you've struck out. Thankfully," Jimmy said and nodded, referring to Jaeren.

"Preaching to the choir. Two is more than enough."

"So, what happened?" Chief sat at the end of the bed. Jimmy and Jason just stayed in the doorway, looking all hunky.

"I drank his blood and I downloaded the zip file of Shea's life."

"What?"

"Close the door."

They all gave me ominous looks.

"Let Shea back in when he knocks. He's bringing me feel betters."

Jason nodded and took up position. Jimmy wandered around to the other side of the bed, plopping down next to me and propping his head up with his hand as he lay facing me.

"This stays between us. I drank and his *entire* life flashed before my eyes. And before you ask me if I mean everything, I fucking mean everything. Not just what he saw, what he was feeling, thinking, everything. The guy has been in love with me for the better part of my life. Here's the crazy part, he *protected* me from everything, too. Attempts at taking me hostage, you name it."

"Woah." Jimmy's usually wiggling eyebrows almost disappeared into his hairline.

"Yeah. But he never even really introduced himself. He was about to when Derek and I started dating. He even stayed close for our entire relationship, still vigilant. When he saw Derek break my heart, he never said a word, just watched from the shadows. Though, he probably would have if my mother hadn't used him to keep me safe.

"Your mother… She is not a nice person."

I blinked at Jason. That was very brave of him to say. She was probably listening. "She has her moments. Like

170

every other super blue blood moon eclipse, she donates to a charity for homeless puppies in Africa, or something."

"We should have her nominated for sainthood." Jimmy ran his finger over my comforter in front of him. He was paying attention, but thinking about something else...

"You okay?"

He looked up and saw we were all staring at him. "Yeah? Why?"

"You seem lost in thought."

"I was just wondering why you were telling all of *us* this before Shea came back into the room. You want to add him to the relationship mix, don't you?"

Busted. "Yes. Which is why I told him I needed to talk to all of you before I made any commitment. It was very fortuitous that you just happened to fall into the room when he opened the door."

I cocked my eyebrow and turned my head slowly, staring at all three of the perpetrators. They all, at least, had the decency to blush. Well, Jimmy didn't blush, but he looked around the room, avoiding my eyes. His method of almost blushing.

"We were worried about you," Chief reiterated.

"Uh huh. Worried he and I were naked in my bed?"

"Maybe a little," he answered honestly.

"I wasn't worried so much as I didn't want to miss the show," Jimmy said forcibly.

Chief gave him a disgusted look. "There's something very wrong with you."

"Please. You enjoyed seeing *him* naked almost as much as me."

"Hardly." He defended himself, but blushed a little, too.

"You could hardly see him? You're telling us you want a *better* look? Jeez, Bill. You call me a pervert."

"That's not what I meant!"

171

I started laughing. "So. Jimmy says yes. Chief?"

"Are you asking for our permission?" He tilted his head.

"Yes?"

"Why?"

I sat up in the bed a little, making sure the comforter covered my breasts. If we were going to have this conversation, I wanted them to pay attention to my words, not my boobs. Chief could probably muddle through. Jason hadn't seen enough boobs in his life to even *begin* to ignore them. And Jimmy…boobs. Shiny.

"Think what you want, but I am not in a relationship with any of you." I paused a moment for effect…and to make them squirm a little. "I am in a relationship with *all* of you. This is one big, gloriously wonderous thing. There aren't three separate relationships in this room, there is, and always will be, *one*. If one of us has a problem, we all suffer. Do you understand what I am saying?"

They all, wisely, chose to nod.

"So, I *can't* ask for your permission to date Shea. I'm asking all of you if we can bring him into *our* relationship. Now let me ask all of you again… How do you feel about this?"

"Absolutely," Jimmy answered without any hesitation.

"It's a yes from me," Chief said and gave me a little smile, almost as if he was proud of me.

"Yes, for me, too. Does this mean Bill can't shoot me now?"

My head hurt, I laughed so hard. "Yes, Jason. He can't shoot you now."

"I do have a big nightstick, though."

Time slowed and almost stopped. The only two beings in the universe, capable of movement, just happened to be Jimmy and myself. My eyes gravitated to his and our gazes locked. His eye twitched as the muscles in my face became

172

taut like braided-steel cables. Jimmy's slapped the mattress at the precise moment that we both burst out laughing. *Bwahahahaha*, echoed off the four walls of my bedroom.

"Oh, will you two grow up."

"Big nightstick," Jimmy managed to gasp while choking on oxygen.

"I don't get it?" Jason looked at us confusedly.

The laughter started all over again.

"I give up. I need to get back to work, anyway. Call me before you leave, please. And be careful!" He stood up and gave me a kiss on my forehead.

"I will, and don't forget that you're in charge while I'm gone. So, I get to blame you for anything stupid Jimmy does while I'm away." I patted his ass as he walked away, using my other hand to wipe away my tears of laughter.

Shea, still naked, was standing in the door when Chief opened it.

"Oh, go put some clothes on!" He turned his head and closed his eyes, feeling his way through the doorway.

"Is he okay?" Shea glanced over his shoulder.

"I just want to know why it's funny getting beaten by a nightstick?" Jason was still waiting for someone to explain.

∞ ∞ ∞

Jason's tongue parted my lips and slipped inside as I pressed myself closer to him. My hands slid down his back and I grabbed a cheek of his ass in each hand, pressing my lower extremities into his. I felt him grow rigid in his tight jeans. That had to have been uncomfortable, but there was little I could do to alleviate the pressure while we were standing in the wide-open door.

I pulled back and kissed his top lip one more time. "You sure you can't stay a while? We're not leaving until sundown."

"Trust me…There isn't another place in the world I would rather be right now. Unfortunately, I got the notification that the very first shipment of books should be at the store shortly."

"Look at you. Putting work above carnal pleasure."

"Carnal?"

"Very carnal."

"Dot…"

"I'm teasing you. Just so I could see that cute ass reaction on your face right now."

"You're evil."

"More like chaotic neutral, with evil tendencies."

"Probably why you're so much fun and so perfect."

"Um. I think you're perfecter."

"That's not even a word."

"Should be." I kissed him again. "Bye, Jason. Lock yourself in the office and look at porn on the computer if you have to."

"Yeah."

"Are you really?"

"Going to look at porn in your workplace?"

His blush told me everything I needed to know.

"That's hot. I want pictures."

"Really? Woah."

I kissed him one last time and pushed him out the door. "Have fun."

"You, too."

I chuckled, checked out his ass one last time, and closed the door behind him. The guy had an ass like sculpted marble. He had a nice chisel, too.

I sighed and put my back against the door, ignoring Yuki and Jaeren standing there staring at me. I needed a moment. His ass deserved a moment of reminiscing.

"What?" I asked after sighing happily.

"I am going to go eat before we go. Jaeren couldn't tell me how long we'd be gone."

"It's still daylight. Will you be able to?"

"I was going to hit the blood bank first, but I wanted to ask if you minded if I borrowed Candace as a front man. If that doesn't work, I'll raid the vampire house as a last resort."

"Why a last resort? Shouldn't they have stock?"

She blushed.

"Yukina Abernathy, what aren't you telling me?"

"Nothing major. I just want a front man to get the blood for me because vampires aren't supposed to be walking around during the day. Same reason I don't want to raid the vampires' fridge."

"You haven't told them yet about being diurnal."

"No."

"Not even George?"

"Especially not George."

"You don't want word to get back to your father."

"Yes."

"Why?"

"Two reasons. One, he already thinks you're too powerful. I don't want any more friction between you two because of me."

"What's the other reason?"

"I don't want vampires flocking to you to make them your familiars…"

"That's not going to happen. I already promised your father."

"If you were forced to walk an eternity at night or become the familiar of a powerful witch who had the means to protect you, would you stay away?"

"Good point. If Candace is uncomfortable going, tell Josie I'll buy her a ten-pound bag of gummy bears if she goes. Or take both of them and buy them lunch. Take my card."

She reached out and wrapped her arms around me. "Thanks, Dot."

"Welcome, sweetie."

She took off to make her plans. Jaeren stood there staring at me, thoughtfully.

"What?"

"You are many things, most of which I find disdainful, but you do care about your people. You have my respect."

I fake gasped. "That might be the nicest thing you've ever said about me, or to me."

"Well, apparently there is much more to you than I initially thought."

"Thank you."

"That wasn't a compliment. When I first met you, I expected very little."

"You weren't the first, and you won't be the last."

"Apparently, you are also humble."

"Me?"

He nodded and leaned against the wall, crossing his arms.

"Well, if you knew my mother and grandmother, you would understand why. Hard to be full of yourself when you are consistently compared to them, even by them."

"Try being the brother of the future king."

"Ouch. I'll give you that. You win. Did you need anything? Or was it just time for your sexy-stance practice?"

He looked down at his posture and chuckled. "At least I know you do find me sexy."

"No. I just said you needed practice."

It was the first time I heard him belly laugh.

Okay. Maybe he is a little sexy.

176

"I will say, you are *much* more attractive when you laugh." I cocked my eyebrow at him.

"My thanks. I shall endeavor to…laugh more heartily in the future."

"You do that. It's the best medicine."

He nodded. "I was just letting you know I was going to be leaving for a short time, too. I need to gather my things and close my camp."

"Camp?"

"Well, it is difficult to check into motels when you do not have human currency."

"Good point."

"I shall return well before our time for departure."

"Flight leaves at six."

"Flight?"

"Never mind. Human thing."

"Ahh. I still do not understand, but I shall pretend and give you a soft chuckle for your effort."

"See? You do know how to play nice with others. Oh, wait!" I ran over to the counter and grabbed my wallet, opening it and grabbing the small pack of kiddie crayons I had forgotten to give him. "These are for you. It was all I could find, and I promise to buy you the sixty-four-crayon set next time I'm at the store."

He reached out with a shaking hand, tears welling in his eyes. He gave me one last glance to make sure it was okay.

"Go ahead. They're yours."

"You have my undying gratitude. I shall treasure them always."

"Yeah. You're welcome, Jaeren."

Chapter 14

"How the hell did you find enough stuff in my pantry to make all of this?" I stared incredulously at the three heaping plates full of steaming pasta with vegetables, chicken, and a heavy cream sauce.

"Don't thank me until you try it. It might suck for all I know."

I gave Jimmy a doubtful look. "There isn't a single thing of yours I wouldn't eat."

"Ditto."

I dropped my fork and gave him the look. He just smiled and shoveled a forkful of food into his gaping maw.

It is very *good,* Dar said beside me, eating his portion.

You just like that he cooks for you.

Well, somebody should. There is less likelihood of death for me when he does it.

You making fun of my cooking?

What cooking? Spaghettios don't count.

They should. That, my friend, is a gourmet delicacy.

Not even in Gehenna.

"This is very tasty. You are quite a cook, James."

I blinked. Shea was the first person I had ever heard use James instead of Jimmy. Not going to lie, I kind of liked it, but Jimmy just suited him better. Jimmy the Perv, not James the Depraved. It just didn't have the same impact.

"Thanks, Sheamus."

"Sheamus?" Maybe they were secretly bonding when I wasn't looking.

Quiver.

"It's a joke. He called me James earlier, so I called him Sheamus. It was the first time I'd seen him smile."

"It's beautiful, isn't it?" We were having a conversation about Shea like he wasn't even there.

"It is. I gushed." He winked at me.

"Do I want to know in which way?"

"Little bit of both."

"You sure you haven't ever slept with Dennis? Because Derek's accent gives you a chubby. Shea's smile makes you gushy. I swear I'm going to have to keep an eye on you."

"That should be easy to do. You know you want to watch."

He did it again. I didn't know how, and just chalked it up to being Jimmy's superpower. I could make familiars and healed unnaturally. Chief was a dick. Jimmy was a perv, but not any normal run-of-the-mill pervert. He could sense the kinks of the people around him, but instead of using his powers for good, he chose to be a super villain. "Your kinky-sense is tingling?"

"A lot of things are tingling right now. Want a list?"

"Not while I'm eating."

Shea was chewing his food and watching our exchange. "That conversation made no sense to me, whatsoever. But it was entertaining to watch."

"Jimmy has a thing for guys and he thinks you're cute."

"Oh. I see." Without batting an eye, he took another piece of penne off his plate and nibbled on it. Jimmy wasn't the only one gushing, I could watch Shea nibble on things all day…

"Want some wine?" I wanted to watch him sip things, too.

He nodded at me. "Would you like some more elderberry?"

"Fuck yea! That stuff was like liquid crack."

"Elderberry? Wine?" Jimmy looked at me.

"Yeah. Had some over at Shea's place. Wow."

"I shall return in a minute." Shea pushed his chair back and headed straight for the darkest shadow in the curtain covered kitchen. He disappeared without a sound.

"I don't think I'll ever get used to that," I said with more than a little bit of wonder in my voice.

"It's freaky but cool. Know how much fun I could have with that power?"

I looked over at Jimmy. Images of him being arrested for suddenly appearing in girl's locker rooms flashed through my brain.

"This is why I don't teach you things like the pleasure spell."

"Cuz you're mean?"

"No. Because you would do nefarious things with them, super perv."

"I cannot deny this." He grinned at me. "At least I'm not boring."

"This is true."

Shea suddenly reappeared, two bottles of elderberry wine in his hands.

"You trying to get us drunk?"

"What?" He frowned a little. "No, Lady. One is for now, one is for you as a gift."

"Aww, thank you."

"You are more than welcome." He set both bottles down on the table and I got up to get us some glasses.

"I apologize, this might be a little too sweet to go with your hearty meal, but the Lady seemed to enjoy it."

Jimmy chuckled. "No worries. I can drink anything."

181

I got back to the table to watch Shea whip a knife out from somewhere, and deftly cut the black wax off the top of the bottle. "Need a corkscrew?"

"She calls me the kinky one," Jimmy muttered.

"Yes, please."

I should have asked before I got the glasses. Ignoring Jimmy, I went back and pulled one out of the drawer and handed it to Shea as I took my seat. He was amazing to watch, and not in a sexual way, either. Okay, that way, too, but he was a wizard with a corkscrew and a bottle of wine. If Cedar Falls had a fancy enough restaurant, he could have easily found employment as a sommelier.

Instead of pouring the wine into the glasses, he lifted each one and delicately poured enough of the dark purplish liquid to fill each one half-full. He handed me mine with a twirl of the liquid inside the glass.

"Thank you."

"Most welcome." He handed Jimmy his and raised his glass to us both in a quick salute.

As soon as the liquid hit my tongue, I groaned in ecstasy. I'd had the elderberry before, but looking at the bottles, you knew in a moment, this was no mass production. The bottles themselves were black glass, frosted with red runes etched into the surface. I had suspicions they might not even be from our realm.

"Holy shit."

I nodded at Jimmy. "See?"

"Wow."

"I am glad you like it." Shea set his glass down and nibbled again on a piece of chicken.

Jimmy wasn't guzzling it, but I could tell he wanted to. He took sip after sip, his food long forgotten.

"You're gonna get hammered if you don't eat."

"Sweet wines like this don't have enough alcohol in them to worry about it."

"Yeah. Keep telling yourself that."

Shea chuckled.

Jimmy wisely set the glass down and started eating again. "Thanks for sharing the wine with me."

Instead of answering, Shea gave him a shy glance and smiled slightly.

I hit the corner of my mouth with my fork. *Don't tell me Shea thinks Jimmy is sexy, too. My heart can't take that much hotness.*

"You okay?"

"Yes?"

Jimmy's eyes narrowed. He was scanning me with his perv sensors. "You missed your mouth."

"Boy, if I had a dime for every time someone told me that…"

Shea choked on a noodle.

"What's the matter, Sheamus? Something get stuck in your throat?"

His eyes widened and he frantically reached for his wine, washing down whatever it was, but knowing that's not what Jimmy meant.

"It is dangerous to eat around you both," Shea rasped.

"Yep. Dot's appetites can quickly shift from the food to those around her."

I swatted him in the arm.

"But to be devoured by her…" Shea closed his eyes, relishing in the vivid image running through his brain.

"Yeah. It's wonderful."

Shea lowered his head, seemingly to gaze at his food, but I could still feel his eyes on me.

"Is it getting hot in here, or is it just me?" I wasn't kidding. I was melting inside.

"That is the effect of the wine. It is made to warm you on the coldest of days, igniting your internal fires."

"You brought…aphrodisiac wine?"

"No. It is made for travelling."

"Oh."

"I thought it an auspicious start to our journey."

"Oh."

"Why? Are you feeling…"

"No. Maybe. My fires are definitely kindled." I shifted in my seat.

Jimmy chuckled softly and gave up on the food, putting his hands behind his head and watching me. It wasn't helping. "Maybe it's not the wine, but the company," he said with a smile.

"Maybe." I ate another bite. Shea was right, the food was delicious. So was the wine. So was the company.

"Maybe you should lie down? Or step outside to cool off?" Shea offered helpfully.

I took another sip, unable to stop myself. "Yeah. Maybe." I took my wine with me and headed for my bedroom. After drinking Shea's blood that morning, I had finally started to feel better, hopefully I was just a little dizzy and needy from that.

Jimmy got up and slipped a hand under my arm. "Maybe you shouldn't finish your wine," he said and reached for it.

"I'm okay. Just a little…"

"Okay."

He helped me get to my room and sat me down on the bed. "Thanks," I said with a smile.

"I'll go clean up the kitchen."

"You don't have to."

"Don't worry. I'll send Shea in to keep an eye on you."

I narrowed my eyes in suspicion.

"Don't you trust me?" He grinned.

"Would you trust you?"

He leaned down and placed his hand under my shirt, making gentle circles over my belly. Everywhere he touched, the heat seemed to spread, and I gasped. "With you, yes."

"That was the best answer, ever."

"You want him. Take him."

"I don't have to. He's already mine. Just like you."

"Forever and a day."

I reached up and grabbed the back of his neck, pulling him down close enough to kiss. I wanted forceful and toe-clenching. He gave me soft and delicate. I wanted to scream.

He slid his hand up my shirt, between my breasts and moved it over, lightly grazing my left nipple with his thumb. "Why are you teasing me?"

"Because I am leaving the room. I want you to devour him and really make him yours."

"But I want you, too."

"Oh, don't worry. I'll be back."

He pinched my flesh between his fingers, and I groaned

"Shea, Dot wants you," he called over his shoulder. "Have fun," he whispered to me and licked my lips. He stood and handed me my glass of wine.

I gulped it greedily and he took the glass with him as he walked away. "Jimmy?"

"Yes?" He cast a sexy glance over his shoulder.

"Hurry."

"Yes, ma'am."

Shea slipped into my room as Jimmy left. "Are you all right?"

"You keep asking me that."

"My apologies," he said with a bow.

"Shea?"

"Yes?"

"Come keep my company."

"If you wish."

185

"So, how much of the conversation with they guys earlier did you hear?"

"I heard mumblings, but not much more than that." He blinked and looked down. "If you wish for me to be honest, I was afraid to hear their response."

"Well, let's just say it was unanimous."

"Could you please indicate a direction?" He looked like he was about to cry in frustration. I reached out and gently stroked his hand.

"Who could say no to you?"

"They accept me?"

"More than accept. They *wanted* you. Some, in more ways than one," I said and winked, pointing at the kitchen.

All that pent-up fear, loneliness, and regret crashed down around him. He almost choked as he sucked in a relieved sigh. A tear even rolled down his cheek.

Not wanting to waste a single more moment, I reached down and grabbed the bottom of my shirt, lifting myself off the bed and pulling it off in one motion. I lay back down, my breasts fully exposed and a hungry look in my eye.

"Beautiful," he managed to whisper as he slowly walked toward me.

"Overdressed," I told him.

He nodded in understanding, pulling the homespun tunic over his head, exposing himself in all of his tattooed glory. He looked delicious.

He sat down next to me and I shook my head. "I'll get a kink in my neck looking over at you like that."

"Where would you like me to sit?"

"On top of me." I patted my waist.

He stood again and slipped his boots off. He began unbuckling his pants, but I stopped him with my hand over his. Blushing, he gave me an apologetic look.

"You're misunderstanding me. They're coming off, just not yet. I seem to have a thing for leather pants…"

"Oh."

He lifted his leg, bringing his knee over me and gently sitting on top of me. My hands instantly slid over the soft doe-skin covering his thighs.

"See, this is much better. Now we can talk."

"Talk?"

I nodded, head rubbing against the pillow beneath me. "Talk about all the things I want to do to you."

"Oh."

"First, I want you to kiss me."

He leaned over and his lips met mine. He tasted of elderberries and shadows. He was unsure and gentle until I slid my hands behind him and up his back, pulling him into it.

His hips shifted back, leveling himself above me as I felt him through his pants, rubbing against my stomach. I grazed his flesh with my nails, sending shivers down his back as my tongue writhed against his. I could feel the gentle rumble of his chest as he moaned into me.

I was burning from the inside out. The front of my leggings became an instant sodden mess as I gushed from the pleasure of holding him in my arms. All the other guys were much larger than me. Having a man who fit in my arms was a new, completely wonderful experience.

I gripped his shoulders, pulled him away from the kiss, and smiled at the dreamy look on his face.

"That was amazing," he whispered.

"Lean back."

He did as I said, his hands bracing himself against the bed. My eyes and my fingers traced lines down his chest, his tattoos igniting beneath my fingers until I reached the edge of them over his chest. His belly wasn't rippled with muscle, further enhancing his feminine appearance. In fact, if he had breasts, he could have passed for a young, petite woman. Until you reached his hips. They were too narrow, but I traced the delicate bones above his pants.

I smiled as my hand caressed the outline of him. He was rigid beneath the soft leather, pointing toward me down the leg of his pants. I curled my fingers and ran them down the length of him, watching his eyes flutter as I did.

"Untie your hair."

He reached behind him and undid the leather thong keeping his hair back. It cascaded around his shoulders as soon as it was free, wavy strands of chocolate-colored silk.

I cupped my hand over him and began stroking him as I bathed in his beauty. People *told* me I was beautiful all the time. I could never see what they saw and just accepted myself for what I was. I hoped Shea didn't suffer from the same affliction. He was *too* beautiful, and I wished he could see it.

His hips began rocking from the pleasure. The leather pants had lost their amusement factor. I wanted to feel his flesh in my hands…and other places.

"Would you take these off for me now?"

He nodded, his hair falling and covering his right eye. I wanted to squeal and die from the sexiness of it. He slid across me, nimbly standing beside the bed. He reached again for the buckle on his pants, but I got there first. Lying on the bed, it wasn't easy to undo the buckle, but I wanted the honors.

As soon as it was undone, the leather separated and hung loosely on his hips. He looked like a tiny rock-star and I definitely wanted to be his groupie.

He stepped closer, knowing I wanted to undress him. Rolling on my side, I grabbed the sides of his pants and slowly pushed them down over his hips, moaning as he sprang free. He stepped out of them when they were low enough and I grabbed his ass, pulling him closer to my face.

He smelled almost as good as he looked, a hint of spice, a hint of musk, and leather. Kissing the tip, I let go of half of his ass and grabbed the base of him, steadying him as I kissed all around his crown.

"Lady…"

"Let go if you need to. We have time to enjoy this for a while."

I brought him into my mouth and wrapped my tongue under his throbbing cock before slowly dragging him out of my mouth with a little *pop*. "You," was all I could say as I grinned up at him, enjoying seeing him looking down at me with his cock in my hand and wanting nothing more than to be back in my mouth.

"What?"

"You have a *very* nice cock, Shea."

He blushed. "Thank you?"

"Where do you want to come, Shea? Do you want to explode in my mouth?" I leaned forward and sucked him back in, rolling my mouth around him as I pulled him back out. "Or do you want to come inside of me, Shea? Do you want to plunge this inside me and fill me?"

He groaned, nearly going crazy with desire.

"Why not both?"

I peeked around Shea and saw Jimmy in the doorway, shirt off and cock in hand, slowly stroking himself as he watched us.

"That is a damn good idea, Jimmy." I looked back up at Shea. "Do you think you can do that? Can you come for me twice, Shea?"

"I could come a thousand times if you keep looking at me like that."

"That's a damn good answer."

"It is the truth."

189

"Is it all right if Jimmy joins us? He was practically begging earlier."

"I do not mind."

Smiling, I pulled him back with me as I leaned back against the pillows. He lifted his leg over me, knowing exactly where I wanted him. He straddled my chest and knelt above me, close enough to let me take him back into my mouth.

His hips began a gentle motion, and my hands found his ass again as I guided him and out. It was one of the hottest experiences of my life, and when he reached down and pulled himself from my mouth to graze my nipple with the tip, I nearly came.

He made small circles over my hardened flesh and shifted over to the other one. I could feel the heat of his cock and the wetness from my mouth spreading over them and it sent quivers of pleasure straight into my pussy. If I weren't wearing leggings, I would be leaking all over the comforter.

Another pair of hands slid under the elastic around my waist before pulling them down over me, exposing my wetness to the cold air. Jimmy was joining the fun. I spread my legs for him and pulled Shea back into my mouth, looking straight up at him.

Jimmy's tongue plunged inside me and the pleasure ripped through me and out of my throat, vibrating my mouth around Shea's throbbing hardness.

"Lord and Lady. I have never before felt such pleasure." Shea's hips bucked involuntarily.

I pulled him from my mouth and licked him from the base to the tip. "Neither have I."

He noticed my bucking hips behind him and glanced over his shoulder at Jimmy performing his oral administrations. He turned back around and smiled at me. "As it should be."

"It should?"

"Yes. You are our Lady. You should have multiple men surrounding you, pleasuring you in every way possible."

A shudder ran through me, liking that thought. "Brilliant and sexy."

"The view is good from back here, too," Jimmy said from between my legs.

"Less talkie talkie, more lickey lickey."

He sucked my clit into his mouth and proceeded to let his tongue ripple against it, sending wave after wave of pleasure washing through me. I began moaning in tempo and bobbing my head until the effects ran through me and I saw them amplified in Shea.

"I cannot hold out any longer..."

I sucked him harder. Rhythmic throbbing began to build at the base of his cock, and I could feel him pressing upward with each clench. With a small moan, I felt the first rush of warm, stickiness splash against my tongue. His orgasm and Jimmy's tongue became too much for me to bear and I opened my mouth, letting loose with a howl of pleasure. Shea was still coming, and it splashed against my chin and down my chest.

"Jimmy..." I managed to let out his name with a throaty chuckle.

He took the hint and let me go with a gentle kiss. A kiss that sent a new ripple of pleasure through me.

"Lady, that was amazing."

"Yes. Yes, it was." I kissed him again. He wasn't as hard as he was, but it wouldn't take much to bring him back to full strength.

He groaned again a little as my lips caressed him. I could still taste him as fluid still leaked from the tip. I ran my tongue across it. Either I was getting used to the taste, or he tasted different from the others. Sweeter and not as…strong, for a lack of a better word.

"You…um. You taste good."

"Thank you?" I tapped his leg and he slid off me. Jimmy was grinning at me like a fool, his chin above my sex. A chuckle escaped my lips.

"Did you have fun?"

He nodded and saw most of Shea's come on my face and neck. His goofy grin washed away and was replaced by…something else.

"You want a kiss?"

He nodded, vigorously.

"Come here."

He got on to his hands and knees and crawled over me until his lips were pressed firmly against mine. His tongue darted inside, and I swear he sighed a little. "It's all over you," he whispered breathlessly. "You're covered in his come."

"It doesn't bother you at all, does it." I didn't even make it a question.

"No. It's hot."

"And sweet for some reason."

He licked a good portion of it off my chin, and held it with his tongue, forcing it back into my mouth with a kiss. With my guys, I always feel like, "This is it. I couldn't possibly be turned on any more than I am, right now." They consistently prove me wrong.

Sharing that kiss with him was the hottest thing I'd ever even dreamt of. Jimmy reached down and positioned himself before plunging inside me. His cock inside me was exactly what was missing, and I gasped as he drove himself against me with a need and want, he'd never shown before. His name became a litany of syllables as he pounded into me.

I pulled away from the kiss, head thrown back in pleasure. I caught Shea stroking himself next to us as Jimmy fucked me with a hungry need. Reaching over, I gently reached under Shea and cupped his balls in my hand, rolling them around gently.

"Goddess…"

"Do you like that?"

"Yes."

I pulled him closer. The tip of his cock was right next to Jimmy and me. Jimmy turned his head and pressed his cheek against mine as his pounding slowed. Together, we watched Shea stroking himself.

"That's hot, isn't it?"

Jimmy nodded against me.

"Do you want to touch it?"

There was a pause and another, much smaller nod.

"Shea, can Jimmy touch you?"

"Please," he almost whimpered. My pussy spasmed around Jimmy's shaft.

"Go ahead, Jimmy. He shouldn't be jerking himself off when there are two other people in the room."

My gut clenched in anticipation. I wanted to see this. I wanted to see him handling another piece of wood. My insides screamed with how badly.

He turned his head and gave me a gentle kiss before turning back and reaching out. Shea let go and his prick bounced before Jimmy slid his hand down his length and began stroking him.

"First time? Are you *really* sure about that, Jimmy?"

"Um. I've done this a billion times…just never to anyone else. I swear. If I'd ever done this before I would have told you about it a long time ago. I would have watched you touch yourself as I entertained you with the story."

"Fair. I would have been fascinated by it, too. I probably would have come twenty times just from the story alone."

"This turns you on that much?"

"You have no idea."

"What about this, then?"

He pulled Shea even closer, giving him a questioning look. Shea must have understood it because he nodded, almost imperceptibly. Jimmy's tongue flicked out and licked the few drops of moisture that had formed at the opening and then his lips wrapped around Shea's head.

I grunted as Jimmy plunged inside me as he suckled on Shea's cock. I peaked again and lay back, trying to bury myself in the pillow behind me as I bucked against the man on top of me. My orgasm brought Jimmy to the edge as he brought back his hips and slammed himself inside me, emptying himself with repeated undulations of his hips.

Jimmy began sucking in earnest, reaching around Shea and using his hand to push him against him. Shea reached down and ran his fingers through Jimmy's hair. It was sweet and hot to watch that gentlest of gestures.

When Jimmy pulled away, I thought embarrassment had overcome the mood, but I should have known Jimmy better than that. He reached under me and rolled us both over, his cock still inside me swimming in our combined fluids.

"You want in on this?" He grinned up at Shea.

"I do not understand."

"I want you to fuck her while I hold her."

"But… Aren't you still inside her?"

"Yep."

"Jimmy?"

"It's up to Shea. Not me. I was asking him if he wanted to."

"I've… I've never had anything in my ass before."

194

"Who said anything about your ass?"

"Wait. You want him to stick his dick inside me with yours already in there?"

"Yeah."

"Okay. I'm game if Shea is." I was almost shaking. *Holy fuck.*

"Lady?" Shea asked to be certain.

I nodded. My eyes telling him I was completely okay with it and that I actually might be a little excited about it.

He smiled.

"Only if you want to."

"Oh, I do and do not need to be asked again."

Jimmy spread his legs and I did the same, giving Shea a place to kneel. "I love you," he whispered beneath me.

"You sucked a cock for me. I love you more."

"Might have sucked it a little bit for me, too. Kinda always wondered…"

"Did you like it?"

He just grinned and then frowned. "Wait a minute! I sucked a cock for you. I get to love you more."

"I might have said yes, but you said you liked it, so it doesn't count. I love you more."

The tip of Shea's manhood shut us both up as it touched us in all the right places.

"Go slow. I don't know if you're going to both fit in there."

He gripped my hips and pushed in. There was *an abundance* of lubrication. Jimmy had never pulled out so most of it was still in there. Shea forced it out and I felt it as it dripped down over my already sensitive clit and judging by the astonished look on Jimmy's face, landed on him.

"Now you know how I feel."

"Happy?" He stared into my eyes.

195

All I could do was nod, the sensation of Shea overfilling me was all I could comprehend. When his hips pressed against me, all I could mutter was, "Full."

Thankfully, he stayed that way for a moment, letting me adjust. I breathed through a small orgasm, my forehead pressed against Jimmy's.

"Feels good, doesn't it?"

"Yes. How are you still hard?"

"Um… This is like the fucking hottest thing ever? I'm probably going to have an erection that lasts more than four hours. I'll probably have to consult a physician."

"Or, I could just continue to take care of them for you."

He groaned. Jimmy, the shit, curled his hips pushing *himself* inside me further. As he did, Shea pulled back a little. Jimmy pulled and Shea pushed. They slowly worked together to get the basic movement down before they utterly destroyed me with pleasure.

"Oh, my Lady. Holy fuck." I couldn't even breathe, I had no idea how I formed the words.

Jimmy grunted beneath me. "Not going to last long."

"What? You literally *just* came."

"His cock…it's sliding against mine. The undersides… It feels too good."

And just like that, he exposed his weakness to me.

I looked over my shoulder, and judging from the look on Shea's face, he was having the same experience. Another orgasm crashed through me and I lost my train of thought. And reality.

Oblivion is such a pretty color.

They slowed their movements as I fought my way back. I was lying on Jimmy and panting. "Woah."

"Welcome back."

"Give me a second. Stop moving, completely." I could feel myself clenching them both together as the pleasure still rippled through me.

196

"Stop that. You're going to make me come," Jimmy grunted.

"Stop what?" Clench.

His grunt turned into a whimper. "That!"

I chuckled softly. "You mean this?" Clench.

"Shea! Damn the torpedoes, full steam ahead."

"Aye, Cap'n."

Now I know how an oil field feels. The two bastards inside me drilled me, see-sawing me from the inside out. Another orgasm hit me. And another one after that. Quite possibly a third, but it was hard to tell where one stopped and another one started. I was in heaven and hell. I didn't know how much more I could possibly take and then Shea called out, drove himself against me and spasmed as his hips bucked. I felt the rush of come escape me, dripping down, and I was filled again as Jimmy exploded inside me.

We collapsed into a wet, sweaty, exhausted heap.

I didn't even care when I heard clapping from the doorway.

Okay. Maybe a little.

Chapter 15

"Good luck and be careful," Jimmy said and gave me one last, lingering kiss.

I inhaled the smell of my shampoo as he pulled away and gave him a dreamy little smile. "Gonna miss you."

"I'll miss you, too. Seriously though, be careful. For me."

"I will."

"Call me when you get back."

"I will."

"Bring a change of underwear."

"You are so frigging weird."

"Yep." He chuckled and headed toward the door.

"Bye."

"See you later."

I smiled at his retreating back. I hadn't lied. I *really* was going to miss him. Chief and Jason, too. In fact, I was looking forward to going to Faerie like having a barium enema and a colonoscopy for kicks.

"Ready to go?"

I turned and immediately averted my eyes. I couldn't seem to look Josie in the eye. In our ninety-nine years of friendship, she had caught me in some pretty embarrassing situations. Passed out on top of my boyfriend, yes. Passed out on my boyfriend with another boyfriend on top of me, both of them still inside me. No. I sighed, and said, "Yep."

"You okay?"

"Gee. I don't know."

"Well, it wasn't your fault the door was open."

"Seriously, did you have to clap?"

"Well, as soon as we pulled into the driveway, your vampire familiar started writhing around in the back seat and screaming. I thought you were being murdered in here."

"Did you have to *clap*?"

"That performance deserved a standing ovation. I would have whistled, too, but you looked sleepy."

I nodded appreciatively. "It kind of did."

"That…was the hottest fucking thing I've ever seen. Two dicks are better than one."

I blushed and grinned at her.

"Was it as amazing as it looked?"

"Better. Like exponentially better."

"Woah."

"Yeah."

"Might have to switch teams again to try it once."

I narrowed my eyes at her. "Don't you dare hurt that precious thing!"

"Candace?"

"No. Your vagina. Of course, I mean Candace."

"Pshah. Like I'd ever hurt her."

"Good girl." I patted her on the head and headed for the kitchen. "Think they have coffee, Underhill?"

"Yes, we do. Unfortunately, we have to use French coffee presses since there is no electricity and electronics do not fare well. I suggest leaving your communication devices here." Jaeren stood by the counter, pack slung over his shoulder. He was ready. Dar stood next to him. Yuki was still in the shower. She had given me an angry glare and practically ran to the bathroom as soon as she was able to walk again. She'd been in there for an awfully long time.

"No magic coffee makers?"

He shook his head. "Though, we do heat the water with magic."

"So, you're not complete barbarians."

"No. We even have chocolate."

"Okay. Let's go."

"We are just waiting on the vampire."

"Shea's still not back?" I looked around and didn't see him, either.

"Nay."

He'd run home to get cleaned up. His shadow walking was too convenient for words. He was unsure if he could walk between Faerie and home, though. He was also unsure if he could shadow walk while *in* Faerie. He said he was afraid to try, and I didn't blame him. I wouldn't want to get lost in the shadows, either.

"I am here," he said and stepped from the wall.

"Welcome back."

"Thank you, Lady."

"Josie, tell Candace to come on."

"She's right behind you," she said with a chuckle and pointed. I turned around and she was sitting on the couch, little pink backpack next to her. She gave me an embarrassed wave.

"Sorry, Cand."

"It is okay."

"Yuki! Hurry up, we're going to be late," I shouted toward the bathroom. The light clicked off and the door opened, the vampire stepping from the mist of the extraordinarily hot shower she had taken.

"I'm ready."

"Let's go."

Everybody stood. Josie walked over to Candace and gave her a hug and a gentle kiss. "You be careful. Stay behind Dot."

"I will."

I grinned at the scene. "Where are we going?" I asked before turning to Jaeren.

"I believe the public house was called O'Malleys."

"The portal to Faerie is in a pub?"

He nodded.

I shook my head. "I guess that kind of makes sense."

"I know the place. We can shadow walk there if you wish to leave your car here?"

"That would be awesome." Sounding braver than I felt, the whole situation was setting off my nerves. Faerie, the shadow realm. I wanted my bed and my boys, not go on an adventure.

Shea moved over to the wall, stuck one hand into it, and grabbed my hand with the other. He nodded to everyone else. I grabbed Candace's hand, she grabbed Yuki's, Yuki made a face and held the elf's hand. I stared at Jaeren expectantly.

"What?"

"Touch the dog."

"Oh, my apologies."

He reached out a hand and put it on Dar's neck. Shea moved forward and we chained our way through the wall into the shadow realm.

My mind was having trouble processing what I was seeing. There were no colors and my living room was still there, but it was backwards and behind us. We weren't floating in darkness, but I couldn't see the ground either. I nearly panicked when Shea released my hand.

"It's okay. We just had to touch to get everyone here. We will have to do it again to leave the shadows. Everyone, do not lose sight of the person next to you."

Candace refused to let go of my hand. I didn't blame her and took comfort in her touch, too. Even Yuki grabbed the back of my shirt between her fingers. Dar moved around us and nosed the invisible ground.

I smell demons.

"Shea, Dar says he smells demons."

"All kinds of creatures get lost in the shadows. Not to worry." He stepped forward and was suddenly thirty feet away. I quickly stepped forward to catch up to him and with one step was beside him.

"Okay. That's kind of freaky."

"Time, distance… They mean nothing here."

He took another step and another after that. We followed him and I kept glancing back to make sure we didn't lose anyone. Nobody wanted to be left behind and kept pace, step for step.

"We're here."

"Where?"

"That's the shadow in the corner of the bar."

I peered through it and saw the pool table. The bar was unusually packed. "Won't they see us?"

"People naturally shy away from the darkness. We will be fine."

"Even walking through the bar with a dog and an elf?"

"That they may notice, but we will be quickly forgotten."

"If you say so."

"I can glamour us to not be seen if that is your wish?"

"Please, Jaeren. I don't need anyone talking."

"We need to get to the basement anyway. This will ensure our stealth."

We all linked hands and I felt the glamour as it settled over us like spiderwebs. I resisted the urge to brush them off. Barely.

Shea looked back and nodded, satisfied everyone was ready, and stepped through the darkness. I followed him and blinked my eyes, trying to focus. When they did, I smiled at seeing Dennis and Alista sitting in a quiet corner and laughing. I guess he had assuaged her not-so-far off the mark observations. Giving them a silent wish for luck, I followed Jaeren behind the bar and down the ancient wooden stairs.

We emerged into a dusty storeroom of sorts. The ancient waitress who had served us our drinks our second night in Cedar Falls stood before a bare spot on the wall.

"I've been expecting you."

"Drucilda."

Her glamour faded, her back straightened, and she grew twelve inches. I gasped at her beauty. She smiled at my surprise.

"You're Carol."

"That is my human seeming."

"You're an elf."

"Yes."

"Why did it take you a hundred years to bring our drinks?"

She chuckled. "An elderly lady racing about the bar would arouse suspicion. My apologies for my lethargic service."

"You work here because of the portal?"

"Nay, I *own* this establishment because of the portal."

"Well, I'm glad to see business is picking up."

"Aye." She gave me one more smile and turned to Jaeren. "You are ready, my prince?"

"Yes."

She turned around and ran her hand over the wall. It shimmered, the illusion blasting apart in a shower of silent fireworks.

Cool.

There was a hole in the stone wall, filled with vertical purple liquid, or light that looked like liquid. "That's the gate?"

Jaeren gave me a brief nod.

"What's the purple stuff, and don't say magic because it's not."

"That is the veil between our worlds. It is thinnest here, allowing us to pass through. The arch around it keeps it stable."

"Oh. Nifty."

"Are you ready?"

Not that I have a choice but, "Yes."

I instinctively reached out and grabbed his hand. He stopped just before stepping through and looked down, staring at the offending appendage.

"Sorry. It's just a door. No chance of getting lost, right?"

He looked up at me and lifted his hand. I let go and he sighed, shook his hand, and stepped through the veil.

You just wanted to hold his hand.

Shut your face, Yuki.

Hehehe.

Shea was giving me a curious look. Not exactly jealous, but not exactly happy, either. I leaned over and kissed him on his forehead. The smile he gave me back was enough to make my heart skip a little beat.

Turning back to the portal, I stepped through and my stomach spun around in sixty circles before my feet touched the ground in the middle of a blue-grassed clearing in the woods.

Quickly glancing over my shoulder, I sighed in relief as the rest stepped through the veil. This side, it was encased in a stone arch with elvish runes. We'd done it. We were Underhill.

Other than the clearing, nothing else was visible save for the purple-hued sky above us. It had been dark when we left, but it was still midday in Faerie. "What time is it here?"

205

He pointed at the fiery disk directly above us. "Noon in this elfhame."

"You have time zones?"

He shook his head. "Immortal, and yet still so human."

"Thank you."

"The royal grounds are this way, " he said and strutted toward the woods.

I don't think he meant that as a compliment. Dar nosed my butt to get me moving.

I know. I just like keeping him on his toes. Still not letting go of Candace's hand, I followed behind him, looking at the trees that were almost like the ones back home. Some kind of Cedar, but fluffier with reddish sprigs.

"Witch! Witch!" I stopped and looked around, not seeing anybody, but wincing as the declarations of my lineage kept erupting around the clearing.

"Begone!" Jaeren glared at the trees around us.

A murder of crows, mostly black with the odd white one, rose from the branches and flew away from us.

"Freaky."

"I do not like it here. I feel…smaller."

I looked down at Candace. "Nope. You're still taller than my belly button," I told her with a wink. She actually came up just past my shoulder, but I wanted to see her smile. She didn't disappoint me.

"I feel the same," Shea said softly, rubbing his arms. "I may have elven blood flowing through my veins, but not enough to keep me from feeling that I don't belong here."

"You're standing at my side. Where else would you belong?"

He blinked at me, and I swear to the goddess, his eyes got a little moist. It was only fair, he did the same thing to parts of me, too.

I'm going to throw up.

Shut up, Yuki.

206

A group of elven archers separated themselves from the trunks of the trees around us and knelt in formation before their prince. He raised his hand in greeting.

"Welcome back, my liege," the foremost said and stood.

"My thanks, Allendyr."

"The king received your message."

"Renlynn is not king as of yet."

Allendyr blushed nervously and noticed me watching their exchange. "You have brought the guests."

"Aye."

He turned and gave a signal to the elvish guards behind him. I wish I could have said I was surprised when the back two rows drew their bows and pointed at them, and the front row drew metal shackles from bags slung at their waists. With the way things had been going for me lately, I wouldn't have been surprised had they fired.

"Jaeren…"

"Allendyr! These are my guests. Stand down."

"I have my orders, my liege. Your brother has been crowned, and it is him I must obey."

"You know not what you do!"

"Only what I must."

The manacle-bearing elves surged forward. I sighed in resignation, holding my hands out before me.

Want me to teach them a lesson?

I thought about Yuki's request and decided against it. Twenty bows with arrows were pointed at us. The slightest provocation might set them off. I could probably stop most of the arrows, but somebody might get hurt. Or dead. *No. We'll play along for now.*

I didn't like the smirk of the elf striding toward me. Something felt off about the whole situation. I changed my plan.

Yuki?

Yes?

Run for it, but only if you think you can move faster than the arrows. At least one of us will be free.

I do not wish to leave you.

I know. But do it anyway.

As you wish.

One moment she was standing behind me, the next she was in the woods and gone.

"That was most unwise, witch," Allendyr said and strode forward, drawing his dagger. He was stopped by a wicked right cross from Jaeren.

"You will *not* harm her."

"My prince?" He rubbed his jaw, and stared at my elf in shock.

"I am now her protector, as commanded by the *goddess*. The goddess who bade her journey into our lands. You wish to raise her ire?" Jaeren nearly frothed in anger.

Allendyr was smarter than he looked. He shuddered and shook his head, sheathing his blade.

The elf with the manacles stopped moving toward me. He didn't seem too keen on locking me up, either. "Sir?"

"I will not resist. You may bind me."

"Bind her friends and keep your weapons upon them. Kill the dog," Allendyr snarled to the guard.

Dar shifted into his hellhound form and growled, stepping in front of both of us. Things were not going well for the elves. Jaeren chuckled and stepped back next to my familiar.

"You would defy the king, my prince?"

"The king has been misinformed. I will deal with him when I return to the castle. You are dismissed."

"I am sorry. I have my orders," he said and turned. "Kill them all, spare the prince. If possible," he added almost as an afterthought.

I guess he would rather risk angering a goddess than pissing off his king. Jaeren's brother must be a real peach.

But, just like that, my elf's world came crashing down around him. His own brother had cast him aside for some reason. I almost felt…bad…for him.

Dar gutted the unarmed guards holding useless shackles in front of him. It was enough to draw the brunt of the fire from the elven archers. It gave me enough time to throw shields over us. I wasn't in time to completely protect Dar, but he didn't seem to mind the few arrows that had gotten through and pierced his chest and face. The wounds weren't deep enough to kill, until they exploded.

Elfshot.

Jaeren pulled his sword from the air in front of him and pulled the dagger from his belt behind him with the other hand. His intended target had been Allendyr, but Yuki got to him first, ripping his throat from his neck in a spray of blood. He did cleanly slice through the arrow that had been about to stick into her unshielded back, though.

When I saw Shea, my first instinct had been to jump in front of him, thinking his stature made him an easy target. I'd spent a lifetime in his memories, I'd seen him deal with those who intended me harm. I shouldn't have been surprised when he lifted his arms and shadows rose up and wound around the elves closest to him, dragging them down screaming through the earth beneath their feet. Their own shadows had become their undoing. I shuddered and made a silent note never to piss him off…

I looked around for something to use. The one thing my mother and grandmother had failed to mention about Faerie was the abundance of magic in the realm. It was literally everywhere. Witches lived in the human world and generated the very magic they used within their bodies. We had something not unlike a battery inside of us, a well of power. If we used it all, it became empty, but we slowly refilled it over time. There…standing, surrounded by limitless power, I felt like a god.

I drew the power into me and split the sky above us while reinforcing our shields.

Faerie had been referred to as Underhill since the dawn of time. Its plane literally sat below ours, sandwiched somewhere between the mortal realm and Gehenna. I'm sure there were literally thousands of planes, most of which had never been seen or explored.

With the human realm above us, when I unthinkingly split the sky above us, I literally tore through the veil separating the planes. A good portion of a largish building, two cars, a fire hydrant, and several tons of asphalt and concrete came crashing down upon the elves. Our shields were enough to save us from the edge of the urban shower. The elves, however, weren't as lucky.

"What did you do?"

"Looks like I squished 'em," I answered Jaeren in a state of shock. "Or, most of them." A few archers in the back line escaped death, but not injury. I debated finishing them off but decided to let them go. There was no way the king didn't know we were here, anyway. The limitless power thing was more than a little scary. I was kind of glad the mortal realm had little to no magic to speak of. Witches would be monsters.

"How? How did you rip through the veil?"

"I don't know. My only intent had been to split the sky above us in a show of power. I didn't realize that Underhill was really *under* a fucking hill. My bad."

"You can touch the magic."

"Around us?"

He nodded.

"Um…yeah." I reached out and scooped a handful out of the air in front of me, setting it alight in a flare of fire. "It's everywhere."

"No witch–" His sentence was cut off as he fainted to the ground in front of me.

What the hell am I and what the hell is going on?

∞ ∞ ∞

I silently vowed not to cause Jaeren to pass out around me as a joke anymore. Unfortunately, that hadn't saved his consciousness this time. He was staying asleep longer each time it happened. I was afraid he wouldn't wake up sometime in the future if it kept happening.

The elven sun had gone down over the horizon and the rest of us were huddled around a campfire in the ruins of Elm Street for warmth. After Jaren had passed out, I sealed the veil with a bit more magic and some serious intent. I didn't need any humans falling into Faerie. I'd even sent Dar through the rubble, looking for any survivors, human or elf. Luckily no humans had been above us. I brought new meaning to the name Cedar *Falls*. Hopefully, they would just chalk it up to a sink hole and move on with their lives. The insurance companies were going to be pissed, though.

The second thing I'd done, was draw forth a foot-thick shield around the clearing. Nobody, elf or crow, would be getting through that until I let it go, and that wasn't happening until Jaeren woke up and we came up with a game plan.

"I think we should go home."

I nodded at Candace. Our welcoming wagon had been less than welcoming. "I wish we could. We *will* be avoiding the castle, though. The Lady bade me go to Faerie to see something I needed to see. However, she did *not* say it was in the castle."

"Unfortunately, there is little else in this elfhame but the castle and the surrounding city." Jaeren sat up with a groan, shaking his head.

"Welcome back," I told him, skipping the teasing.

"Thank you."

"I'm sorry, Jaeren."

"It would seem that power has changed my brother somewhat. We have never seen eye to eye, but this… This I cannot forgive."

"I'm sorry I wrecked your clearing, too," I said, motioning to the half of a building sitting skewed on the grass beside us.

He chuckled. "How is your familiar?"

"Which one?"

"The beast."

"Which one?"

Har har, Yuki said in my head.

"Dar?"

"He's fine, but cranky. The elfshot exploded and left some nasty wounds, but he healed."

"Good. He is a far better protector than I."

"You didn't do so bad yourself. I know Yuki appreciates you."

"Yep. I'da been a vampire on a stick. Thanks, elf."

"You are welcome."

"So, what do we do now?"

"I would agree with your little friend. We should go back to the human realm."

"I wish I could, but I'm afraid the goddess would just send me back until I do what she wants."

"It is not for me to decide what you do. I merely guide," an amused voice said from behind.

"She's right behind me, isn't she?" I couldn't feel her behind me, not with all the magic surrounding me.

Jaeren and Yuki nodded, wide-eyed. Even Shea gave a quiet gasp and bowed low.

I sighed and turned around on the clump of sidewalk I'd been sitting on. "I'm sorry," I said and bowed my head to a glowing Candace.

She chuckled musically and strode forward, bending over and kissing my forehead on my once-again invisible mark. I just hope it didn't flare up again.

"I see you are enjoying the power that should be rightfully yours."

"What is up with that? My mother and grandmother never mentioned it."

"Because they are not you. It is not theirs to touch."

"I'm not an elf?"

"No. Nor are you fae blooded. I wish I could explain to you, but all of us who know have been bound to silence."

"Even you?"

"Even me. We are simply powers in the grand scheme of things. There are those that even gods answer to."

"So, there is nobody who can tell me what the hell is going on?"

"I'm sure if you thought about it, you would find the answers you seek."

"You can't just tell me who to look for?"

"I may not. Think. Ask those of your coven to help you to find that which you lost before you even knew it. Use your magic to find it. You have all the pieces, save one. You just need to find it and put them all together."

"That's why I am here."

Candace's face smiled and nodded.

"Can you at least tell me if it's in the castle?'

"Sadly, it is. But, between you and your guardians, you should have more than enough power to stride in and take it. Once you have it, I shall deal with the obtuse Renlynn."

"But not before?"

"No. This is your journey, I may only aid you so much."

"I understand. Thank you."

"For what, Child?"

"Guiding me as much as you have, aiding me as much as you could."

She reached out and caressed my cheek. "You are dear to me for so many reasons. You will know the truth one day."

I nodded and the light faded from Candace's eyes.

"We strike at dawn," I said to my little raiding party.

"How long has the sun been set?" Jaeren moved a little closer to me.

"A couple of hours, why?"

"I would suggest that we infiltrate the castle tonight, before the sun rises. There will be minimal guards."

"That's not a half-bad idea. We attack at midnight!"

He shook his head. "Too early. The court fools may still be in attendance, leeching from the wine cellars of the king."

"We attack at three-ish!" I looked over at him.

He nodded.

Sadly, nobody applauded my decision. Decisions. Whatever. I was just glad Jaeren had been there to help me strategize. At least I had the military sense to wait until he woke up to start planning shit. Otherwise, we might already be dead or in elf cuffs, rotting in a dungeon.

"So, we have to wait like seven hours, sitting in a clearing?"

"Sorry, Yuki."

"I'm going to check the perimeter and make faces at any elves on the other side of the shield."

"That sounds like fun."

"Better than staring at a fire."

214

I glanced over at Shea, a way of passing time springing to mind. I doubted the others would appreciate it. A little conversation might not be a bad idea, though.

"Sit," I told him, pointing to the slab of concrete next to me.

He gave me a worried glance.

"I'm not going to yell at you. Sheesh."

"Sorry. I am a little on edge."

"Why?"

He sat and motioned to the clearing around us, pausing a moment and pointing at me.

"I'm setting you on edge?"

He nodded shyly.

"Why on the goddess' green earth would I be setting you on edge? I'm supposed to take the edge off. Make you happy and stuff."

"You do. But, I am also afraid you are going to think that what happened was a mistake. That you realized you acted impulsively in the heat of passion."

I sighed in frustration, but let it go. He had waited so long to be with me, I shouldn't have been surprised he would worry I would take it away. "Let me clue you in on a little somethin'. I may act rashly. I may charge into things with both horns pointed at the red cape, but I *never* would when someone might get hurt from it. Do you understand?"

He shrugged and nodded. A little. Almost unnoticeably.

"That was kind of half-hearted."

"Lady, I'm afraid. I lay no claim to you, and yet I am petrified that you will leave."

I wrapped my arms around him. "What did you think, that I would fuck you and leave you?"

He at least hesitated before he nodded, head against my chest.

"You, silly bastard. You're mine. I'm keeping you."

215

"Forever?" The whisper of hope in his voice nearly broke my heart.

I nodded. "You're part of us now. I told you we had a big long discussion about it. Did you think I was kidding?

He shook his head.

"I'll reiterate once more. They all wanted you to be a part of us. Do you believe me now?"

"What about you?"

"I wouldn't have had it any other way," I said softly and leaned over, pressing my lips against his and making him forget about everything else.

Chapter 16

I pressed my hand against the pulsating energy of the shield I'd cast around the clearing. Normally, I would have pulled all that precious magic back into me, letting it fill my well. But here, in Faerie, things were different. I'd pulled the magic straight from the earth and that's where I sent it as I burst the shield in a silent shower of glimmering strands.

"That was beautiful," Candace said with a hint of wonder in her voice.

"Magic to burn gives me the opportunity to do things a little flashy."

"Let us hope the guards did not notice," Jaeren added chidingly

Oops.

Instead of heading directly for the castle, Jaeren, my master strategist, decided on an alternate route that would take us through one of the outlying villages. The main road would be well watched, totally ruining our element of surprise. Hopefully, any elven watchers of the clearing would report that we had disappeared back through the gate to the human realm.

"Let us go." He strode forward and slipped between the closest trees.

You could smell their fragrant boughs in the clearing, but threading through their trunks and under their branches, the smell of cedar was almost overwhelming. I rubbed my nose and fought off the sneeze.

Candace didn't have as much luck. "Choo!"

I giggled and rubbed her head. She even sneezed cute.

Jaeren was less than impressed and shot a reproachful look over his shoulder. "Lord Bless."

Candace flashed him a small smile.

The moon did little to illuminate the forested path. I could see perfectly, and Yuki, Shea, and Dar seemed to have little problem. Jaeren was definitely moving slower and Candace was practically stumbling beside me, tripping over roots and branches. I reached down and grasped her hand.

She gasped.

"What?" I whispered.

"I can see!"

I let go of her hand and she stared back up at me blankly. I touched her again and her eyes refocused. She grinned up at me, excitedly. "It's you."

"When I touch you, you get my night vision?"

She nodded.

"That's cool as fuck."

"Lady, *please* keep your voice down. Please." Jaeren was practically begging.

I pulled Candace forward to catch up to him. "Can you see in the dark?"

"Our eyes are different from humans and witches. We cannot see in the dark, per se, but we can see the flames of life dancing. Even in the darkest of nights. Far superior to–"

I reached out and touched him to shut him up. "We call that thermal imaging, but this might be a little better."

He stared at me in disbelief. "That is. I thank you. You may let go now."

"Up to you, but you won't be able to see as well. Which do you prefer?"

I could see him struggling to answer. "You have to touch me to impart this gift?"

"Yep."

"I shall make do on my own, for now. Easier to spot any sentries. If I struggle, I will let you know. Is that acceptable?"

"Of course." *Didn't really want to hold your hand, anyway. Stupid elf.*

He gave me a quick nod, retaking his position in the lead.

Dar ambled up to me and nudged my hand with his nose. *I'm smelling wood smoke. Up ahead about half-a-mile.*

"We're getting close to the village," I hiss-whispered to Jaeren.

He nodded, not even deigning to look back, let alone say thanks.

He is proud.

He is a dick. I absentmindedly scratched Dar between his ears.

Not compared to most elves I have met. They are a haughty people and look at those of other races as lesser. Do not take it to heart.

Yeah, well... He doesn't have to be so snobby with me. It's not like I want *him around.*

Even here in Faerie?

Okay, maybe here, but definitely not at home.

If you acquire many more guardians, you shall need a larger dwelling.

Preachin' to the choir, Darling. I should gift the house to Josie and Candace and build a hotel.

You are under the assumption that they would leave your side. You are incorrect. They both adore you and would see your gift as abandonment.

You're pretty smart for a dog.

You're pretty smart for a witch.

I chuckled as softly as I could.

A few minutes later, Jaeren stepped from the trail and motioned for us to do the same. Candace and I wound around a tree and came up behind him as he stared in the direction of the village.

"Is somebody coming?"

He shook his head. "Just judging if it is safe to travel through. The way around would take us through a river and stealth with sodden boots and clothing is not advisable."

Want me to scout?

I nodded at Yuki, who had come up behind us without a sound. At least I didn't jump when I saw her. *Please. Don't be seen and don't hurt anyone.*

She nodded and disappeared as silently as she had come.

"I could shadow walk into the village…"

I looked over at Shea. "I thought you said you weren't sure it would be safe to shadow walk in another realm?"

"The shadows still seem to be mine to command, I do not think it will be an issue."

"No. I don't want to take the chance. Try if it's absolutely necessary. Right now, it's not."

"Yes, my Lady."

"Hey, Shea?"

"Yes?"

"We're together. Call me, Dot."

"Yes, my Queen," he said with a smile and backed into the shadows. Even my vampiric eyes couldn't see him, but it was just camouflage. I could still feel him. It was like he draped the shadows over him like another cloak.

220

Show off.

It is clear. Everyone seems to be asleep for the night. I wouldn't march through the center of town, but if you are quiet, you should go unnoticed.

Thank you, Yuki.

I passed the information along to the others, Jaeren leading the way as soon as the words left my mouth. I watched him as he walked, using the cover of darkness to check him out a little more. He was much taller than Shea, and his shoulders were far broader, but he still had the stereotypical elven thinness. His waist was just a little bigger than mine, but that was the only similarity between us. His ass was even nicer than mine, not exactly small, but extraordinarily well-muscled. Even his hair was television shampoo-model worthy. I hated him just a little bit more.

Bet he looks amazing naked though...

I wanted to dip my brain in a vat of frying oil. That would teach it a lesson it wouldn't forget.

I nearly ran into him when he stopped suddenly and held up his hand over his shoulder. A goat stepped out from behind one of the closest buildings, took one look at us, and screamed. It didn't bleat, it screamed like a human.

Fuck. A damn sentry goat?

If I had blinked, I would have missed Yuki's goat-punch. She didn't kill it, but she did knock its ass out. I felt bad for the animal, but it was better than having its screams wake up the entire village. However, I did *not* envy it the headache it was going to wake up with.

She looked up at me and I nodded my thanks. She shrugged her shoulders apologetically, and I shook my head. It wasn't her fault she missed a sentry she didn't know was a sentry. I probably would have tried to pet it if I saw it first. Wouldn't have been the first time something screamed at me for trying to pet it.

A few lights in the surrounding houses flickered to life. I pulled Candace's hand, we needed to get out of there fast. Yuki picked up the goat and took off toward the opposite side of the village.

"Keep to the shadows," Jaeren hissed, unnecessarily.

One of the shadows of the buildings under the bright moonlight broke away and settled over us like a blanket. I smiled at Shea running beside me.

We hit the edge of town and Yuki tucked the goat beneath a tree as we made it safely into the forest beyond. I chuckled trying to picture the villagers' faces when they discovered poor Billy passed out beneath the tree, trying to figure out what had happened.

The trail headed deeper into the woods. A break in the tree line showed the castle on the hill ahead of us. The pink moon illuminated it and the elven city below. It looked straight out of a fairytale.

"It's beautiful." Candace squeezed my hand.

I nodded. "But not really someplace I want to be."

"Me neither."

"I'm sorry to drag you into this."

"It is all right. I'm sure the goddess has her reasons."

There was no way I was letting Candace know her role seemed to be that of celestial cell phone. "Here, keep this adorable fae blooded witch by your side in case I need to contact you…"

Ouch.

"I'm sure she does, but we may never know."

She nodded, emphatically.

We walked for thirty minutes before the town appeared at the edge of the trees. If I were the elves, I would have put the gate a hell of a lot closer. Or the castle to the gate. Either way, travelling for an hour to get to the closest mode of transportation seemed a little silly. But then I realized I lived over an hour to the airport by car. Doing seventy. Maybe the elves weren't so dumb after all.

"How are we going to sneak through an entire city?"

"I am more concerned about getting through the gates, undetected," Jaeren answered me.

"Anybody know any good Jedi mind tricks?"

"What is a Jedi mind trick?" Shea pulled his cloak a little closer. It was getting chillier in the wee hours of the morning and dew was starting to settle.

"It was a joke."

"Oh. Pity."

I could leap over the wall in my hellhound form and cause a distraction. Close enough to the gate to ensure they would be the ones to take action.

Can you guarantee your safety to me?

No offense, Lady. But I can't even guarantee my safety to you right now. We take our risks and minimalize the danger. It is part of life.

Quit being all logical. But you have a point and a good idea...just be careful.

Always. Somebody needs to keep you alive.

"Dar is going to be a distraction. Shea, can you cloak us through the gate?"

"Yes."

"Good plan?" I actually asked Jaeren for his opinion. Surely, Faerie was about to perish.

"Nay, but I cannot think of a better one."

At least he gave me an honest answer. Surely, Faerie was about to perish, twice.

"All yours, Dar. Be careful."

He *huffed* and shifted. I never got tired of watching it. In his hellhound form...he was pretty scary. I'd have given him a nine on the distraction scale. If I saw something like that leap over a wall next to me, I'd probably have shat myself.

223

He took off, full bore, a black streak in the pinkish-hued night.

"There's no way he's going to clear that wall. It's twenty-feet tall," Yuki said, doubtfully.

We all tensed in anticipation. When he was about ten feet away, he launched himself into the air.

He cheated. I expected him to try and high-jump over it. He didn't. His claws hit the wall and he practically ran up the side of it, propelling himself over it when he ran out of wall.

"He did it!"

"Amazing," Jaeren acquiesced.

The shouts and screams of the guards could be heard from where we stood.

"Let's go," I said and ran along the open road, ditching the cover of trees behind us.

The tree-shadows followed us and enveloped us. We were still visible, but much harder to see under the moonlight. It would be much more effective in the city, but I gave silent thanks to Shea for the effort.

There were no visible guards at the gate. Unfortunately, an intricate metal grate in the shape of ivy vines blocked our way through. It was my turn to be useful. I reached out with the magic around me, grasping the vines, intent on creating an opening large enough for us to squeeze though.

The portcullis had been spelled to resist magic. It was like using my hands to grab it and pull, only to find the bars had been oiled. I couldn't get a grip.

We were close enough to need a plan B. I gave up on the gate, reached my hand to the stone wall beside it, and bored a hole through it with my magic, melting the stone into a puddle.

"Go!"

Candace, Shea, and Yuki slipped through.

"Can you repair it?" Jaeren hissed his question as quietly as he could.

"Why?"

"Once they lose sight of your familiar, they shall take up their post again. If they see the hole, the alarm will be sounded."

"But they didn't sound it for the hellhound jumping over the wall?"

"A single animal intruder is much different from a breach in the city's defenses," he said impatiently.

"Okay. I'll fix it."

We went through the gate, and when I was on the other side, I repaired the wall, sparing a moment to pray we wouldn't need the hole to get *out* of the city.

Jaeren nodded. "Good. It looks perfect."

"Thanks."

"You have a future in mason work, should you wish."

I couldn't tell if he was joking or not. He spun and lead us toward the castle without so much as a smile, so I wasn't going to find out anytime soon.

We'd actually made it halfway to the castle when they sprang their trap. There was a small bridge over a glowing blue stream we needed to cross. As soon as Jaeren's foot touched the silver brick paver, bursts of magic above us illuminated the square, turning night into day. The rooftops of the buildings around us became a bustle of activity as dozens of archers aimed their weapons at us as they lined the edge of the rooves.

Four elven mages crested the bridge lowering staves in our direction. From behind them, stepped an elf in metallic armor, not quite full-plate, but shining crimson in the bright light above us. He wore no helmet and he grinned evilly as he stepped in front of the mages. He gave a small clap and struck a pose on the bridge.

What a douche.
"Greetings, brother." His eyes narrowed at Jaeren.
King Renlynn.

Chapter 17

For the first time in my life, I wished making Jaeren into a guardian had given him the ability to speak to me as my familiars did. I didn't know what to do.

I decided to take stock. Dar still hadn't rejoined us. I prayed he was okay. *Dar. If you can hear me, stay away.*

Why?

They ambushed us. I might need you, but not yet.

I have just lost the guards, I shall remain hidden.

"Shea, get ready to shadow walk everyone back to the camp." Apparently, I had a plan in my head, I just didn't know what it was yet. The only thing I was certain of was that I needed to get to the castle. I could let myself be taken prisoner, but everybody else… That wasn't happening. Renlynn was too much of a sociopathic unknown to risk the lives of my family. And the elf next to me.

"But," Shea started to protest.

"I trust you. This is one of those times where the outcome outweighs the risk."

"Yes, Lady."

"Welcome to Elfhame Autumn Glade. I must say, I should be surprised to see you walking freely through my kingdom. A situation that is now remedied. You are now my prisoners. What say you?"

"Everybody, touch Shea."

Renlynn looked at me confusedly. "Pardon?"

"Now, Shea."

I didn't have to turn around to know they disappeared into the shadows. Renlynn was going to have to be satisfied with just one prisoner and judging from the look he was giving me, he was disappointed.

"That was…most unwise."

Instead of giving him a witty retort, I held out my wrists like I was returning a volleyball serve. The universal symbol for, "I give up, please shackle me."

Sure, I could have fought. I might even have won, but I needed to get to the castle anyway, might as well go with an armed escort.

Renlynn stomped forward, his metal boots hardly making a sound against the stone road. "Where? Where did my brother go!"

He was pissed and nearly foaming at the mouth.

"Back to the human realm. They were merely an escort."

"And the demon dog you unleashed upon my city?"

"That was an illusion to get your guards away from the gate."

He narrowed his eyes in suspicion. It didn't make him any less unattractive. I'll admit it, his features, had he been remotely sane, probably would have been prettier than Jaeren. The anger and hatred had completely distorted them, making him look sinister, evil, and crazy.

"I'm to assume it was you?"

"Me? Me who?"

"Opened the rift, destroying half of the castle and killing my father?"

"No. That was some sort of freak accident. I'm the one who closed it."

"Pity. I was going to thank you for ridding me of my father and giving me the throne."

"Uh…okay."

"As thanks, I was going to free you."

"Still wasn't me." I didn't trust him. 'Freeing me' probably meant freeing my head from my shoulders. I'd seen too many movies to fall for that shit.

He snarled in outrage.

Called it.

"Bring her," he said to someone, I'm assuming more elves, behind me.

I was grabbed roughly from behind. An elven mage stepped forward and stopped before me. Holding his staff out before him, he touched my wrists and blue smoke coalesced at the tip, encircling them and binding my hands in blue crystal. I was encased from fingertip to forearm. Surprisingly, there was little weight. It had the density of Styrofoam but was probably much stronger than that. I'd bash it against a wall later to test my theory.

By then, every resident in the sleepy city was leaning out their windows or lined up in the streets to witness the spectacle of the king himself arresting the treacherous intruder. It was in front of them that I was unceremoniously paraded and marched past as we made our way through the winding elven streets.

Are you okay?

At least I had Dar to keep me company. *Yes.*

Thank the night. Yuki joined the conversation.

Shea's shadow walk was successful?

Yes. We're back at the clearing.

Don't stay there. It's not safe without my shield and I'm sure that will be the first place they look. Renlynn isn't as dumb as I expected.

Where should we go?

Home. Go home. If I'm not back in a day or so, we'll worry about mounting a rescue. Dar can stay with me. I could feel her formulating the words of an argument. *This is not a request, Yukina. I command you as your master to go home and take the others.*

That's not fair, but I will. No promises on the elf, though. He…isn't happy.

This is his world, his king, and his people. Let him stay if he wishes.

As you wish.

Thanks, Westley.

Huh?

Never mind. Tell Shea thank you for saving everybody.

He's crying. So is Candace.

Tell them I allowed myself to be captured. I'll be okay. I needed to get to the castle so we could all go home.

There was a moment's pause. *They nodded, but that didn't shut off the water works.*

Best I can do for now. Take them home and put them to bed.

Okay. I'll take care of the Keeblers.

Oh, that's funny.

I know.

I'll see you soon.

You better. Because if I have to bust a hole into fairy and knock down a castle to come get you, I'm gonna be pissed. Judging from her tone of voice, she would do just that.

Thanks, Yukina.

Don't die. And don't take too long, or I'll die.

I won't.

Without another word, she was gone. I don't mean out of the conversation, I meant I couldn't feel her anymore. They had gone back through the gate and would be home in time for margaritas. I sighed in relief. Which ended up with me getting pricked by the pointy end of a sword behind me. I glared over my shoulder and the elf just chuckled.

I bumped him up to the number-two spot on my squish-list.

I am guessing you do not wish to be rescued.

No, Dar. I'll holler if anything changes. Stay hidden for now.

No need. I am wandering the streets in my dog-form. There are many animals about. In fact, I can see you.

I glanced around and saw him beneath the awning of the building we were passing on our right. He seemed to be watching the procession with little interest.

Geez, talk about hiding in plain sight.

I turned my head back to the front and cast a seething glare at the elf king. He turned and gave me a grin. I couldn't wait to wipe the smirk off his face with his severed arm.

Not soon enough, we past the last building and the street faded away, becoming a winding crystal pathway supported with white marble pillars leading up another fifty feet to the gates of the elven castle. All I could picture is how it would make an awesome waterslide if it ever rained.

The landing would suck. Does it even rain in Faerie? Inquiring minds wanted to know.

I needed to stop talking to myself. Dar was one thing…

The castle portcullis rose when we were close enough, and instead of a draw bridge, a path of light extended from the castle connecting to the crystal walkway. I was completely in awe and debated the feasibility of installing one back home. I'd never have to shovel a driveway of light. Plus, a moat would be nice to deter nosy neighbors.

"Take her to the dungeon," King Renlynn said to the guards as soon as we were inside. I didn't even get a chance to gasp at the shimmering alabaster glory and blue-hued tapestries before Mr. Pointystick started jabbing me in the back, ushering me to a staircase off to the left of the main entrance.

He jabbered something in elvish.

"I don't speak, Legolese."

"Move, bitch."

"Oh."

Jab.

I was going to need a new hoodie and he was going to need a new sword because I had grand designs of smelting it into a big silver dildo-sword and I knew exactly who the sheath was going to be.

The glimmer walls became darkened stone as we approached the massive wooden door at the end. I thought it was kind of funny they put an entrance to the dungeon right off the main room of the castle, and I wasn't wrong. We were at the servants' level. Elves, brownies, boggles, fairies, and everything else imaginable were scrambling about, preparing for the day. I tried not to stare as we walked along the wall to another staircase leading further down into the bowels of Castle McDickhead.

This one didn't even get the musty gray stone of the servant's level. Black, green-mold covered, wet looking rough-hewn rock was the motif. Either the servants had servants, or we had reached our destination.

When one of the guards broke ahead of us to unlock the iron door, I kind of figured this would be the last staircase. As soon as I was alone, I would try to break free of my crystal cuffs, find a way to break out of the dungeon, search the entire castle for an unknown something, hopefully undetected, kill the King, and be home in time for biscuits and gravy. Piece of cake.

When Pointystick pushed me into a cell, he whacked me across the back of the head with the flat side of his sword and I fell to the ground unconscious.

∞ ∞ ∞

Candace woke me up with coffee. When I was in the mortal realm. Underhill, some asshole with pointy ears

232

figured a bucket of water was all I deserved. At least I hoped it was water. I sniffed my arm as I got to my feet. Thankfully, my vampiric healing took care of any headache I might have woken up with.

"Thanks," I said to bucket woman.

"You are thanking me?" An elf in a pretty pink dress stared at me incredulously.

"Yeah. I didn't want to sleep too long. I might have missed breakfast."

"You are a strange creature."

"Hi. I'm Dot. And you are?"

"Glabrielle."

"And you just threw water on me, why?"

"I wished to speak with you."

"Oh. Pull up a chair," I said sarcastically and leaned against the wall. Two guards I hadn't noticed yet stepped closer to the elven lady. And a lady she was. She was even wearing slippers.

Some kind of royalty.

"I only seek news of my brother."

"Your brother?"

"Jaeren."

"So, you're Renlynn's sister, too."

"Unfortunately," she said with a little more ire than I was expecting. Apparently, she was just as appalled by his behavior as her brother was. Relaxing, I slid down the wall and sat on the floor.

"Are you unwell?"

"Just exhausted. Getting arrested and hit in the head takes a lot out of a girl."

"You will stand before the princess!" Guard one stepped forward, but she stopped him with a hand on his arm.

"We do not have much time, Thoryn. Let her be."

"As you wish."

I kind of liked the princess. Out of respect, I stood up. "Sorry, Princess. I should be a little more respectful. Just haven't had many pleasant dealings with your family."

"Jaeren went to kill you. Apparently, he did not succeed. Is he still alive?"

I nodded.

"Where is he?"

"I sent him back to the clearing with the rest of my friends when Renlynn ambushed us."

"He got away?"

"Yes."

Her sigh of relief was genuine. One of the guards steadied her as she swayed on her feet. "You have my thanks. He is our only hope."

"Why?"

"Renlynn has… He's gone insane."

"He wasn't always?"

She shook her head. "He was a good brother, the eldest of us. A few moons or so ago, he changed. Started arguing with father. Drinking. We watched him turn into a monster before our eyes. When father was killed… He couldn't wait to be coronated and begin his rule."

"I'm sorry."

"You are the witch responsible?"

I shook my head. "Jaeren thought so, too. It was an accident that tore apart the town where I live, as well. My coven and I fought very hard to seal the portal."

"Is that why he let you live?"

I wasn't sure how far to trust her, but it wasn't like I had anything to hide. "He had me, but the goddess herself intervened and told him what had happened. She sentenced him to be my guardian for a hundred years."

"She did?" I saw the life drain from her face.

"It's not that bad. I'm not mean to him or anything. Most of the time."

"It is not that. Without him... Even if Renlynn fell, we would be without a king."

"But not a queen? What's wrong with you?"

"I am... I am, not a suitable candidate. Not fully elvish."

"Daddy had fun with a human? You don't look like a half elf. You look just like your brother, but prettier."

She smiled in thanks and let the illusion drop.

Her skin looked minty, a greenish tinge that even affected her eyes and hair. She was still absolutely gorgeous, just kind of unripe.

"Woah."

"My mother was a dryad. My father an elf."

"Why the illusion, though? You're still beautiful and obviously elvish."

"Father feared the court would not take kindly to a mongrel, but he loved me. I've worn that illusion since birth."

"Well, we'll think of something. I won't be here long, I just need to find something and get out of here."

"I cannot help you. My brother, even if we share the same blood, would kill me without hesitation if he even learned I had questioned you. I must be going."

"Take care, princess. I'll help you find a solution if I can."

She nodded and gave me a small, sad, and doubtful smile before leaving me alone in my cell. The guard even closed the door with a small *click*.

They could have at least 'forgotten' to lock it.

Chapter 18

I sucked at planning *anything*, a fact that had become abundantly clear during our foray into the land of elves. Thankfully Jaeren had been there to help guide me, but at least I had become painfully aware of my weakness.

Finally, a permanent solution presented itself to help me combat my shortcomings. I learned to deal things with one step at a time. Work on one problem, usually the largest, and then tackle the one after that when it was done. I'd figured that one out on my own. I was a little proud of myself.

Right now, my most pressing problem, other than being locked in a castle in a foreign world, was the crystal encasing my hands and wrists. I had a horrible itch on my nose that wasn't going away despite rubbing it against my soft hoodie.

I gathered some of the magic around me and tried to liquify it. No luck. It was magic resistant, just like the portcullis at the city gate. It was almost like a shield. Any magic directed at it, curved around it, not letting it take hold.

When I beat my hands against the floor, a chip of stone flew and hit me in my noggin. My brain must have just needed a little nudge, an idea formed in my head. They were obviously magic…maybe I could pull the magic *from* them. Even if they were ordinary crystal after, it was better than unbreakable *magic* crystal.

I closed my eyes and concentrated on the material enveloping the hands I desperately needed. The magic was there, swirling purple around me, and I could see it, but when I tried to pull it into my palm, the crystal prevented it from escaping.

Damn it.

There was only one other way.

When I was a child, we had gotten ahold of some human fireworks during the towns Fourth of July celebration. Not knowing what they did, I held a firecracker in my fist as I lit the fuse with the finger of my other hand. It had been the dumbest thing I had ever done. Luckily, I was young and had many, many more years to do much stupider things. My screams had brought the entire coven rushing to my rescue. My fingers were charred and black, one of them had been blown completely off, and there was blood all over my red, white, and blue witch's outfit. The strongest of our coven had me healed before my mother even saw the damage. She changed my name to "Statistic" for a year after that, though.

Now, staring at my bonds, I was going to willfully do the same damn thing to both of my hands. I just hoped my vampiric healing including growing fingers back…

The other concern was the noise.

I walked over to the door and couldn't feel any protections cast upon it. Guess they weren't worried about any magic users busting through it if their hands were encased in crystal. Instead, I cast a quick reinforcement on it, not wanting it to blow off into the corridor and bring half the castle down to the dungeon. Once that was dealt with, I whispered, "*Ciúin,*" to keep the sound of the explosion inside the room. Hopefully I wouldn't have to heal my *ears*, too.

I braced myself and concentrated on my hands, gathering magic from around me and trying to judge how

238

much power I would need to blast the crystal apart from within. I *really* didn't want to have to do this twice.

"*Pléascadh*!"

If I were a smart girl… I would have put some sort of protection between my hands and my face and chest. It worked. Holy shitballs, did it work. The crystal cracked and exploded, sending razor sharp shards at my face, neck, and chest.

I lay there on the ground, broken and bleeding, with two charred stumps smoking heavily in the air above me. I didn't smell yummy, barbequed. Nor did I make a relaxing incense.

I groaned, sputtered, and spit as my nerve endings were *literally* on fucking fire. Finally, I passed out from the pain but eventually came to, still alone and wholly healed.

"That wasn't so bad." I cried just remembering the pain.

I stood up and felt the crystal that had been shot into my body slide down the inside of my still bloody shirt and collect in the elastic waistband of my hoodie. Flipping the bottom open, I danced around getting them all out. Getting jabbed in the stomach every time I moved wasn't an option. Plus, I didn't want any of the little bastards working their way down into my jeans. Ouch.

And just like that, I was free. Of my handcuffs. Now I just needed to sneak my ass through two levels of castle, find what I needed, and get my ass through the city and back home.

I needed a tank.

Dar, you still with my buddy?

Yes.

How goes it in the city?

Now that I can use my front paws again, quite well. What did you do?

I had totally forgotten they could feel my pain through our bonds. If she felt even an inkling of what endured, even across the realms, Yuki was going to be quite vexed with me upon my return home. To put it mildly. She was going to bite my ankles off.

Sorry. Blew my hands off getting the shackles off.

Idiot.

It's not dumb if it works. Hello.

If you have to regrow appendages, it's still stupid.

I'm just glad they grew back. Stumpy is not an attractive nickname.

Shut up and get out of there or I'm coming in to get you before you blow something else off.

Geez. Grumpy.

Grumpy is better than Stumpy. You passed out. I did not. That is twice in the past two hours that you have been unconscious. A record, even for you.

It's still early. Okay. I'm melting the lock. Let me concentrate.

I touched my finger to the door, right on the keyhole. A quick word and a push of power and my finger went through the door, the metal glowing around it. I hooked my finger on the other side and pulled it open.

At least elves kept their hinges oiled. The door didn't even squeak.

The hallway was empty. At least they didn't think I was a big enough threat to post guards outside my door. I wasn't a fan of combat magics.

I padded as silently as I could toward the stairs and stopped cold at the sight of a guard standing just outside the grated iron door to the dungeon.

Shit.

I probably looked like an idiot tiptoeing toward his back, but I had little choice. I was three-feet away when my foot scuffed the stone beneath me.

Shit.

He turned around slowly. I leapt at the door but couldn't reach him through the bars. He cocked an eyebrow at me.

"Uh. Hi."

"How did you get out of your cell?"

He drew his sword and pulled out the key, unlocking the door with one hand and pulling it open while leveling the sword at me. I backed away slowly.

"If you do not go back to your cell, willingly... Let us just say it shall not end well for you."

An image of Bill caught in the middle of Jason's trailer floor sprang to mind. "*Poll oscailte,*" I said with a smile.

He disappeared through the hole in the stone. I'd only meant to drop him a short way, but peering over the edge, there was no end in sight. The castle had been built over the edge of a large underground cavern. I waited for the sound of him hitting the ground, like when you toss a coin in a well. Fortunately, he either silently splatted or landed in something soft.

Oops. At least he left the door open.

I slipped up the stairs and peeked around the corner into the servants' floor. It was nearly empty save for a couple of brownies cleaning the floors. I quickly stepped across the open entrance and stopped.

Servants could go anywhere in the castle. Nobody paid attention to them...

I'm a motherfucking genius!

Peering around the corner again, I waited and prayed nobody came down the stairs behind me. The room was gigantic, held quarters, storage, and had several other staircases leading up to the back. If I could judge by the smell, even the kitchens were on this level. It easily took up the entire base of the castle.

I caught the first break I'd found since coming to Faerie when the brownies finished the floors and headed away from me. Slipping inside, I padded to the closest set of quarters to the entrance.

I opened the trunk at the foot of the bed and grimaced. The quarters belonged to a maid. I wanted something a little less prestigious. Like a scullery captain, or silverware polisher. There was no way I could pass myself off as a maid.

I closed the lid and headed further back, hoping their rooms were based upon rank. I found what I was looking for about halfway-down. A simple green knee-length tunic, apron, and kerchief for my head. Perfection. I could even use the kerchief to cover my ears.

Dressing as quickly as possible, I stuffed *my* clothes under the straw-filled mattress and slipped out of the room. I just needed to find something to dust with. Or maybe a nice broom. Then, I could really start my search.

Lady, I just wish I knew what the hell I was looking for.
You will know it when you see it, Daughter.

It was the first time she had ever answered me in my head. Not going to lie, it freaked me out…a lot. I needed to be a little more careful in invoking her name in the future. Especially during sexy times.

Keeping my head down, I went in the direction the brownies had gone. I'd find a broom, someplace. There had to be a broom closet, *somewhere* in the servant's area.

I decided to check the storage rooms first. Mostly they were supplies of the kitchen kind. Finally, in the fourth one, I found a pile of new brooms just waiting to be swept off their feet by Cinderella.

Heading the way I'd come in, I marched up the stairs like I belonged there, still keeping my head down to avoid anybody getting a good look at my face. I might have been a witch, but I looked human enough and illusions weren't my forte.

The entryway was empty, and I swept my way around, trying to get my bearings and a feel for the layout. Twin staircases lead up. They were probably the private rooms of the castle. Straight ahead from the entrance was the throne room and dining halls. I doubted I would find what I was looking for there and decided to head to the private quarters. It just felt…right.

I swept my way slowly up the stairs, not being an actual housekeeper, I didn't know enough to start at the top. A brownie started cursing at me in Irish. Thankfully slow enough for me to understand she was telling me I was sweeping in the wrong direction, and I was a moron for not having a dust bin with me. She stomped off and retuned with a flat, lidded can and shoved it at me before stomping off again.

I did it. I passed myself off as a slightly stupid housekeeper!

I was so proud.

Marching up the stairs, I started again at the top of the steps, glancing around while I did the hallway at the top.

The second floor wasn't nearly as open as the servants' floor. Two hallways went off in different directions, doors lining both corridors. Suddenly my task seemed much more overwhelming. It wasn't like I could check each room. Sooner or later I was going to get busted and end up back in a cell, or dead.

Which way?

Trust your instinct.

I sighed. I hadn't even said her name this time.

Lowering my head, grabbing my trusty broom and dustbin, I headed slowly down the hall leading toward the back of the castle. There was another housekeeper ahead of me. She lifted her bin off the floor and turned around, nearly squawking in surprise. She prostrated herself on the floor and I immediately saw why.

King Renlynn and another elven soldier were imperiously walking down the hallway. Fearing discovery, I prostrated myself much the way the other servant did but glanced up at him from under my eyebrows.

Please turn...please turn.

They didn't and were walking straight toward me. I kept looking up at his shoes, praying they would turn before they got to me. Luckily, they didn't. As I stole one last glance, I found what I was looking for. It wasn't Renlynn, it was the chained jewel around his neck. If he hadn't been covered in crimson armor the first time I saw him, my journey to Faerie would have been much, much shorter.

The bastard was wearing what I was looking for the whole time. I should have figured that one out much sooner.

Dumb, Dot.

The closer he got, the more I started to cringe and shake. It wasn't from him, either. It was the power emanating from the jewel. It was almost pure magic. It wasn't black magic or evil on its own, but it was driving him insane with its power, and absolute power corrupts absolutely. His own paranoia, and thirst for more power, had burned all of his redeeming qualities away, leaving an insane villain in its wake.

The necklace itself felt like the goddess. The warm, powerful feeling she wore like a cloak.

I'm proud of you.

The king passed by me without so much as a look. I chose my disguise well. Now I just needed to figure out how to get the necklace off him and get the hell out of there.

The housekeeper down the hall had already righted herself and was busy working now the king had passed. I got to one knee and slowly stood. Pain blossomed across my back as an arm draped in finery swept around my shoulders, pulling me tightly against the blade. The dagger's tip ripped through the front of my uniform and blood quickly poured from the wound, staining my green tunic brown.

"Did you not think I wouldn't notice you in that ridiculous outfit? Did you not think I couldn't smell your human *stench* as I walked past you? Did you not think I could *feel* your power? Those were the mistakes you will pay for with your *life*. Look at the bright side, I give you release. I had planned on letting you rot away in my dungeon. You're welcome."

He twisted the blade in my chest, and I screamed as my ribs spread, the metal grinding against the bone. Searing blackness that even my vampiric eyes couldn't see through, filled my vision as he shredded what was left of my heart. My last sight was falling forward, crashing into the floor, and Renlynn saying, "Clean up this mess," to the housekeeper at the end of the hall. He hadn't even had the decency to pull the dagger from my back.

Chapter 19

I came to in a pile of garbage. Not the first thing you want to see when you come back from the dead. Gagging and retching from the smell, I left the remnants of my last meal on my chin. It blended well with the other liquids I had woken up covered in.

Rolling over on my back, I scrambled away as another body slid closer to me, her dead eyes staring, and mouth locked in a silent scream. At least I had been dumped wearing clothes, the faerie hadn't been so lucky. Whoever killed her had done it after using her.

"May the Lady's blessings find you in the next life." I reached over and closed her eyes, touching her body preferable to being stared at in death.

Dar?

Welcome back.

Yeah. Good to be back, but the situation sucks.

Where are you?

I looked around. I was in a cavern much like the one I had dropped the guard into. They had built the castle on a mountain, which was apparently riddled with caves. *Garbage dump.*

I shall refrain from making jokes. Can you move?

I twisted my back, testing my wounds. I'd been worse, but I'd also been much, much better. *I can. Slowly.*

Can you get out?

Not unless I can grow some wings. I can see a trap door, but it's like fifty-feet above me.

I'll try to get into the castle.

No! Too dangerous. I'll figure something out.

Dot... I have sat here and felt every time you were injured, stabbed, and exploded... I am coming. You can order me not to, but I shall be very angry. Let me be by your side.

Fine. Chances are I'm below the servant's floor. Probably below the kitchen judging from the amount of animal carcasses around me.

That was the last I heard from him. If I closed my eyes, I could feel him getting closer to the castle and feel his relief at *finally* being able to do something.

My plan sucked.

I should have just blasted my way through the castle and killed the evil little, pointy-eared fuck-nugget. The world, this one, would be better off without him. I know I would have, too.

I sat up, balancing on the back of something I didn't want to know and hugged my knees to my chest. The smell wasn't getting any easier to deal with, either.

Looking around, I could barely make out a patch of ground at the base of the pile and the mouth of another cave. Wherever it led, had to be better than the king of the hill-of-shit position I was in.

I slowly crawled to the edge and slid down the side, hanging on to goddess knows what as I stopped myself from shooting down a slip-and-slide of decay. When I got home, I was going to take a long hot shower. Fifty of them. And twelve baths in rubbing alcohol.

When my feet finally touched solid ground, I lurched forward and gave it a quick pat as I got to my feet and headed for the cave.

I found a cave out of this dump. Going to see where it leads.

Be careful. That much refuse is bound to attract things that would love a free meal.

I could use a free meal right about now, too.

I'm in the castle.

Nobody is questioning a stray German Shepherd? I found that a little hard to believe.

I did not say I was in my canine form.

Oh, so nobody is going to notice a hellhound or horny, naked blue-demon?

Recall our past conversations. Not once, did I ever state that those were my only forms.

Dar?

Yes?

Please tell me one of them is an extension ladder.

I could feel him roll his eyes.

A really long rope?

You are disrupting my concentration.

And the conversation is keeping me from losing my mind and throwing up from the smell. What are you?

I will not say, but I can show you when you are free.

Okay. Long talk after I get out of the pit of misery.

I rounded the corner of the cave and stopped. Dead in my tracks. The entire cave was blocked by some sort of worm. As I backed up slowly, it lurched forward, its mouth splitting into three sections, displaying row after row of wickedly curved teeth that disappeared all the way down its gullet.

Found one of those things.

What things?

Things that like to eat garbage. It's looking at me like it hasn't eaten in a while.

I would suggest running.

I was already doing so. Worms should *not* be able to move that fast, but it was. I barely made it from the mouth of the cave when it sailed past me, diving head first into the mountain of trash. Ideally, I would have run into the cave as it came out, but its body was still inside. The thing was huge.

It pulled back and started waving its bulk from side to side. I was safe but stuck. Roaring in frustration, it brought more of its bulk into the cavern, giving itself enough leeway to curl around. It might eat trash, but it knew a fresh meal when it smelled one.

The part of it sticking out of the cave was starting to taper. I needed to get more of it into the cavern. It was the only way I would be able to squeeze by it.

Taking a chance, I ignited the air beside it.

In a cavern. With decomposing corpses. Releasing methane gas…

I started a fire.

Genius.

The worm monster screamed, I screamed, and the entire cavern went *poof.*

In an instant, the giant worm-beast was curled up on itself in the middle of the flaming garbage pile, writhing in circles to extinguish the flames burning it. I stopped, dropped, and rolled, rubbing my hair to put out where I was burning. Luckily, most of me was covered in decomposing corpse goop. It kept most of the flash fire from burning me too badly.

Getting back to my feet, I ran for the cave.

What the hell just happened?

Don't ask.

I'm to assume whatever it was caused the kitchen to explode?

Oops. Maybe.

Are you all right?

250

Peachy fucking keen. I'm heading through the cave. I'll let you know where I end up.

I ended up at a lake. An underground lake, glowing softly in the cavern it completely filled. It was beautiful and offered me a place to wash the muck off. Heedless of the danger, I jumped in, scrubbed, and crawled back out. I felt a thousand times better, but still smelled like ass.

Standing on the edge, I took in my new situation. Cavern full of glowing water, check. Cave on the other side, check. It was sink or swim time.

Or get eaten.

I was in a crouch, ready to spring when I *finally* noticed the ledge. The glow from the water had almost completely camouflaged it. Only by putting myself lower did I see its reflection.

I went with plan B.

The going was slow, but I only almost fell into the water twice. Thankfully the cavern wasn't *that* large. When I reached the other side, I dropped to my knees in exhaustion.

How are you doing, Dot?

Made it past the monster and around the lake. About to go through another cave.

Lake?

Yeah, a blue-glowy lake. Pretty, but not something I needed right now. I just want to get the hell out of here.

It's blue…and glowing?

Yes?

There is a fountain in the courtyard, between the kitchen and the dining hall. It is glowing blue as well. The lake must be the water source.

I fail to see how that is relevant.

Is there a hole in the cavern above the lake?

Maaaybe. I don't know. Let me look.

Turning around, I walked back and glanced at the roof. This lake cavern wasn't fifty-feet high like the garbage pit. Maybe a little less than half of that. There was a hole, a little off center.

Yep. There's a hole. How did you know?

Because, right next to the kitchen is a well.

Oh. Cool.

You have no idea where I am going with this, do you?

Nope.

A well, Dot. With a bucket. I know you humans with your modern plumbing take things like this for granted, but surely, you've seen a well on television.

Like a bucket and cranky thing?

Yes! With a very long…rope.

Dar?

Yes?

I fucking love you, man.

I heard the crank of the winch before I saw the bucket. Finally, it came into view and I resisted the urge to shout and pump my fist into the air.

Looks like I'm going swimming after all.

I'd only gotten halfway there when the bucket finally dipped into the water, sending ripples toward me. A *very* large shadow passed beneath the bucket.

"Oh, come on," I sputtered in the water. I'd had enough. Enough of fucking Faerie, enough of getting hurt, enough with the monsters at every turn. I was *done.*

I put on a burst of speed and practically did a dolphin-leap that Flipper would have been proud of, grasping the rope in both hands and shoving a foot in the bucket.

Pull, crank, whatever. Just get me the hell out of here!

Your wish is my–

Dar. Big monster.

The slack went out of the rope and the bucket started lifting me out of the water. As soon as I was a few feet in the air, I could see it. It looked like a giant catfish with horns.

Catfish are bottom feeders. They don't eat live things. Right?

In the human realm. This is Faerie.

You were just supposed to say yes.

The twenty-foot monstrosity surfaced, its giant dorsal fin flopping in the air, and gazed at me curiously. For once, the monster left me alone.

Looking up, I could see daylight and smell freedom. It smelled much better than the garbage pit, and I nearly bounced in my bucket.

Reaching out I threw my hand over the stone ledge of the well. Another hand, the same shade as mine, reached out and grabbed it while an elven face peered over the ledge. I screamed.

Shut up! It is me.

Dar?

The elf nodded and gave me an apologetic look.

Oh, Lucy. You got some splainin' to do.

I shall. But not right here. You're not exactly light.

And now, you're just in fucking trouble.

Seriously, pull.

I grabbed his hand and the ledge and hoisted myself up over the edge. The courtyard was completely empty.

"Where is everybody?"

"The kitchen blew up, remember?"

"Good, now you have time to tell me why you are an elf."

"Do you really want to know?"

"Very much so." I nodded for emphasis.

"I can… I can assume the form of any creature whose flesh I have consumed."

"Ew. You ate an elf?"

"I was also in dire need of a uniform…"

253

"Wait. You *just* ate an elf?"

He burped, and I could have lived without the nod.

"Never mind. I changed my mind. I want to *un*know that little fact."

"I did try to warn you."

"I remember."

"Should we go?"

"Yeah. I have a king to kill."

"Well, now would be a good time to do it. That explosion blew the kitchen up and the entire castle caught the shock of the blast."

"Good. Let's go."

"Want some elf clothes?"

"Depends. You gonna eat another one?"

"Too stringy."

"Ewww."

He led me to the entrance to the kitchen and had me sit down on a stool by the door. "Wait here for a few minutes."

"Okay?"

"The moment you step into the palace, kitchen or not, dressed like that…"

"Gotcha. Waiting." He was just lucky I was way too tired to argue. I started to doubt my sanity and my need for this mysterious necklace around Renlynn's neck. Letting past wrongs, and living and letting live, sounded like a much more plausible plan. Much. Showers and bed were all I really needed.

Have faith in yourself, Daughter.

I sighed. I didn't need a pep talk, even if it was from the goddess. I needed a bazooka. Maybe even some surface-to-elf missiles. Those would be pretty handy.

Is that not what you are? You split the sky of Faerie on a whim. You are surrounded with limitless power. Stop hiding from what you are and who you are.

254

What am I?

That is up to you to discover. Go home and have a shower or find the answers to your questions. The choice is yours.

I just bought that new bottle of pomegranate body wash...

I will.

She must have felt my determination. I felt her ethereal arms for a moment as she hugged me, warming me from within. They vanished as the kitchen door burst open.

"Here. It was all I could find."

I reached out and took the rolled-up dress from his outstretched hand. Anything would have been better than what I was wearing. I stripped naked and pulled the dress over my head.

It was definitely made for an elf.

The material felt like silk, but stretched, thankfully. It was far too tight in the chest and hips, but with a wiggle here and there, I managed to get everything of importance covered.

"I suggest you wear that home. You look stunning..."

I stopped looking at the white dress and stared at Dar in shock. He wasn't staring anywhere *near* my face. "I do?"

His eyes finally met mine and a blush crossed his elven features. "You do. Most definitely."

"You say the sweetest things. Like woof. And bark. And I look pretty."

His eyes narrowed, not appreciating my doggy jokes. "Now if we could just do something about that intoxicating mouth of yours."

I chuckled and gave him a kiss on the cheek. "Not kidding, though. I didn't think you saw me like that."

"A demon would have to be blind not to."

"Thanks, Dar. For the dress and making me feel better."

"You are welcome, Master."

When Yuki called me Master, it kind of freaked me out. When Dar did it, it made me feel a little…warm. In his elf body. Maybe even in his demon body. The horns had possibilities.

It was my turn to blush, and I motioned to the kitchen door. He looked around the door, paused for a moment, and motioned me in.

The fires had been mostly contained. Brownies, sprites, and other creatures were using magic to smother the rest. Everyone else was cleaning up the destruction that had started at the trap door in the corner. From there, sacks of flour had ignited and burned the rest of the giant room. Nobody paid us any attention as he pulled me across the stone floor and into the main room of the servants' floor.

"We need to find Renlynn."

"There is no need. He sits upon his throne, receiving reports as to the state of the castle."

"How do you know?"

"While you were traversing the caverns, I listened in."

"You're wearing a guard uniform."

He nodded.

"Good. One guard down, two-hundred to go."

He nodded, grimly.

"I'm going to go panzer in there. Hopefully most will scatter."

"Panzer?"

"It's a type of tank."

"I'm surprised you know this."

"I was alive during dubya-dubya-I-I."

"Do I even want to know?"

"World War Two."

"That sounds…destructive."

"Watch the History Channel."

"We can discuss this later. You are stalling."

"You see... America wanted to avoid going to—"

He pushed me toward the exit. I gave up.

"You can do this. Bring down the castle if you need to."

"There are innocent people."

"Who?"

"The Princess. The kitchen staff. That nice catfish beneath us that *didn't* try to eat me. Fuck that worm though. He's an asshole."

He sighed and pulled me into a hug. "You can do this. You need to do this. Do not forget all that he has done to you. Remember the feel of the blade in your chest. Remember the pain you endured to free yourself from prison. Think of that to fuel your resolve, but most of all, remember who you are, High Priestess of the Coven of the First Moon." Before he let me go, he kissed the mark on my forehead, and it flared beneath his lips.

"Dar?"

"*Ze'ni m'fal torrein j'aa bokthu m'ren.*"

"What?"

His arms went limp and dropped to his sides. He stepped back and drew the dagger at his belt.

"Um... Whatcha doin?"

His eyes were black. Entirely. There was no iris, no pupil, no bloodshot anything. They were inky wells into his soul.

He held his hand out in front of me, palm down, and nodded to it. "Place your hand upon mine."

"Not until you tell me why."

"Trust me," his voice took on an otherworldly quality. The resonance behind his voice sent shivers down my back. For the first time since I had met him, I was afraid of him. But... I trusted him. I reached out and put my hand on his.

He struck so fast I didn't have a chance to flinch. His other hand was at his side one moment and in the next a blade was through our hands, pinning them together. I winced, but managed not to cry out.

"Do'vorth h'maal belen da, vokuth dormal di'edra."

I invoke the fourth rite, as is our right. Somehow, I understood the words flowing from his mouth. It wasn't any language I had ever heard before. It was far from pretty, sounded like you would need an extra tongue in the back of your throat to pronounce half the words, but was still comforting.

"*Melan portu viie p'al vodru b'lek.*"

This is the choice we have made.

"P'daal gotru s'med boraan, molak da'bor ju."

From this day forward, we are one.

Wait. What?

Fire flared from the wound and flowed through my veins, and when it hit my heart, my senses exploded. I could hear *everything,* I could smell *everyone,* and I could taste the flesh in Renlynn's skinny little neck. My mouth started watering and I knew I would never be satisfied with any meal, ever again, until I had tasted that sweet flesh.

The world snapped back into focus.

The world was the demon in front of me.

He blushed and nodded, pulling the dagger from our hands with an arc of glistening crimson that splattered the white wall next to us.

"Do you feel it?"

"The burning need to extinguish his life and feast upon his flesh?"

Dar nodded.

"Yes."

"Good."

"What did you do?"

"Invoked the rite of... It's probably best if you do not know. I have given you focus. I have given you reason. The rest is up to you."

"You're not coming with me?"

"I cannot. This is your rite, your trial, your task."

"I wouldn't have it any other way."

"Feast upon your enemies."

"Keep the hearth fires warm," I answered automatically, without reason or knowing what the words meant. I could tell they meant something to Dar, his sudden smile nearly ripped his face in two and he bared fangs that were far from elvish.

"You look fierce," he said proudly, darting forward and licking my lip.

I blinked at him in shock for a moment. "I'm not the one sporting fangs."

"Are you sure about that?"

Wait, what?

I reached up and sure enough... "We will discuss this...later."

He nodded and motioned toward the throne room, leaning back against the wall and crossing his arms as I took the first step toward the end.

The double doors were closed. I felt like a kid at Yule, unwrapping my presents as I lay my hands against the gilded white wood. "*Bheith ar dóiteáin.*"

The doors exploded inward in a ball of fire.

I should have rushed in and rendered the flesh from their bones, but I waited. It only took a few moments for the cloud of dust to settle and the smoke to billow up to the thirty-foot ceiling. I wanted my entrance to be dramatic. I wanted Renlynn to see that which he could not kill, coming for him.

I was death.

In a pretty, white dress.

259

I strode forward, my bare feet making no sound on the seafoam green runner leading to the ornate oaken throne centered upon the dais at the end of the room.

A snarl escaped my lips as I felt my nails split as talons slid from the tips of my fingers. I needed no sword, no dagger, no weapon. Not even my magic. It was with my hands, I would tear the flesh from his neck.

Twenty archers took fire as the King grinned at me from his seat. It quickly quelled to a smile before becoming a frown and then turning into open-mouthed shock as the arrows bounced harmlessly away from my shield.

"It can't be. I killed you myself."

His fearful whisper was like music to my ears. I felt the stirring in my groin as his terror excited me in ways unimaginable. It was the sweet song of a serenade, it was the hands of a lover caressing me in places it shouldn't, but I liked it. A lot.

"Renlynn…"

"No." He sprang from his throne. "Kill the witch!"

"That's not very niccce, Renlynnn…" I was having trouble speaking words through the fangs in my mouth. They seemed to be getting longer.

"Kill it!" His voice had become a shrill scream as he pushed his guards in my direction and made to run.

He was rounding the throne toward, what I assumed was, a hidden exit. I held out my hands, and without the need for a canting, used the magic around us to pull down the back wall into a mass of rubble. He barely escaped the onslaught. Now, if he wanted to leave, he had to go through me.

He fell to the ground and whimpered, seeing his death in my eyes. Eyes that I had no doubt, were shining like orbs of obsidian, just as Dar's had been.

The archers dropped their bows and charged at me with swords they pulled from the air, blades glowing red.

I danced at rituals. I danced at hand-fastings. I danced under the moon in spring, summer, fall, and winter. Until that moment, I had never known what true dancing was.

I wove my body between their blades, twirling and striking with my new claws, dipping and disemboweling them, one by one. A few got a nick in here and there, but I was healed before the blade swung back around. One elf snuck up behind me, and I could feel the heat of the blade just before it struck my neck. It was more than enough time to spin and duck, lifting him up off the floor by his bottom jaw as my fingers drove through the soft flesh beneath. I dropped him to the ground and kept fighting, until only the king's personal guards remained.

They dropped their blades and stepped away.

"You." I curled a claw and motioned for him to come to me.

"No. No. No. Stay away! I am *King!*"

He wanted to play hard to get. It was cute.

I crouched low and used my hands to crawl across the floor, never taking my eyes from my prey. The tension in my legs threatened to propel me across the room in a single bound.

His eyes widened, but his gaze shifted above me. I could feel an overwhelming presence behind me and the gentle caress of his clawed hand, lovingly over my back. It wasn't the touch of a lover, it was the encouragement of a father.

I sprang and Renlynn screamed. When I hit him, we rolled and he slammed against the rubble of his throne. My hands were in his chest, clutching his heart in one hand as he stared at me in disbelief. I roared and with the last wave of sound leaving my throat, I slammed my face into his neck and tore out his throat. With my pound of flesh in my jaws, I pulled my hands from his chest and smiled as the light left his eyes.

261

I looked down at my gore covered hands and opened them, dropping the heart with one, and smiling at the gem in the other.

Chapter 20

"Y̲ou did well, Daughter."

I fell back against the floor, looked up at the Lord above me, and smiled. He had come for Renlynn's reckoning, just as the Lady had promised.

As I stared in awe at his massive frame, he reached down and scooped me up in his open hands, turning me toward him. His hands smelled like blood and sage and I resisted the urge to rub my face against them.

"You are quite the little hunter."

"I had a little help."

"As it should be. Nothing should ever be shouldered by oneself. That means you have failed in life if you do not have friends to share your burden." He nodded at Renlynn.

"I know it wasn't his fault," I said sadly and lifted the gem for the Lord to see. It winked under the massive chandelier of the throne room as the Lord's antlers continually cast shadows across it. "This drove him insane."

"As it was meant to."

"You mean someone gave it to him to drive him crazy?"

He nodded.

"Who?"

"That is for you to discover."

"Nothing is ever easy."

"Nothing worth *having* is ever easy."

"True story, my Lord."

He chuckled and the sound echoed off the remaining walls of the massive room. "I shall return you to your friend. Good luck, our Daughter."

"Thank you. Both of you."

He kissed the tip of his finger and touched it gently to the mark on my forehead. It flared again, blinding me for a moment, and when I could see again, I was standing before the ruined throne room doors. Dar stood there, staring at me with a look of disbelief.

"Let's go home," I told him.

He held out his arm and I wrapped my arms around it, the gem clutched tightly against my chest. "How are you feeling?"

"Sated."

He chuckled.

An elf blocked our exit. I would have been more worried if she weren't dressed head to toe in a flowing green dress. I nodded as she and her guards stared at me in horror.

"You're alive," was all she said.

"Yes."

"My brother?"

"Dead."

A sister should never sigh in relief at the death of a sibling, but she did. It spoke volumes of what she had suffered at Renlynn's hands. It might not have been his fault, but he was irredeemable and better off in the next life. He had ruined this one for far too many people.

"What of Jaeren?"

"I do not own him. He was commanded by the goddess, but I shall not hold him to it. The decision is his."

She nodded grimly, knowing which path her brother would follow.

"A suggestion?"

She tilted her head.

"If you do not wish to be queen, you would be a fair and honorable *regent*. Keep your illusion and rebuild a kingdom befitting Jaeren."

Her guards smiled at my suggestion. I briefly wondered if they were more than guards…

You go, princess. Now you just need a few more!

"It is all I *can* do. I thank you for your sage advice."

"Least I could do. Since you have to rebuild the castle again because of me."

She chuckled. Elven laughter should be bottled as a cure for depression. I felt better about everything just listening to it for a moment. "It sacrificed itself for a worthy cause."

"Well, I'm going home. There's a hot shower and a warm bed waiting for me."

"Take care of my brother?"

"I will."

"Wish him well for me. Should you ever want to visit, I promise a more…welcome time."

Mmm. I might if I ever need a recharge. I could get used to all this magic. "Let me know when things have settled. If you need anything…"

She held out her hand to the guard on her left. He reached into a pouch at his side and pulled a key from its depths.

"Take this with you. You shall have the ability to return whenever you wish."

Did she really just give me the key to the city? I looked at Dar.

That's what they do for heroes. I'm sure it is a key to one of the broom closets. Maybe the privy.

"My thanks, Princess."

"Fare thee well."

"Come on, Dar. Take me home."

∞ ∞ ∞

The clearing still had the ruins of Cedar Falls littering it, but it was part of home and I smiled. We were almost there.

Our guard left us, disappearing back into the forest. It was the last kind gesture of the Princess. Or, she wanted to make sure we went home without breaking anything else. I was good with either of her possible motives.

At least Dar and I finally had a chance to speak.

"What was all that?"

"What?"

"The Fourth Rite?"

He blushed and shifted into his Shepherd form. Just when I was getting used to the elf. *Nothing.*

That was not nothing, Darling. I grew fangs and claws and turned into a big kitty thing.

The Fourth Rite is… It is a challenge.

What kind of challenge?

A hunting challenge.

Did I pass?

Is Renlynn dead? Did you not feast upon his flesh?

Yes.

Then yes. You passed. With flying colors.

So, what do I get? Money? A condo in Miami?

Nothing so grand.

Dar. You have three seconds to tell me what the hell happened to me.

He gave a mental sigh. *The Fourth Rite is kind of like a mating ritual. A challenge is issued. If the female of the species hunts and kills an apex predator of the male's choosing, she wins.*

Wins what?

That is up to her…

266

"What the actual fuck? You issued a mating challenge to get me to kill the king?"

He shifted again but chose his blue demon form. "Well. You were being a pansy. I had to do *something* to get you motivated."

"So, you used a mating ritual?"

His cheeks turned purple. "It was all I could think of."

"You *don't* want to mate with me? You just used it as an excuse."

"I... I..."

"You *do* want to mate with me? Until today, you have never even once complimented me on my looks. I actually thought you were gay."

He turned to me, shocked and sputtering. "I am not," he finally managed to stutter.

"Oh."

"Yes."

"Yes, what?"

"I do find you beautiful beyond words. It is why I spend most of my time in the form of a canine. It is easier to deal with."

"So, you were afraid of walking around with a demon boner."

"What?"

"Boner. It's an erection."

"I know what it means. Why would you assume I would walk around with one?"

"Cuz I'm naked a lot."

"This is true." He gazed at the ground, thoughtfully.

"Why do I get the feeling you're not telling me the whole truth?"

His aversion to my eyes told me everything I needed to know. There was a *lot* more to this Fourth Rite than he was telling me.

"We better not be legally married in Gehenna or something stupid."

He swallowed, but shook his head, not elaborating further. I'd get the truth out of him, eventually. Even if it killed him.

Deciding to let it go for now, I bumped his naked blue hip with mine. "I'd totally mate with you."

"You would?"

"Yeah. You're hot?"

"Which form?"

"Well, not the dog's, obviously. But this one, definitely. The elf one is kind of hot, too."

"Which do you prefer?"

"This one. The handle bars have promise."

"Handle bars?"

"Horns."

"Why would you refer to my horns as handlebars?"

"Because that's what you hold on to when you're riding something."

"Oh. *Oooh.*"

"Caught my drift?"

"Yes, Master."

"Good boy. Let's go home."

"Woof."

Epilogue

Reaching out, I wrapped my hand around the door handle and blinked when it was ripped from my hand. There was a blur of motion and then I was suddenly engulfed in vampire. We landed on the ground outside my door as she buried her face in my chest and whimpered. Dar chuckled above us, but managed not to get any shepherd slobber on me.

"You are in so much trouble, but I've never been happier to see *anybody* in my entire life."

"I missed you, too, Yuki." I patted her head and let her get a recharge of master-juice. It had been well over a day since she'd seen me. Her batteries must have been pretty low.

"I felt *everything*. Even though you were in another world, I could still feel your hands. I even felt you die."

"Yeah, but you didn't die. So, I wasn't *really* dead."

"Not funny, Master."

"I know." I ruffled her hair.

That's when I saw Candace and Shea standing in my doorway, tears flowing freely. Josie came up behind them, wrapped her arms around them, and started with the waterworks, too.

"Yuki. The ground is cold and hard. And I need coffee."

She sniffled, rubbed her nose against me, and lifted herself off me. At least she offered me a hand and hoisted me up off my back. Giving one last glance around, I waved at the two neighbors who had paused unlocking their door to witness the spectacle of me getting sacked by my vampire. They *quickly* finished unlocking the door and ran inside.

I chuckled and went up my steps again.

Shea was next in the hug line. He threw in some kisses, but winced when he noticed the smell still emanating from me.

"Sorry. Long story."

"One I am sure you will be repeating numerously before the night is over. The others are on their way. Josie informed them of your return."

She shrugged over Shea's shoulder. "I was threatened with pain of death if I didn't let them know you were back the *moment* you returned."

"I was only gone a couple of days. Sheesh. They're addicts."

"Dot… It's been a week."

"What?"

"You left last *week*."

I looked down at Dar.

Time travels differently in different realms. The same is true for Gehenna. A day in the mortal realm was akin to three days there.

No wonder everybody was having shit fits.

I looked at Yuki. "You went that long without me?"

"Barely. And you would not believe the amount of blood I imbibed to still be able to move." She blushed, embarrassedly. "I used your card to pay the blood bank. I'm sorry."

"Don't be. Well, if the rest of you will excuse me, as you can smell, I need a shower." I left them standing there and headed for my bathroom. The coffee could wait fifteen minutes.

Unsurprisingly, Yuki followed me, stripping as we headed for the bathroom. I guessed I was getting my back washed, or she hadn't fully recovered from the separation anxiety.

"Sorry I was gone for so long," I said as I lifted the dress over my head. It was a shame it was covered in blood, I might have worn it again. Maybe I could magic it back to its former glory.

"I'm just glad you are safe. I don't feel so bad about leaving you back there."

"You didn't leave me, I commanded you to go."

I turned on the shower and didn't wait for it to warm up before plunging under the spray. Yuki silently washed my hair, while I scrubbed the stench of the past week away. She even scrubbed my back for me when I was done. I was definitely keeping her. She even dried me when we were through.

Sweatpants and hoodie were donned before I left the sanctity of my bedroom. Candace handed me a cup of steaming coffee as soon as I walked out. A cup I almost spilled, as Jimmy wrapped me in his arms, sobbing silently.

"You, too?"

"A week, Dot. It was a fucking week."

"I'm sorry," I said and kissed him, soundly. Letting him get it out of his system.

Finally, he pulled away, and everybody was standing around me, just watching me. "What?"

"Did you win?" Josie motioned to me to tell the story.

"Yes. Wait. Where's Jaeren?"

"He delivered us here and then headed back to rescue you. Did you not see him?" Candace sounded confused.

"No?"

"That is strange. He did not really wish to return to our world to begin with. It was only your wish that we get

271

home safe that drove him here. We were barely through the door when he vanished."

"Must have just missed him. His sister will fill him in."

"So, what happened?" Josie was getting impatient.

"I'll tell you when everybody else gets here. I'm not telling and retelling the tale over and over again. I'm sorry."

She sighed but nodded. Luckily, there was a knock at the door.

"That must be them," I said and walked over, carrying my mug and opening the door.

There was an elf standing there, blinking under the bright sunlight.

"Delron?"

"I see you have returned. I was expecting an arrow."

"I literally just got home."

He closed his eyes and tilted his head. "I see you have returned with the gem."

"You mean the one you sent as a betrothal gift to the seleighe court?" Everything started to make a little more sense. "You sent it to create havoc."

"Yes. We figured it would be easier to get the princess to marry our prince if her father was out of the picture. We did not expect the brother to intercept it."

I felt the flames of anger flare inside me. He was two seconds from getting scorched from the mortal realms. "Do you have any idea of what you have done?"

"Yes."

"Why?"

"I was not speaking in jest when I said we would not stop at nothing to find a new queen."

"Even asking a witch?"

"Do you have the gem?"

"I do."

"Then the betrothal gift has been accepted. Would you accompany me to the unseleighe court?"

"The gem was not yours to gift in the first place. But nice try."

"You know what it is?"

"No. But I have an idea. It belongs to me."

"You could come to the unseleighe court to find out what we know…"

"Or, I could just do some research here. Sorry for not trusting you after you nearly destroyed a kingdom."

He smirked, amused at the outcome. I really didn't like Delron.

"I think you shall."

"I think you've been smoking crack rock if you think I'm going anywhere with you."

"We have your elf."

"Say that again?"

"Jaeren, Prince of Elfhame Autumn Glade. He is in our dungeon as…insurance."

I fucking hate elves.

Bonus Scene

Enjoy this scene from chapter 14 in Jimmy's point of view!

A Feast of Plenty

"How the hell did you find enough stuff in my pantry to make all of this?" Dot was staring at the three plates of food with something like admiration in her eyes. She should have known that a fireman could cook, even when the supplies were limited. She was lucky I loved her enough not to make her my four alarm chili.

"Don't thank me until you try it. It might suck for all I know."

She gave me a doubtful look that I couldn't help but find sexy. There wasn't a look in her repertoire that I didn't find sexy. Or a body part. I found myself in a place that I never expected to be, or wanted to be, in. I was in love with a witch.

"There isn't a single thing of yours I wouldn't eat."

I loved that she had meant it in the most innocent way possible. It made my retort that much sweeter. "Ditto," I said and wiggled my eyebrows.

That earned me *the look.* I tried not to chuckle as I took a bite of my dinner.

"This is very tasty. You are quite a cook, James."

"Thanks, Sheamus," I said with a smile and tried not to stare. He was as confusing as Dot was frustrating. Sweet as anything you could imagine, which is a rarity in a guy, but prettier than ninety-seven-point-nine percent of the women in the state, too. I'd never considered myself bi-sexual. I mean, sure, I liked looking at cocks in porn, but I'd never had the desire to see one up close and personal in my life. Sure, I'd seen them at the firehouse, and Dennis', but it's not like we did circle-jerks or buddy-sucks on Thursdays and Sundays.

But, then there was Shea. He looked like a flat-chested, tomboy supermodel jedi. I wasn't sure if he *had* a lightsaber, but every time I stared into his overly large dark eyes, let's just say the force was strong in little Jimmy. I hadn't told Dot, I *couldn't* tell Dot, that I'd had two dreams about him already. I woke up screaming from the last one. Screaming and ejaculating in my boxer shorts. In my dream, he had male and female sex organs and he knew what to do with both. It was horrible. And wonderful. And very, very confusing.

"Sheamus?" Dot raised an eyebrow and flashed me a sexy little smirk.

"It's a joke. He called me James earlier, so I called him Sheamus. It was the first time I'd seen him smile," I answered honestly.

"It's beautiful, isn't it?"

Shea looked kind of uncomfortable with us talking about him like he wasn't even there. Of course, I had to up the level. "It is. I gushed."

"Do I want to know which way?"

"Little bit of both."

"You sure you haven't ever slept with Dennis? Because Derek's accent gives you a chubby. Shea's smile makes you gushy. I swear I'm going to have to keep an eye on you." She even added a little exasperated sigh. She didn't look worried at all. Not even a little bit. Maybe a little hopeful. Just like that, she let me see her tell. She had exposed another one of her kinks to me. The foolish immortal.

"That should be easy to do. You want to watch."

She stared at me for a moment. "Your kinky-sense is tingling?"

"A lot of things are tingling right now. Want a list?" I opted for the truth.

"Not while I'm eating."

Shea, the beautiful bastard, was chewing his food and watching our exchange. "That conversation made no sense to me, whatsoever. But it was entertaining to watch."

"Jimmy has a thing for guys and he thinks you're cute," Dot told him without a hint of reservation.

"Oh. I see." He took another bite of food like it was the most normal thing in the world. Maybe for him, it was. But, I'll be damned if watching him eat pasta wasn't one of the most sensual things I'd ever seen. I felt myself stiffen in my pants.

Dot looked at him. "Want some wine?"

He nodded at her. "Would you like some more elderberry?"

She lit up like a Christmas tree. "Fuck yeah! That stuff was like liquid crack."

I was confused. "Elderberry? Wine?"

She nodded at me. "Yeah. Had some over at Shea's place. Wow."

"I shall return in a minute," he said, stood, and disappeared into the shadows by the door. I didn't think I would *ever* get used to seeing him do that.

"I don't think I'll ever get used to that," Dot reiterated my thoughts.

"It's freaky but cool. Know how much fun I could have with that power?" I wasn't lying. I *wanted* that power.

She turned and stared at me, narrowing her eyes. "This is why I don't teach you things like the pleasure spell."

"Cuz you're mean?" I was trying to phrase it as a question. I was more accusing in my heart.

"No. Because you would do nefarious things with them, super perv."

She was so cute when she didn't have a clue. "I cannot deny this. At least I'm not boring."

"This is true." She had barely gotten the words out when Shea made his entrance, two bottles in his hands.

"You trying to get us drunk?" She stared at him incredulously.

I didn't get it. It was just wine.

"What?" Shea flashed her a cute little frown. "No, Lady. One is for now, one is for you as a gift."

Well, we definitely ain't getting drunk off one bottle…

"Awww, thank you."

"You are more than welcome."

He set the bottles down and Dot got up to grab some glasses. I used the opportunity to check out her butt. It never ceased to amaze and mesmerize me. Shea was watching me watch her…and whipped out a knife, cutting the glob of black wax off the top.

"Need a corkscrew?" Dot asked Shea from the kitchen.

"She calls *me* the kinky one," I muttered to Shea.

"Yes, please," he answered and gave me a small smile.

She handed him the corkscrew and sat back down, never taking her eyes off him. I might have been a little jealous if I wasn't watching him, too. He turned opening a bottle of wine into a sexy ceremony. My mind kept flashing back to the dreams…

He broke me out of my reverie with a final twirl of burgundy liquid in the glass as he handed it to me, flashing me another one of his smiles. He might have meant it as a friendly gesture, but it was having a thicker, longer effect than being reassuring.

"Thank you," I managed to say.

"Most welcome," he said and lifted his glass to the both of us.

I tilted the glass and let a little splash across my tongue. "Holy shit." It was like liquid sweetened fire, burning like booze and warming me like magic.

"See?" Dot gave me a nod.

"Wow."

"I am glad you like it," Shea said and nibbled on some chicken.

I was focused on the wine instead of Shea, wanting to gulp it down but taking sip after sip to prolong the experience and not seem like a junkie.

"You're gonna get hammered if you don't eat," Dot warned.

That was the thing about wine. It was like beer. I would get full and hurl before I got drunk off it. "Sweet wines like this don't have enough alcohol in them to worry about it."

"Yeah. Keep telling yourself that," she answered dryly.

Shea just chuckled.

They knew something I didn't. I decided to take their advice… "Thanks for sharing the wine with me," I told him.

Shea lifted his eyes, but not his head, flashing me another of those shy smiles that made me question my sexuality at that moment. He was *way* too beautiful to be a guy. I kind of wanted to see what he looked like in a dress. Maybe some of Dot's leggings. Or a bikini. My cock went from stiffening to rigid with that smile and looked over at Dot. She stabbed herself in the mouth with her fork.

"You okay?"

"Yes?" She asked innocently. Too innocently.

I narrowed my eyes, trying to read her. She was avoiding looking at Shea. She had noticed my discomfort and was completely mesmerized by it. "You missed your mouth." I gave her the opening for the innuendo bus to pull out of the garage.

"Boy, if I had a dime for every time someone told me that…"

She took it. She was turned on. If she hadn't, she would have gone for the innocent reply.

Shea choked on a noodle. At least he had caught it.

"What's the matter, Sheamus? Something get stuck in your throat?" I wanted to judge his reaction, too. The night might have just gotten infinitely more interesting. My cock throbbed in my pants.

I might have dreamed of Shea. But I'd never *wanted* to do anything with another guy. A few times, in my younger days, I'd been involved in a couple of threesomes… Mostly with multiple women. One time, Dennis and I had fooled around with a girl from high school at the same time. She wasn't up for the old double penetration, but that didn't stop us from each taking opposite ends. One time, the opportunity *did* present itself. Jared, another fireman, had invited me to his house for dinner. It had ended up a drink fest and he shared his wife with me. She rode me and I had gotten the surprise of my life when he slipped inside her ass, standing over me. It had been one of the most erotic experiences of my life. The thought of sharing Dot with Shea…

Shea set his wine down after washing away the noodle. "It is dangerous to eat around you both," he rasped.

"Yep. Dot's appetites can quickly shift from the food to those around her."

She swatted me in the arm and blushed.

"But to be devoured by her…" Shea closed his eyes and a small smile spread across his face.

"Yeah. It's wonderful," I told him.

He lowered his head, but was still staring at her under his long lashes.

"Is it getting hot in here, or is it just me?" Dot even fanned herself.

"That is the effect of the wine. It is made to warm you on the coldest of days, igniting your internal fires."

"You brought…aphrodisiac wine?" She looked almost afraid.

"No. It is made for travelling."

"Oh."

"I thought it an auspicious start to our journey."

"Oh." She was repeating herself. Things were about to get *more* interesting.

"Why? Are you feeling…" I almost laughed as he looked at her expectantly. *He delivered the death stroke. Best wingman in history!*

"No. Maybe. My fires are definitely kindled." She shifted in her seat. The sure sign that she was getting turned on. I could almost picture the wet spot on the front of her leggings. *Lady, I love this woman!*

I chuckled softly, leaning back to watch the show, and put my hands behind my head. "Maybe it's not the wine, but the company."

"Maybe," she answered, taking another bite and looking everywhere but at us.

"Maybe you should lie down? Or step outside to cool off?" Shea offered her a means of escape. *The fool.*

"Yeah. Maybe," Dot answered, taking her wine and heading for the bedroom.

I wanted her hot, but not drunk. "Maybe you shouldn't finish that," I said worriedly, reaching for it.

"I'm okay. Just a little…"

"Okay." I stood up, just to make sure she didn't fall, and helped her to the bedroom.

"Thanks," she gave me a smile.

"I'll go clean up the kitchen."

"You don't have to."

"Don't worry. I'll send Shea in to keep an eye on you."

Her eyes narrowed. She saw through me in an instant. She was the only woman who ever had or could and it made me love her that much more. Because she *knew* and still agreed.

"Don't trust me?" I flashed her a grin to let her know I knew I'd been caught.

"Would you trust you?"

I reached down and slid my hand up under her shirt, letting the heat of my hand ignite her skin as I made lazy circles over her stomach. "With you? Yes."

"That was the best answer, ever." She smiled.

"You want him. Take him."

"I don't have to. He's already mine. Just like you."

"Forever and a day," I told her, meaning every word.

She reached up and grabbed my neck, pulling me in for a kiss. I knew if I let her, she would have pulled me down on top of her and the fun would have started prematurely. I forcibly kept it slow, soft and delicate, just to build her frustration. That was the key of getting her over her inhibitions. She shouldn't have them. Not her.

I just needed to stoke her fires a little more. I slid my hand up higher, lightly grazing her nipple.

"Why are you teasing me?" Her voice cracked. She was ready.

"Because I am leaving the room. I want you to devour him and really make him yours."

"But I want you, too," she practically whimpered.

"Oh, don't worry. I'll be back." I meant it. Every word. I pinched her nipple. "Shea, Dot wants you," I called over my shoulder. "Have fun," I whispered to my Dot, letting my tongue flick over her lips.

I handed her the rest of her wine. The heat inside her had burned away the effects of what she already had and she might need a little bit more courage. She gulped it down, stared at it for a fraction of a second. "Jimmy?"

"Yes?"

"Hurry."

"Yes, ma'am," I answered with a little chuckle, heading for the kitchen.

I gently touched Shea's shoulder in passing, giving him a bit of fair warning.

I abhorred doing dishes, but with the dessert that I was about to feast upon, I did them in record time. Dar reaped the benefits of the uneaten portions of our dinner and he gazed at me lovingly. "You're welcome, Dar."

Walking over to the table, I sat and slowly sipped the rest of my wine, trying to judge the atmosphere and the sounds coming from the bedroom to time my return. It wasn't *anything* but my inability to stay away a moment longer that *finally* drove me to the door.

Shea was sitting on Dot's chest, completely naked, hair freely flowing down to his waist. I was shocked to literally see him covered in tattoos. My second shock was that, completely naked, he could never be mistaken for a woman. His shoulders were too broad, his hips too narrow. I may have even been expecting to see tiny breasts and almost sighed in disappointment as I caught a glimpse of his chest as he bent over to kiss her. As he threw his head back, I knew she had his cock in her mouth. It was so hot, I couldn't stop myself, I took off my shirt, pulled my cock out of the front of my pants, and began lazily stroking it.

"Where do you want to come, Shea?" She asked him. "Do you want to explode in my mouth? Or do you want to come inside of me, Shea? Do you want to plunge this inside me and fill me?"

He groaned, unable to form the words.

I answered for him. "Why not both?"

Dot leaned over and saw me stroking myself in her doorway. "That's a damn good idea, Jimmy." She looked up at him. "Do you think you can do that? Can you come for me twice, Shea?"

"I could come a thousand times if you keep looking at me like that."

"That's a damn good answer."

"It is the truth."

"Is it all right if Jimmy joins us? He was practically begging earlier," she said to tease me.

"I do not mind."

My cock surged and I had to stop myself from coming, not before a little leaked out of the tip and fell to the floor. I kept myself there, at the edge as he knelt over her and fed his cock into her mouth. I was almost jealous…of her.

I almost yelled, "No," when he pulled himself from her mouth and used the tip to tease her nipples. Involuntarily, her hips began lifting off the bed as he continued to tease her.

It was time for me to join in. I crossed the empty space between us and reached down, grabbing the waist of her leggings and pulling them down over her legs, nearly groaning as her pussy became exposed to my eyes. I had never told her, but her patch of red hair drove me absolutely insane with desire.

As I lowered myself to her, I don't know what came over me, but my lips found Shea's spine and planted three gentle kisses on my way down. That shocked me more than anything, and I had to fight the urge to let my tongue drift over his skin. I needed a distraction and found it between Dot's wet lips as I plunged my tongue inside her, drinking in her wetness.

Her hips began bucking against my mouth as she pleasured Shea with hers. He looked over his shoulder at me pleasing our Lady. "As it should be."

"It should?" I heard Dot's quivering voice.

"Yes. You are our Lady. You should have multiple men surrounding you, pleasuring you in every way possible."

She shuddered. "Brilliant and sexy," she said to him.

"The view is good from back here, too." I called out, not lying. Shea's ass... Dot's pussy. They were equally as beautiful.

"Less talkie talkie, more lickey lickey." She bucked her hips impatiently.

I sucked her clit into my mouth and let my tongue undulate against it. She began moaning and must have been pleasuring Shea with each moan. He began to roll his hips in tempo.

"I cannot hold out any longer..." You could practically hear the orgasm coming from his voice.

I doubled my efforts with my tongue, wanting her to come at the same time. And she did. Tenfold.

"Jimmy..." Her voice became a throaty chuckle as I refused to relent until she was happy.

Giving her a gentle kiss, I pulled away.

"Lady, that was amazing."

"Yes. Yes, it was."

He groaned a little more and I knew she was teasing him. My cock had leaked all over the bed, and I was lying in a very wet spot, not caring in the least, and resting my head against her leg.

"You...um. You taste good," she told Shea.

"Thank you?" He slid off her, over the edge of the bed. I grinned at her, my mouth nearly touching her pussy.

"Did you have fun?"

I nodded in answer. Her face and neck were splattered with Shea's come. My grin washed away as curiosity took hold.

"You want a kiss?" She cocked an eyebrow as she asked. Almost as if *she* knew.

I nodded. It was all I could do. I wanted to taste his come on her lips.

"Come here."

I got up and crawled over her, mashing my lips against hers and letting my tongue taste him in her mouth. It was more erotic, sexy, and right than I'd imagined. Sighing happily, I pulled away. "It's all over you," I whispered. "You're covered in his come."

"It doesn't bother you at all, does it."

"No. It's hot."

"And sweet for some reason."

I had only gotten a hint of flavor from our kiss. I found myself wanting more. There was a large glob of it on her chin and I flicked my tongue out, scooping it off her and kissing her again, letting his seed play between our tongues.

While we shared that kiss, I lifted my hips, letting my cock align with her entrance and thrusting myself inside her. She enveloped me with more heat, more wetness than I had ever thought possible.

My name became unintelligible syllables as I began thrusting in her, fucking her with a need that almost scared *me*. I wanted her, but more than that, I wanted to explode inside her.

She pulled away from the kiss, eyes rolling in pleasure until she spotted Shea stroking himself beside her. She reached out and cupped his balls, rolling them gently between her fingers.

"Goddess…"

"Do you like that?" She asked him.

"Yes."

She used his soft flesh to pull him closer. His cock was barely inches from our faces. "That's hot, isn't it?" She was asking me, but never taking her eyes from him. Neither was I. All I could do was nod.

"Do you want to touch it?"

A million thoughts raced through my brain. The one that emerged victorious was, "Yes! Fuck yes." I gave a smaller nod, not wanting to seem too enthusiastic.

"Shea, can Jimmy touch you?"

"Please," he whimpered causing Dot to spasm around my cock.

"Go ahead, Jimmy. He shouldn't be jerking himself off when there are two other people in the room."

And just like that, she made up my mind for me. I'd have to thank her later. She'd have to settle for a kiss for now.

I reached out, my hand practically trembling as it was about to wrap itself around another man's cock. There was no denying it. He was definitely a man. And his skin felt smoother in my hand than mine did. My hand practically glided over the velvety smoothness of it.

"First time? Are you *really* sure about that, Jimmy?" Dot teased me, and it turned me on even more.

"Um. I've done this a billion times…just never to anyone else. I swear. If I'd ever done this before, I would have told you about it a long time ago," I told her and meant it. It was hot.

"Fair. I would have been fascinated by it, too. I probably would have come twenty time just from the story alone."

"This turns you on that much?" I asked, but I already knew the answer. The hunger in her eyes, the wetness of her pussy, gave it all away.

"You have no idea." She was practically quivering, watching me stroke Shea.

"What about this, then?" I watched her face as I pulled Shea closer, not stopping to think about what I was about to do. Sparing Shea a glance, I wanted his permission, and he understood, giving me a small nod. Flicking my tongue

287

out, I let my tongue catch the drops of moisture leaking from his tip and then pulled the tip of him into my mouth.

Dot went absolutely wild, spasming beneath me. I'd have to admit, I did too. Between having a cock in my mouth and Dot's pussy squeezing my own, I erupted into her as I sucked Shea into my mouth as far as I could. I let my orgasm flow through me as his cock twitched in my mouth.

When I finished emptying myself inside her, Shea reached down and ran his fingers through my hair in thanks. I was just sad he hadn't come with us, but I let him go. I had better plans.

I kissed Dot, reached under her, and rolled us over. "You want in on this?" I grinned up at my new partner in crime.

"I do not understand."

"I want you to fuck her while I hold her," I told him.

"But… Aren't you still inside her?"

"Yep."

"Jimmy?"

"It's up to Shea. Not me. I was asking him if he wanted to."

"I've never had anything in my ass before." She sounded almost worried.

"Who said anything about your ass?"

"Wait." She stopped to think about it. "You want him to stick his dick inside me with yours already in there?"

"Yeah."

"Okay." She didn't bat an eyelash, seaming almost *eager*. "I'm game if Shea is."

"Lady?"

She nodded and gave him a sultry look. My cock, still inside her, hadn't really gone soft but surged back to attention. Looking back up at Shea, I nearly laughed at the smile on his face. "Only if you want to," she said one last time.

"Oh, I do and do not need to be asked again."

I spread my legs, and Dot did the same, giving Shea a place to kneel between them. "I love you," I told her as she stared at me lovingly.

"You sucked a cock for me. I love you more."

I couldn't, wouldn't lie to her. "Might have sucked it a little bit for me, too. Kinda always wondered," I said, finally admitting the truth. Even to myself.

"Did you like it?"

"Wait a minute. I sucked a cock for you. I get to love you more."

"I might have said yes, but you said you liked it, so it doesn't count. I love you more."

And then we were both rendered unable to speak as we both felt Shea's cock nudge Dot's entrance, just above my cock.

"Go slow. I don't know if you're both going to fit in there."

Luckily, I had exploded inside her. The abundance of lubrication made it almost easy for him to slide inside, his cock rubbing against mine until his balls touched mine. He displaced my semen and it practically poured out of her, landing on me and it kind of turned me on more. If that was even possible.

Dot had noticed. "Now you know how I feel."

"Happy?"

She nodded, smiling. "Full."

"Feels good, doesn't it?" I asked her.

"Yes. How are you still hard?"

"Um… This is like the fucking hottest thing ever? I'm probably going to have an erection that lasts more than four hours. I'll probably have to consult a physician."

"Or I could just continue to take care of them for you."

289

I groaned as I pushed myself even further inside of her. When I did, Shea pulled out. He knew what he was doing, and the thought surprised me. He was far from innocent. How far, I would have to determine later. When I could think clearly. Between her pussy and his cock, this wasn't going to last much longer.

"Oh, my Lady. Holy fuck." Dot was grunting as we seesawed inside her.

"Not going to last long."

"What? You literally *just* came."

"His cock…it's sliding against mine. The undersides… It feels too good."

She turned around to look at Shea. As soon as she did, the orgasm hit her like a truck. She started panting, unable to even make sounds as she lowered her head next to mine, breathed into my neck, and lost consciousness for a moment. Shea slowed his movements.

"Welcome back," I told her as she looked up at me dreamily. She clenched around me, almost triggering my orgasm. "Stop that. You're going to make me come."

"Stop what?" She asked with a grin, purposely clenching her insides around us.

"That!"

"You mean this?" Clench.

"Shea! Damn the torpedoes, full steam ahead!"

"Aye, Cap'n."

And we pounded her into submission, his in to my out as we pummeled her with our cocks. She came again. Another time after that, until she lowered her head to my shoulder and just rode the pleasure. Shea called out and I felt him splash over me, just increasing the wetness flowing from her all over me. It was that wet heat that enveloped us that sent me over the edge into blackness…

Author's Note

Reviews are important for new authors and I greatly appreciate everyone who takes a moment to leave one, even a line or two! Thank you so much for reading my reverse harem series! I'm writing away and more books will be out soon!

Follow me on Amazon to be sent updates on my new releases!

Come join my Readers Group on Facebook for news, fun, games, teasers for upcoming books, and naughty shenanigans! 18+ recommended.

Coven of the First Moon

About the Author

A late comer to the writing game, Jacquelyn had always been a fan of romance novels and lately become addicted to the reverse harem category. I mean seriously, who wouldn't? Sitting alone one night she flipped open her laptop and said, "I'm going to give this a whirl." And thus, the Lovin' the Coven series was given life. She has designs on other series as well, but only time shall tell.

As for her, she is five-foot-something, with graying hair, wicked eyes, an eager smile, and an annoying laugh. She lives at home with her dog, a cat, and that is about all she is comfortable sharing.

Other Works

Lovin' the Coven Series
(Reverse Harem- 7 book series)

First Moon
Second Blood
Third Charm
Fourth Rite
Fifth Essence
Sixth Sense
Seventh Seal

The Fox and the Hounds
(Reverse Harem – trilogy)

A Tail of Woah
A Tail of Two Kitties
The Tell Tail Heart